ME & MY DOPE BOY III

SHVONNE LATRICE

Other Works by Me:

Good Girls Love Thugs 1-5
Falling for a Hood King 1-4
Married to a Distinguished Thug 1-3
She's Gotta Have It 1-2
Me & My Dope Boy 1-3
Yazir & Nina 1-3
Forbidden Love with a Thug 1-3
You Needed Me 1-3
Shorty is in Love with a Real One 1-4
I Got Your Back 1-2
My Baby Is a West Coast King 1-4
Our Love Is the Realest 1-3
She Got It Bad for a Heartless Gangsta 1-4
She Got It Bad for a Heartless Gangsta: An AK Christmas
Hood Boyz Fall In Love Too 1-3
Nobody Can Love You Like Them Roughnecks Do 1-4
She Gave Her All to the Hood's Finest 1-5

Visit www.theshvonnelatrice.com for paperbacks!

 facebook.com/ShvonneLatrice

twitter.com/siobhannoir

instagram.com/siobhannoir

My vision was getting blurry as fuck as I tried to nurse all three of my gunshot wounds, which were bleeding out profusely. I was doing this, all the while trying not to choke on the blood flowing out of my mouth. Blood was everywhere around me, and covering my hands, lips, and chin. I was dead; I knew it.

"Tell Aysia..." I couldn't even finish my sentence, and I doubt Kenzie could make out what I was trying to say anyway.

"They're on the way cuz, shit!" Kenzie shouted, but his voice sounded like he was under water. I started to cough up more blood, before letting my head hit the gym floor.

"Kaleeini!" he hollered and I could tell he was right on the floor next to me at this point. "Kaleeini man, come on! Open your eyes!" he hollered again and tapped my face. I couldn't move, and I could only see blurry colors. "Kaleeini!" Kenzie screamed at the top of his lungs, which echoed over the huge ass gymnasium, just before everything went black.

THIS WEEK HAD BEEN crazy as fuck for me, so right now I just wanted to rest my fucking nerves and reset myself. I needed to be on my toes whenever these niggas from Camden decided to show their faces, because losing was not an option. I refused to be caught slipping, therefore I wouldn't be. As the saying goes, when you stay ready you ain't got to get ready. And in order for me to be on my shit when they got into town, I couldn't be stressed and overworked.

"Okay he's asleep," Gianna smiled referring to our son, as she entered the den.

She sat down on the couch next to me, and I draped my arm around her before kissing her soft cheek. I still had some more time to wait before I could slide up in her, and it was killing me. It seemed like everything she did turned me on. The way she walked, talked, laughed, breathed, every damn thing had my dick hard as a rock. Out of all the enemies I'd ever encountered, this six-week post delivery wait was the one I hated most. That shit did not want me to be great. I felt like pussy gave me a new burst of energy, and that's probably why I was feeling a bit drained. Gianna better be prepared when her wait time is over though, because that pussy is gonna get killed, demolished, pulverized, and all that shit.

"What should we watch?" she asked as she surfed the channels.

Her hair smelled so good, and so did her skin. It was like a vanilla or cinnamon scent, and just like everything else about her, it made my dick brick up. She was wearing one of her little short nightgowns, and she knew she was wrong as fuck for that. I would much rather she walk around the house in a onesie, than that little ass gown that showed her sexy ass legs and the bottom of her small round ass when she bent over. Fuck, just the thought alone had me on one. I ran my hand over my face to help mask my sexual frustration.

Ignoring her question about what we should watch, I started to plant kisses down her shoulder. They started off innocent, but then became more sensual as I made it to her neck, chin, and finally her lips. I slipped my hand between her legs, and began to rub very gently and slowly. I don't even know why I was doing this. I guess I was hoping she'd say fuck the wait and let me smash. I was on some thirsty shit I know.

"No Kendrick," she whispered and turned her face. I sat back and stared at the wall frustrated. Head wouldn't even do right now, because I wanted some pussy and nothing could substitute it. "It's not much longer KJ," Gianna rubbed my knee and then kissed the corner of my mouth.

I declined to respond because I needed to collect my thoughts. Fucking another girl wasn't an option, so I needed to get my mind right. Not only did I not wanna cheat on Gianna, but I'd become accustomed to fucking with no cap, and I only wanted to do that with her.

As I stared at the TV watching Gianna continue to channel surf, my phone began ringing. I looked at the screen to see my father's name, so I picked it up and answered.

"What's good Pop?" I held the phone between my shoulder and face, and then slipped my hand into my sweats for comfort and warmth.

"KJ, Kaleeini got shot picking up Kenzie from practice," he replied somberly.

"What?" I sat up at the edge of the couch. This had to be a joke, a cruel one.

My body became hot all over at the thought of someone shooting my cousin and one of my fucking best friends. I was so angry that I'm sure my body was filled with fire. I was somewhat upset with myself, because whenever something happened to someone on my team I felt responsible. I was also a little shocked at Kaleeini for not wearing a vest, knowing that niggas were coming for us left and right. This shit was not cool right now for so many reasons.

"They've got him down here at Mercy right now. We're all just waiting to see what the doctors have to say. Figure out who did it KJ."

"I will. Thanks," was all I said before I hung up. Furious was an understatement when describing how I felt right now. I felt disrespected on top of that.

I stood to my feet abruptly, and began to walk out of the den. I had some planning to do, and I needed to think quickly. I didn't want the muthafucka who shot my cousin to last more than forty-eight hours in Baltimore. If it was them cats from Camden, I would lose my mind at the fact that they'd gotten to us so quickly, easily, and discreetly. *You can't lose KJ*, I chanted to myself.

"What happened Kendrick?" Gianna frowned as we both entered the bedroom.

"Kaleeini got shot-"

"Oh my gosh!" she squealed and then ran towards her closet to get dressed.

She wasn't about to go nowhere, because ain't no fucking telling what might pop off. And if them niggas that got Kaleeini shot her or my kid, I would murder all of Maryland.

"Gianna stay here, I have to go handle some shit."

"When will you be back?" she questioned as her eyes watered.

"Not until I off somebody, so don't wait up."

I rushed around our bedroom for the shit I needed to wear, with Gianna hot on my heels. I wasn't in the mood to deal with her questions and shit. I didn't wanna blow up on her, but with the way she was following me and questioning me, she was about to feel my wrath, verbally.

"Kendrick let me come, I need to see Aysia-"

"No, you need to be here with the baby. You can call Aysia on the phone, or see her once I say it's okay to leave Gianna."

"No-"

"I already told you what the fuck you was gonna do so stop asking me about it!" I roared so loudly that she jumped.

I was irate as fuck, and with the way my dad sounded, it was as if my cousin was fucking dead. I didn't wanna bite her fucking head off, but she was trying me in a moment where I didn't need to be tried. All she needed to do was sit her ass down and wait for me to give her the okay. How fucking hard was that to do?

I changed into my clothes as soon as Gianna left the bedroom angrily. I didn't have time to coddle her or make her feel better. She needed to learn that when I made a decision it was final and to never argue with me about it. I was the fucking man of this house, and she needed to follow along when necessary. That's how shit works when you fuck with a nigga who has his hands in dangerous shit. Wives and girlfriends who don't listen, always end up in some bullshit, and I refused to lose her because she wants to be Miss Independent.

Once I finished dressing, I rushed down to my gunroom and collected whatever I may need for tonight. Someone was dying either tonight, or bright and early tomorrow morning, and that was a fucking promise.

I didn't bother saying bye to Gianna because she probably wouldn't even say it back. She was in her feelings, so, oh well. Right now I didn't care about shit but getting back at my cousin's attacker, so her pouting and stomping her feet were the least of my worries.

I sped to Mercy Hospital, and parked all the way in the back because I didn't care to hunt for a closer park. I wanted to just park my whip and get the fuck out. I jogged the whole way to the entrance of the hospital, and as soon as I got by the waiting area, I spotted my uncle Kendreeis, aunt Morgan, their other two sons Kendall and Kendlan, my parents, Kenzie, and Aysia.

Aysia was lying on Morgan's shoulder crying like a newborn baby. You could tell she thought this was the end for Kaleeini, and that shit made my heart thump. Her body jerked so hard that it looked like she may be hurting the child in her big ass stomach. I knew her current state could not be good for the baby, but I knew she couldn't help it. She loved that nigga. Aunt Morgan was trying to be strong for Aysia, but tears were still spilling down her cheeks.

I walked over by them, and after greeting everyone, I waved Kenzie to come sit by me a little ways away. I wanted to get some information from him, but I didn't want to ask around my parents, aunt, uncle, cousins, and Aysia. They were worried enough, and recounting the events wouldn't do shit but make matters worse.

"Did you see who it was?" I quizzed Kenzie and he nodded slowly after exhaling.

"Tell me."

"That nigga y'all jumped at the club that night, Christian. Adams is his last name, I remember Shannon telling me."

I squinted my eyes and cocked my head. Why the fuck would he choose to shoot Kaleeini of all people? Shooting Kendrin or me would've made more sense, because we're the ones who roughed him up and embarrassed his ass.

"Why did he shoot Kaleeini?" I frowned.

"He had a white boy in the back who pulled the trigger. I'm sure he meant to pop me, but he accidentally hit Kaleeini. That's what I'm assuming."

"Thanks man."

I nodded and stood up to leave the hospital, because I had some muthafuckin heads to blow open. I wanted to see Kaleeini, but clearly that wasn't an option right now. In addition to that, I couldn't stand to listen to Aysia's cries any longer, because it was making me feel some type of way. I think hearing her wail was causing the reality of the situation to sink in. I needed to focus so I could take these niggas out, I didn't have time to sulk.

"KJ!" I heard my mom call after me as I walked towards the exit of the hospital. I stopped and paused for a second before turning around.

"Yes ma?"

"Where are you going?" she asked as she looked up into my eyes with a worried expression.

"I'm gonna go handle some business."

"KJ, please be careful," she sniffled.

I could see that she was worried about me getting shot too. Kendrin getting shot by that bitch nigga TJ really broke my mom's heart, and I didn't think she could deal with another one of her sons getting shot. I was too careful and cognizant to get shot though, and she should know that by now. You would never catch Kendrick Jr. slipping, and that's on everything I love.

I grabbed my mother's shoulder and pulled her closer to me, before hugging her tightly.

"I'm gon' be good ma," I pulled away and then cupped her pretty face. She nodded and then stood on her tiptoes to kiss my jaw. "Go back over there with dad," I half smiled to ease her mind. She nodded but stared at me for a couple seconds like she thought it was the last time she'd see me. "Ma, I'm gon' be good. I will even come to breakfast tomorrow morning alright?" I grinned even though there was nothing to grin about right now. But I had to put on this quick show for my mother.

"You promise?"

"I promise. Have the omelets and waffles ready."

"Okay," she chuckled lightly.

She finally turned around to walk away, so I continued out of the hospital. I wasn't selling my mother wolf tickets. I was gonna murk this weasel ass nigga tonight, and then be at the breakfast table with my siblings, fiancée, and son tomorrow morning. You just watch. I'm not cocky, I'm just confident; nah I'm both.

Once I got into my car, I cracked open one of the burner phones in my trunk to call my boy Oscar.

"What's up?" he answered.

He already knew who it was because this was the normal now. Only people I called from the same number every time were my parents, youngest siblings, and Gianna. Every one else got calls from all types of weird ass numbers. I'd even found a way to text people and have it show up as unknown.

"Get me the address and family member names of Christian Adams within an hour please."

"Got you."

We disconnected and then I called my brother Kendrin on another burner.

"Hello?" he answered and I could tell he was wondering what was going on.

"Don't tell shorty, but Kaleeini got shot. Get dressed," was all I said before hanging up.

I sped to Kendrin's home, and by the time I got there, Oscar had delivered the information I'd requested much earlier than needed. I smiled as I opened the text and read Christian's address, along with his mother's name. According to Oscar, he was the only biological child of his mother's, but she'd adopted a boy named Gunner Reese, who I assumed was the white guy that blasted Kaleeini. She'd be a childless woman after tonight though.

I text Kendrin on my real phone to let him know I was there, and he came outside of his door about fifteen minutes later.

"Who the fuck shot him?" he asked as soon as he got into the car.

"The nigga you put to sleep in the back of the club. It was drive-by style when he went to pick Kenzie up from practice. Kenzie said the Christian dude drove the car, but someone else shot him. It was some white boy with no aim, who I just found out is his foster brother named Gunner."

"How you find that out?" he asked as I peeled down his street.

"Oscar got me his info, so that's where we're headed. We're about to take these niggas out tonight, and if their mama gets froggy she can take a bullet to the dome as well."

"You think Kaleeini gon' be mad he didn't get in on it?"

"Man I don't even know, and I don't care honestly. These niggas need to go, and they need to go tonight. Living more than twenty-four hours is not a fucking option now that we got this information."

"I'm with it. How is Kaleeini though? I wanna see him."

"I don't know," I sighed.

"You didn't ask?" Kendrin frowned. I could see his facial expression out the corner of my eye.

"I didn't wanna know. I can't handle that shit right now. I need a clear head, and seeing him shot the fuck up and possibly in a coma would fuck up my mindset. Right now ain't the time for me to be in my fucking feelings bro."

Kendrin nodded as we continued to Christian's mother's condo in Park Heights. We finally made it, and thankfully no one was outside except for a couple addicts who didn't even know what year it was. I never understood how you could get to that point, and I didn't wanna understand.

I handed Kendrin a Ziploc bag with some gloves, as well as a gun. Once we were both dressed like some damn bank robbers, we climbed out of the car, ready to see some bloodshed.

We passed a guy who looked dirty as fuck, and was walking in a squiggly line singing Sam Cooke. The nigga didn't sound half bad, which made me wonder how he ended up living on the streets getting high. It was sad to see people with talent just waste their lives by getting high. Then again, it kept my pockets fat, so I wasn't about to be an advocate for any *say no to drugs* campaigns.

Kendrin and I rushed up the steps of the porch, and easily lifted the window. It had no lock or anything, making it easy for Kendrin and I to just crawl through. The only reason I knew that was because I'd smashed a many of bitches on this same street, and had to sneak out when their daddies came home. I laughed on the inside at the fact that them niggas really thought they had virgin daughters. Little did they know, I had them faced down ass up almost everyday after school. My mind began to drift to the time where I had a threesome with two best friends about two houses down when I was in twelfth grade. This six-week wait needed to hurry the fuck up, because it was starting to fuck with my concentration!

Once Kendrin climbed in after me, I looked around outside to make sure everyone was still inside their houses. We had masks on and shit, but still I liked to cover my tracks as if we didn't.

We crept around the house, and followed the sound of the TV. Walking into the living room, we spotted Christian chilling on the couch, knocked the fuck out. As if God was on our side, the white dude was chilling adjacent to him on a smaller couch.

Kendrin eased his gun from his waist, and pressed it against the back of Christian's head. His eyes flew open, and when he tried to get up, Kendrin locked his forearm around his neck, choking him. He was bucking his eyes and squirming like the dramatic bitch that he was. I put my silencer on as tears spilled from Christian's eyes. That shit didn't faze me, just like it didn't bother him to shoot my cousin. This nigga was big chilling as if he'd done nothing.

"I'm wondering if I should kill you here, or torture your ass a bit," I grinned.

"You ain't ready to die yet, right nigga?" Kendrin asked him, still holding him in a headlock. The white boy was still knocked the fuck out with his head cocked back and his mouth open.

I text Blade to find out if he was outside, and once he let me know that he was, I went and answered the door for him and four other niggas.

"Now follow them Christian," I pointed to Blade and his people with my gun. Kendrin released his neck from his grip so that he could stand up.

"Come on man," he cried, with snot coming down and everything.

"Go," I stated sternly, but calmly.

I didn't feel like looking at his ugly punk ass any longer. I had a somewhat weak stomach, so seeing all that snot coming down was enough alone, to make me shoot him.

Finally the snow-nigga came to, and I had the gun pressed to the middle of his forehead. He blinked lazily about three times, before he finally realized what the fuck was happening.

"You killed my cousin?" I quizzed. He just stared at me stunned, letting me know he did the shit. I knew it was him most likely, but he confirmed it for me by going temporarily dumb when I asked him about it.

"Get him too," I told Blade's boys.

Christian and the white guy walked out with no problem, just like some idiots. I told them that if they didn't make noise, I wouldn't kill them. Yeah right, what the fuck would I be taking them for, if I wasn't gon' kill their asses? If they put up a fight they were getting dropped, and if they didn't put up a fight they were getting dropped. It was a lose-lose situation here.

We made it to the warehouse, and Blade's people tied them upside down so that they were hanging like a piñata. Blade then provided Kendrin and I with bats, before we went to town on these niggas. Their screams and cries didn't rattle me one bit, as I broke damn near every bone in their bodies. By the look on my face, and the calmness of my body language, you would never know that I was going Jackie Robinson on these niggas.

Once I didn't hear any more cracks or snaps when my bat landed on their limbs, I had them taken down. After being released from the ropes, they both laid on the floor crying like some bitches. I swear I have never in my life seen some big grown ass niggas cry like this in my life. They literally looked like some overgrown toddlers.

"Y'all niggas cry more than my fucking son," I laughed as I waited for Blade's boys to come back with the chainsaw.

Once they did, Kendrin and I placed face shields over our faces, grabbed the chainsaws, and then turned them on.

"Ahhhhhh!" the two guys screamed as we each started cutting into their leg. We stopped midway to let the pain sink in. I didn't want to cut it off, I just wanted to slice into the shit to make them suffer.

"Please man, I swear I don't even know your cousin! My brother just asked me to shoot the guy so I did!" the white guy pleaded.

Kendrin and I said nothing in response, before cutting the chainsaws back on to carve into the next leg. They both howled, cried, hollered, and everything else.

"This is my favorite part," Kendrin said, making me laugh as he lit a match.

Blade covered them with gasoline, as they tried their best to scoot away on their asses. The shit was funny as hell, making me wish I had my phone out to record for my personal pleasure.

"I mean if y'all wanna leave go ahead," I shrugged. They weren't tied up, but Kendrin and I had broken their bones with the bats, so it'd be a miracle to see them walk.

"No, no man! I'm sorry! For real! Come on! Nah nah ahhhhhh!" Christian pleaded to Kendrin before he dropped the match on him. The white boy had given up, and took the match like a G.

We sat there and watched them burn and scream. They couldn't even drop and roll, because their bones were crushed. These niggas reminded me of an octopus or jellyfish. They were forced to simply sit there and burn the fuck while we watched. I almost wished I had some popcorn.

"Blade, shoot these little octopussies please," I directed.

Blade's men dumped water on them to put out the fire. I stared at the two, as they still clung weakly on to life just like I wanted. I wanted the fire to burn the fuck out of them but not kill them. They needed to feel the burn, feel the revenge, and feel the anger I had towards them.

POP! POP!

Blade shot them both, and then he and his team began to clean up. Once it was all finished, Kendrin and I called my mother to get an update on Kaleeini before I took Kendrin home.

My mom had told us that Kaleeini was in a medically induced

coma, but that he would be coming to very soon. She said that they didn't pierce anything major, but the bullets were very close to vital organs. I was thanking God the whole way home for saving my cousin, and in hopes that the circumstances wouldn't change for the worse overnight.

I walked into my house, and went straight to the bedroom to see Gianna. She wasn't in there, so I went to the den with a heart rate that was a bit faster than the one before. She was gone from there too, so I frantically rushed back upstairs to K-Three's room. He was gone, and I saw his little diaper bag was, too. *Lord please give me the strength to not haul off and backhand my baby mama*, I prayed. The irritation I felt right now was unexplainable.

I quickly pulled out my phone and called her.

"What?" she had the nerve to answer with an attitude.

"Gigi, where are you?" I asked calmly and with my eyes closed. I knew if I cursed or blew up, she wouldn't tell me out of fear.

"I'm at the hospital with Aysi-" I hung up the phone and went back out to my car chanting, *You don't hit women KJ.*

I specifically told her looney-toon ass not to fucking go, yet she did it anyway. She was always doing some shit that I told her ass not to do, and she needed to understand that the shit could get her killed. I understand she wanted to see her friend, but she needed to be smarter than that. Does she honestly think I would tell her not to go see her grieving friend just because I wanna be in charge? Come on now. I obviously have a good fucking reason.

I made it to the hospital in no time, and this time I parked right in front by the entrance because I didn't care. I power walked inside, and I saw Gianna sitting next to Aysia, with K-Three in his carrier. Everyone else was still there excluding Kenzie and my parents, but I still didn't want to act like too much of a fool in front of my aunt and uncle.

Gianna and I made eye contact, and I could damn near see the lump in her throat. I walked closer, picked up the carrier, and then leaned down to whisper in her ear.

"Bring yo' ass on. If I have to ask you twice, you're gonna regret it shorty," I gritted.

I walked off and she was right behind me. I buckled my son in the back, and then opened the passenger side for her. Although scared as hell, she got in the car.

"Fuck did I tell you before I left?" I asked as I pulled out of the hospital.

"Not to leave, but KJ-"

"Exactly Gigi, the next time I tell you not to do something like that, don't do it. I live a dangerous life, so when I tell you something you need to listen. What if someone was trying to kidnap you and you didn't listen huh?"

"I'm sorry Kendrick."

"You should be sorry. Ain't nobody trying to control your hard-headed ass, I'm trying to keep you fucking safe. The next time I give you directions you need to follow them without one fucking swerve or detour aight?" I raised a brow as I sped to the house. I could feel her looking at the side of my face.

"Okay."

I wanted to yell at her ass, but my kid was back there sleep, so I had to stay calm.

"Are you hungry?" I asked as I came to a stop at a red light.

"No."

I gripped her chin and kissed her lips gently and sensually. Once I let her face go, the light turned green so I pulled off. She was still staring out of the window with her arms folded. I didn't care if she was mad; I meant what I said.

We made it to the house, and I took my son up to his room to lie him down. I then went to the bedroom, and immediately turned on the shower to clean off the night's dirt. When I was done, I came out into the dark bedroom to see Gianna sleeping. I slipped some boxers on, and then climbed in bed with her. I cuddled behind her and she slightly recoiled, making it obvious she wasn't comfortable with me touching her.

"I love you Gigi, I just need you to understand why I do what I do," I whispered. She nodded but kept staring straight ahead. "You hate me?" I asked. She finally turned to look at me and shook her head no. "You love me still," I smiled widely.

"Yeah," she chuckled.

"I love you too shorty. And when the wait is over, I'm gonna eat your pussy real good to make up for getting in your ass, okay?"

She nodded with a smile.

I kissed her soft lips, and once it started getting hot and heavy, I pulled away, so that, I wouldn't get my dick's hopes up. Fuck, two and a half more weeks until I could smash. Lord, get me through it.

I STARED at the big ass TV, while laid up in the hospital set-up in Annapolis. It was a medical facility that my family had built for when one of us needed to recoup. It'd been in the family since my grandfather Kairio and his brother Kylin were in the game. It was only known about by family members and not even the homies, because you never knew when a snake would start to slither. No one wanted to possibly get set-up while already out of commission, by a nigga who you thought was your friend.

Aysia was laid out on the little Queen bed in the corner, sleeping good as hell. The upside to being in this room, other than being protected, was that it wasn't a traditional hospital, so it had way better amenities. We had big screen TV's, plush chairs for visitors, and a queen bed in the corner for your woman and/or kids if they wanted to stay with you. There was even a fridge, stove, closet, and a nice ass bathroom. If I was gonna be in a hospital, I was glad it was this one.

I was happy to see Aysia asleep and at peace, because she'd been worrying me all night with her cute pregnant ass. She kept making sure I was alive the whole night, and I could barely get any rest. Two nights ago, I woke up to her weird ass standing over me with her finger under my nose. She was making sure that I was still breathing. I wanted to be mad, but how could you get angry with someone who cared about you so much that they annoyed you? I could finally have some quiet time now that she was knocked out, and I wasn't afraid to admit it. I loved my shorty though.

There was a light knock at the door, before it started to open slowly. I sat up and winced in pain, because my wounds were still very fucking painful. As bad as I wanted to get back to running the streets, I was not in any condition to do so. Getting out there before I was ready would do more harm than good.

KJ walked in, and then closed the door behind himself. He pulled a chair next to my bed after we dapped one another up. My cousin had my back like no other, he and Kendrin, so I was not surprised to find out that they'd deaded that nigga the same night he shot me.

"Feeling better?" he asked.

"Much better every day. And thanks for going after old boy," I responded.

"Don't thank me nigga, that's what I'm supposed to do. I didn't want that nigga living any longer than that day. I made him suffer just for you, too."

"Yeah, I heard you and Kendrin went in on them niggas Hank Aaron style," I chuckled.

"Yes indeed, mixed with a little Leatherface."

"Y'all pulled out chainsaws on them niggas?" I grinned widely as fuck, before putting the side of my fist up to my mouth to laugh. I laughed so hard that my wounds began to throb.

"We had to!" he laughed, and then turned to a knocked out Aysia. "I see your shorty don' calmed the fuck down," he said and we guffawed in unison.

"Yeah, thank God. She was going crazy every damn hour making sure I hadn't died. Every time I closed my eyes, she would slap my face to make sure I was living still." We both laughed but tried to muffle it so she wouldn't wake up. "Kendrin said y'all broke in while the boys' mama was there. I saw her ass all on the local news crying and shit," I nodded getting back to the previous topic.

"Yeah, me too, I wasn't tripping though. Her son was a bitch, and so was his little foster brother." Suddenly the door opened again, and my father came into the room. "Let me give y'all some time." KJ stood up.

My father embraced him, and then let him by. He gave me a look that I didn't wanna see, so I looked away towards the television.

"Kaleeini, do you know how angry I was when I heard you got shot?" he frowned. I wasn't looking at him, but I could see his scowl out the corner of my eyes.

"Nah, I don't," I responded dryly.

"Well I was ready to hit the pavement and go back to my old ways. That's how fucking mad I was," he gritted, making me look over at him.

"I don't know what to say, Pop, it happens in the game."

"It does, which is why I told you I didn't want you in this shit. First Kendrin, now you, who's next, huh?"

"I don't know who is next, but if someone else is stupid enough to come for us, then they'll die just like the last ones," I stated calmly. I wasn't worried about the enemies we had. We would win just like we always did.

"Kaleeini, are you honestly telling me that you still wanna do this shit?"

"Yeah, I am. This is what I know. I'm a street nigga and that's how I'm gonna live my life. It didn't turn out too bad for you," I shrugged nonchalantly.

"But I've only been shot at, I've never actually been hit like yo' ass." I just inhaled sharply and looked back up at the TV. "What if you would have left her and your kid?" He pointed to Aysia lying on the bed as if someone had knocked her ass out with a vase.

"I won't Pop. Look at me, I'm good!" I smiled.

I hated when he did this, acting like he didn't do this shit until I was in my fucking teens. I understood his angle, but right now he was the pot calling the kettle black. He'd admitted to me many times that the street life gave him a rush that he could only otherwise get from pussy. I was the same way.

"I'm recovering and I'll be back to normal in a couple weeks. Ain't nothing to worry about. I'm not getting out of the game. This is what I love to do and a couple bullets ain't gon' stop me from doing what the fuck I wanna do."

"I guess you've made up your mind," he smirked at me.

I could see that a part of him was happy that I didn't bow out like a bitch nigga. Me choosing to stay in the game after being hit was bittersweet for him. He wanted to protect me from harm, but he was happy he didn't have a bitch nigga for a son.

"Yeah, I have. I promise this shit ain't gon' happen again. Watch."

"It better not happen again. If anything happens again, I'm coming back out. If one more of you gets shot Kaleeini, the originals are suiting up," he stated and I knew he was serious as fuck. If we did get shot again, hopefully we'd be like my uncle Kendrick with his nine lives having ass.

"I know," I finally responded.

My mom walked in, and a big smile covered her face once she laid her eyes on me. She was wearing a tight black dress that I didn't like. I hated when she wore shit like that, because niggas thought she was young and ready. I was always willing to let niggas know that she was not in her twenties and very married. She and her friends were always out looking like some twenty-five year olds, knowing their sons hated for these young hustlers to approach them. A part of me believed they wanted to prove they still had it sometimes.

"Move Dreeis," she told my dad, so she could get close to me, and then she hugged me tightly.

As she rubbed my dreads I closed my eyes. It was crazy that even though I was a grown ass man, my mom's touch was still so calming, as if I was a little ass baby. I inhaled her perfume, because she'd been wearing it for the longest. I remember when I used to come home from school, the scent would hit me as soon as I walked in the door, letting me know my mother was home; that shit used to always make me smile.

She pulled away, and then kissed my cheeks a couple times, before sitting down in my dad's lap.

"Mm," my dad mumbled as he looked her small body over, while gripping her waist in his hands. She moved her long hair out of his way, as if she was trying to give him a better view.

"Can y'all please not flirt in front of me?" I turned my lip up.

"Flirting is how I was able to convince your mama to make you," my dad chuckled along with my mom.

"For real Kaleeini, we practiced making you a whole bunch of times," my mom fucked with me further. "That was when your daddy had dreads like you."

"Wasn't this the position that did it?" my dad taunted and kissed my mom's arm.

I hoped he wasn't serious, because I was not trying to find out that my mom bouncing on my dad's dick, lap style, was how I got here. I'd like to think it was a bit more romantic than that shit.

"Alright y'all can leave," I chuckled.

"He's just kidding Kaleeini, he knows it was regular old doggy style."

"Ma!" I bucked my eyes as she and my dad cracked up like this was the funniest shit in the world.

We talked for a little bit more, but once they started kissing and shit, I asked their hot asses to leave. Aysia woke up thirty minutes later all frantic and shit, which made me snicker.

"Relax shorty," I grinned.

She climbed off of the bed, and then wobbled over to me. Once she got closer, I palmed her stomach making her smile.

"I can't wait until you come home," she caressed my face.

"Same shorty, same."

I STOOD in my huge walk-in closet, staring into the wide ass mirror. I had on the skimpiest, sluttiest, lingerie outfit ever. I didn't even get it from Victoria's Secret, because their's weren't revealing enough. I bought it from a sex shop online; yeah, I was serious. It was all black but very see through. My bralette was very thin, and you could see my nipples and everything.

I looked over my body, and admired some parts of it. The baby had given me a little bit of hips, slightly more ass, and more thighs. I still wasn't thick by any means, but I felt more like a woman. My breasts were getting back small, and so was my stomach. I still needed to go to the gym though, because I missed my little two-pack very much. Just a flat stomach wasn't enough for me.

I turned to look at the back of my body in the mirror, and smiled at the little heart shaped opening by my butthole. It reminded me of the time KJ and I tried to do anal, but I chickened out. He didn't want to do it, but I made him try. However, he didn't even get it in, because when he started applying pressure I panicked like a muthafucaka. I guess I was trying to be too freaky that night. I would never try that shit again though. I chuckled and then walked out of the closet after slipping a silk robe on.

Checking my phone for the time, I saw it was nearing 10pm. KJ would be here soon, so I laid across the chaise lounge in our room. I tried to figure out what pose I wanted, and once I felt sexy enough, I did my best to stay in position.

I heard the door alarm beep, letting me know he was home, and a big smile spread across my face. I tousled my long brownish-red locks, and pressed my lips together to make sure my red lipstick was covering every bit of my lips. My baby had no idea tonight was the night, despite him initially keeping track, and I couldn't wait to surprise him.

"Gianna!" I heard him call out. I shook my head at his dumb ass.

I'd told him to stop yelling through the house because the baby could be sleep and he'd wake him. But shit if he woke up K-Three, he'd be the main one upset that he lost out on getting some.

Finally the doorknob twisted and he entered the bedroom. As soon as he spotted me, he was smiling from ear to ear. I'd never seen him so happy. It was the most adorable thing, even though he was a grown ass man. I couldn't help but to blush and chuckle lightly.

"It's over?" he beamed. I just nodded because I felt talking would ruin my sexy. He set the plastic bag in his hand down, and then walked over to me.

"No, go sit down on the bed," I ordered him.

He immediately did as I asked, so I stood up, turned the lights down low, and lit some candles that I'd gotten from Bath and Body Works. I decided to just cut the lights off completely, allowing the candles to be our only illumination, and he watched my every move.

Dropping the robe to the floor, I neared him very slowly. I felt like one of those Victoria's Secret models when they walked around in the commercials. All that could be heard was the sound of my heels clicking against the floor. Once I got close, he gripped my waist and instantly began kissing my stomach. His hunger for me turned me on.

"I missed this baby," he whispered in between kisses. "You are so fucking sexy."

I rubbed his hair, and then stepped back to pull his shirt off without saying a word. My pussy began to drip at the sight of his six-pack, and I couldn't wait to feel it pressed against me as he dicked me down. I got down on my knees, and began unbuckling his Hermes jeans.

"I want you to suck my dick while I'm standing," he said.

I nodded and moved back, allowing him to stand to his feet. Once he had, I yanked on his jeans and Hermes boxers, until they hit his ankles. When he stepped out of them, his long thick dick was already waiting for me. I gripped it lightly, and began licking and sucking on the tip as if it were a piece of candy.

"Mmmm," he grumbled as I made love to the head of his dick.

Once my mouth became lubricated enough, I eased more of him into my mouth. He was so hard that if I bit down my tooth might chip. I bobbed my head up and down, letting his tip hit my tonsils.

"Baby shit, deep throat it just like that," he moaned and palmed the back of my head.

He bit down on his lip as he stared down at me. I kept going, letting his dick get as deep in my throat as I could allow. KJ was calling out to the high heavens, and gripping my hair tightly. I began moaning as I played with his balls and sucked him off.

"Gigi, I love you so much," he damn near cried as I continued to work. "Mmm mmm fuck. Baby I'll buy you whatever you want. Oh my fucking gosh," he groaned and came hard. I licked him clean and then he stood me up. "Once I get your panties off, sit on my face back-wards," he demanded.

He pushed me onto the bed, and then removed my shoes. He kissed up my legs with his eyes closed, and the feeling of his lips made me quiver. Flipping me onto my back, he then kissed where the hole of my panties was, right on my butt making me giggle. Once he got my panties down, he climbed on the bed, and waited for me to mount his face. I got up and brought my pussy to his mouth, and he pulled me closer to begin feasting.

"Grind slowly so I can taste every bit of you," he ordered.

I loved the way he ordered me around. I moved my hips slowly, and wound my pussy on his tongue. Feeling his soft lips between my legs was euphoric. I placed my hands on his six-pack for leverage, as I moved my hips in a circular motion.

"Fuck," I whimpered and scrunched my face up.

"Sit up straight, and spread your legs wider," he lifted me up a little to say.

I then brought my pussy back to his mouth. I sat up like he'd asked, practically sitting on his face like a chair, and began to work as if his mouth was a dick. This shit was feeling way too damn good. He gripped my hips and sucked my clit with all his might, as I continued to roll my hips. It'd been six long weeks and I missed my baby's head game.

"Uuuh uuuh," I screamed and came. He kept going in as I rode his face a little faster, and my body jerked as I exploded. He pushed me onto all fours, and I immediately got scared. "KJ, not like this the first time," I looked back at him.

"Calm down baby, I'm not done."

He dipped down behind me and began eating my pussy some more. This nigga was eating my pussy so ferociously, that I had to grip the footboard. He then ran his tongue from my clit all the way to my asshole, making me shiver a bit. As he went in on me, I felt another orgasm rise quickly. He was putting his tongue everywhere and I loved it. Once I came, he stood up on his knees and unhooked my bra. He laid me on my back, and then began flicking his tongue over my nipples, and sucking them hungrily. I was happy to see he didn't complain that they weren't as big as before. Slipping his tongue into my mouth, he then lowered himself onto me, and placed my legs in the nooks of his arms.

"I love you Kendrick," I whispered as we kissed one another.

Suddenly I felt his dick at my opening, and I jumped. He paused and looked into my eyes frowning.

"Relax baby," He told me and I nodded. "Just relax," he stated in a low tone as he kissed my stomach and pecked my lower lips. He brought his head up and kissed me roughly some more, and then his thick head began pushing into me.

"Aaahh ahhh," I cooed as he kissed me. He began pumping me slowly, until he was all the way inside of me.

"Gigi, fuck," he moaned as he wound his hips into me. The pain quickly subsided, so I spread my legs wider. "Yes, fuck," he said referring to me opening my legs more. He savagely pounded me, making me call out to the high heavens.

"Oooh uuuh aaah," I cried as I exploded.

That didn't stop him, he kept beating it up, tearing my shit to shreds, and I knew it was because he hadn't had any in awhile. I was proud that he didn't step out, because that's when most niggas cheated. And because he'd been loyal like he'd promised, I took the beating like a champ... somewhat.

"Oh shit!" he hollered and twisted his sexy face. His dimples appeared as he bit his lip and continued to fuck the shit out of me. I'd cum so many times it was ridiculous.

"Mmm uuuh aaah uuuh!" I whimpered as I gripped his strong arms.

"Gigi, whose pussy is this?" he grunted and slowed down his strokes. He sucked on my neck, and wound his hips into me, hitting my spot.

"It's your pussy Kendrick."

He picked his head up and began slamming in, but pulling out slowly, making my legs tremble wildly and uncontrollably. He was nibbling on his lip, while staring straight into my eyes as he did it, and that shit was the business. He was too fucking fine.

"I love seeing yo' little ass take this dick," he growled as he pummeled me. I couldn't say anything as my unmanageable moans continued to come through. "Tell me again," he panted before starting to pulverize my pussy even more.

"I-it's y-your pussy Kendrick, and nobody else's," I whined and spread my legs wider again.

"Fuck, you know what to say," he growled and then rammed me a couple more times before shooting off inside of me.

He dropped down closer to me, kissing my lips and bear hugging me. He dropped his head to suck my nipples for a little bit, and then he finally rolled off of me breathing heavily. *My poor baby needed that*, I laughed to myself.

"Damn baby, shit," he said and covered his face, as his chest continued to rise and collapse violently.

My legs were still shaking as I scooted closer to him to cuddle. I could barely lay them together because they were quivering so. It was slightly embarrassing.

"Baby?" I said.

"Yeah?" he inquired.

"I didn't know you ate ass," I chuckled and so did he.

"Just yours shorty," he rubbed my back. I straddled him and then laid down on his chest to listen to his rapidly beating heart. "I love you Gianna," he said and caressed my hairline.

"I love you too, Kendrick."

TODAY KALEEINI WAS COMING home from the family's underground medical facility in Annapolis. I was so happy because I wanted to get home and sleep in our bed, together. The queen was comfy, but there was nothing like being in the comfort of your own home, or sleeping next to your nigga. I missed hearing him tell me I was taking all of the covers, or feeling his dick against my ass. I even missed the nights where I would put my ass against his crotch trying to get some, only to turn around and see he was for real knocked the fuck out.

"Ready?" I smiled up at my man and he nodded.

He was using crutches right now, but the doctor said he wouldn't need them for much longer. His ass was happy about that, because he said he hated to look like he needed help or anything. I hoped he was gonna actually let his body heal before he started running the streets with KJ, Kendrin, and Lenny.

We made it out to my new Porsche truck, and the doctor helped him get into the passenger side as I climbed into the driver's seat. I wished I had brought the car and not the truck, because my big ass stomach was in the fucking way, making this big shit hard to maneuver. If we died, we'd die together at least. Once we were locked and loaded, I pulled off so we could head back to Baltimore.

"Two more months, and then we will officially be mommy and daddy," he chuckled and looked out of the window.

"I know. Are you excited?" I asked.

"Yeah I'm excited, but I just have to make sure that I take extra steps to make sure you two are protected."

"I'm sure you will do a good job of that Kaleeini," I rubbed his hand. He took mine into his, and kissed the back of it.

"That also means that you have to make sure you listen to me when I tell you to do something." I sucked my teeth and he said, "See Aysia. I'm not fucking around with you shorty."

"I know Kaleeini. I'm gonna listen like a good little girlfriend," I rolled my eyes.

"Keep being sarcastic Aysia. You won't be talking all that shit when your ass gets kidnapped."

"You wouldn't let that happen to me."

"I'm actually thinking it'll be good for your smart mouth ass. You need someone to ruffle up them little ratchet feathers."

"Kaleeini!" I chuckled. "If someone kidnaps me, I'm just gonna give in."

"Give in?"

"Let them smash and then they will let me go," I said to fuck with him.

There was silence as I drove. I stared straight ahead out of the windshield, because I could feel his ass staring a hole through me. It was so hard not to laugh, as I pretended to be captivated by something on the road.

"I would murder yo' ass once I rescued you," he finally replied.

"I'm kidding daddy, I would fight until the end."

After about forty-five minutes, we made it to the house, and then I helped him out as best as I could. I couldn't do much because of my big belly though. We finally got into the house successfully, and then both sat down in the den. As soon as my butt hit the couch, I kicked my feet up and let him rub my tummy.

"What do you think it is?" I asked him as I looked down at my stomach.

"I'm hoping it's a boy, but I really have no idea. I wish we could know now, but someone is being difficult."

"I know me too, but I wanna be surprised. Whatever it is though, I'm gonna kiss its cheeks all day," I chuckled.

"If it's a boy don't be doing that shit. I don't want him growing up to be no bitch."

"I'm sure your mom kissed you a lot as a baby Kaleeini, and you're just fine."

"Nah, she didn't shorty. She knew what was up and let me do my thing."

"How the hell do you know?" I laughed.

"I just know," he grinned.

I stared into his green eyes as they sparkled, and then caressed his face. After a few moments I said, "I thought you were dead."

"I know, so did I when it happened. I just knew it was over for me. All that damn blood, and my body was on fucking fire."

"You're not scared to continue on?" I asked.

"Nah, I'm not, baby. That's part of this shit though. If you're scared to die it ain't for you. If a gun makes you flinch, you're in the wrong field as KJ would say," he gave me a half smile.

I didn't like what he was saying. He may have not been scared to die, but I was scared for him to die.

"I would've hated for you to go before I even had the baby," I started to tear up. He moved closer to me, although hard for him to, and then pulled me into him.

"I'm not gonna leave for a long time baby. I wasn't being careful, and that's why I ended up where I am. I should've known better than to be out with no vest or anything. We have some enemies coming for us from every damn where. I should've been smarter."

"Enemies trying to kill you?" I looked up into his face.

"I really don't know what the hell they're trying to do, but it doesn't matter because we Kings always win."

I stared down at the floor as I laid my head back on his chest. I heard what he was saying, but I was still scared. How could he be so sure that he was gonna win this time? Who were these people? Why couldn't he and I ever just be happy and relaxed? I had so many questions circling my mind.

"Why can't we have some peace?" I whispered.

"You can't have peace until you prove yourself time and time again shorty. Everybody has to do that in this game. Do you know how many enemies and shit my father and uncles had?"

"Really?" I picked my head up. Who would be stupid enough to come for them?

"Yeah really, but they kept going and kept winning until niggas just surrendered and bowed down. My cousins and I are doing the same thing. No matter who you are, you have to earn your stripes. People aren't just gonna respect us because we have the last name King. And honestly, I wanna earn respect on my own. I don't wanna ride my family's coattails."

"I know, I just wish we could fast forward," I giggled.

"I know, but don't worry about that shit Aysia. Just chill and enjoy life with me. I love you and I would never leave you. And I appreciate you loving me enough to wanna be with a nigga who lives like me. Most chicks only see my looks and what I could buy them, but they ain't really down for this shit. They're not willing to sit up in the hospital with me, annoying the fuck out of me all damn day. They just wanna spend my money, and brag about me being their nigga."

"I annoyed you?" I grinned.

"Yeah, you annoyed the shit out of me, but I loved it. People don't understand how hard it is to be with a nigga like my cousins and myself. You have to really love a nigga to be willing to spend nights alone, nurse niggas back to health, and possibly hold a nigga down during a jail bid."

"That's true. I would never leave you either. No matter what," I looked up into his face.

"And that's why you're my girl and nobody else. But, I would never put you in a situation where you had to hold me down for a ten year plus jail bid."

"Even if you did, I would."

"I know, that's why I love you Aysia. You love me for being simply Kaleeini, and not just because I'm a part of the Maryland King clan."

"Would you do the same for me?" I smiled.

"Umm, I never really thought about it, but sure, yeah. I'd hold you down if you went to jail," he laughed and furrowed his eyebrows.

"Good, because if I go to jail for killing one of these thirsty hoes that check for you, I'm gon' need you to have my back," I half joked.

I was serious though, because all during my pregnancy bitches were getting stupid with me, and I wasn't having it. My words alone weren't satisfying me anymore. As soon as this baby dropped, they'd better shape the fuck up, because I would be kicking asses and taking names faithfully. If you wanted a piece of Kaleeini, you'd better be ready to lose some teeth, limbs, and weave hair.

"I got you for any jail sentences as long as it don't involve me," he kissed my lips and then my belly.

"So if we argue and I stab you a little, you ain't gon' wait for me to get out of jail?" I sucked my teeth.

"What kind of stab though? I mean how the fuck do you stab someone a little?"

"Just a little one where you only have to get a little bit of stitches," I laughed when his face frowned up.

"Yo, why you always giving me these fucking scenarios shorty? First, you ask me about loving you at five hundred pounds, now you're asking about this shit. I feel like you're telling me ahead of time because you're gon' do all this shit."

"Maybe," I looked over at him mugging me. "I'm kidding baby. I promise not to stab you, and I promise to stay fine and sexy."

"Thank you." He closed his eyes and exhaled heavily. I got down onto the floor slowly, and then unzipped his pants. A cute smile crept across his face as I released his dick. "This is also why a nigga love you," he said as I took him into my mouth. He threw his head back as his chest heaved up and down and asked, "You gon' cook me some food after?"

"Mhm," I mumbled since my mouth was full.

It was hard being with a dope boy, but I would never leave his side.

"Fᴜᴄᴋ, ᴍᴍᴍ," I groaned as I stroked Willow from behind. Her pussy had been on some other shit for the past couple of weeks, and it had a nigga more addicted than before.

"Kendrin, that hurts," she whimpered when I sped up.

That was another thing happening lately, she was always complaining when I put her in certain positions. Willow was never a complainer, and always let me fuck her in any position I wanted, even when I took her virginity. I fucked the shit out of her when I popped that cherry, and although painful, she took that shit. That's one thing I loved about my shorty, she would take the dick even if she couldn't.

"Owww," she whined again.

I stopped, pulled out, and then put her on her back.

"Fuck is wrong with you huh?" I frowned and got down closer to her.

My dick almost got soft until I watched it go inside her. I was right back hard at the sight. I moved in and out of her slowly, and fondled her nipples in the process. Once I saw her getting into it, I began slamming into her until we both came. I fell to the side of her, and she grabbed my face to kiss me.

"What's wrong with you?" I asked.

"Nothing, you're just being too rough. I feel it in my stomach too much. It makes me feel sick after."

"Willow, I fuck you the same way all the time."

"No you don't. And I don't know, my pelvis be hurting when you fuck me doggy style," she pouted. "For the past weeks I've been feeling like I've got food poisoning after we have sex. My stomach feels sour. Stop going so deep."

"You need to go the fucking doctor or some shit, because in a minute I'm gon' put a paper bag over ya head and just bust my nut."

"Kendrin!" She held her mouth open and slapped my arm.

"I'm serious shorty, you're my wife, meaning I'm not gon' have any restrictions when fucking you."

"I know Ken, I just think it's stress because of the wedding. Speaking of the wedding, the lady making my dress sent the bill over."

"Oh yeah, how much?" I pursed my lips.

Her ass was always trying to pretend like she didn't know shit was gon' cost a lot, when she knew damn well it would. Nothing was too expensive for my baby though, so I wasn't tripping about paying top dollar. I will admit that I didn't know a wedding would cost this much. I just prayed that I didn't have any daughters, because like Willow, her nigga would be footing the fucking bill, not daddy.

"It's fifty grand."

"What? For what? You only gon' wear the shit for like fifteen minutes!"

"It has real diamonds on the top part, and it's hand sewn. It's vintage, yet new age. It's really cute Kendrin!" she whined.

"I got you," I scoffed.

I walked around the bed to kiss her lips, and then headed to the bathroom so I could get showered and ready for the day. Hopefully, it would be a good ass informative day.

I'd enlisted this cat named Swiss, to basically be a street informant. He was to mingle and shit with the street niggas, and bring back any information that would benefit my brothers and me. Currently I had him keeping his ear out so we could catch them Pablo and Chef niggas who robbed our trap on Garrison Avenue. Swiss hit me this morning saying that he had some information, so I wanted to get at that nigga.

I cleaned myself up, brushed my teeth, and then put on a Nike Crew neck with the matching joggers and slide-ins. After securing my hat on my head, I kissed my girl goodbye.

Pulling onto Lucille Avenue, I spotted Swiss chilling out in front of his crib. I parked a little ways down, and then secured my heat in my waist. I made it down the street and to him, and he nodded up when he saw me. He looked up and down the street a few times.

"Come inside," he pointed behind himself.

I looked around myself, and then followed him in. I sat down on his couch, and waited for him to get to talking. He better not be wasting my fucking time.

"So what's up my nigga?" I frowned.

"This." He slid a little ass baggie across his coffee table to me.

"Fuck is it?"

"That's y'all shit. I got it from this kid who was working on the corner of Baker and Mount. He told me he worked for Pablo and Chef, and even showed me the trap. I had a base head confirm for me that it was y'all shit."

Them niggas Pablo and Chef were making whatever they stole last. They'd still been selling it despite KJ stabbing up one of their own. We couldn't find them niggas for shit, but maybe having the trap location would help.

"You got the exact address?" I asked.

"Right here." He slid me a piece of paper and I smiled when I read the address. This was way more than what we had at the time. I pulled fifty out of my pocket and handed it to him. "Thanks man. Let me know if you need me to keep looking out."

"I still need you to keep looking out. I need you to do so until we catch these niggas," I explained and stood to my feet. "If this address is bullshit, that's your head Swiss."

"I wouldn't even play you like that Ken."

"I hope not."

I pocketed the piece of paper, then text my brother to meet me at my house, so we could get to work on these niggas. This was the longest that anyone had ever lasted against us, and I wasn't feeling that shit at all.

I WALKED INTO THE GYM, and snatched down the missing persons poster with Christian's picture on it. I trashed the shit and then walked into the area where my team was stretching. I was happy that nigga Christian got murked, because I was tired of his bitch ass. He had me thinking that Shannon had actually fucked with him, with the way he was acting. How do you get that possessive over a couple of text conversations? Having my cousin shot at all over a girl you've never even kissed? Who does that? I don't know, but I'm just happy that now I can focus on making it to the NBA and my woman.

"What's up man?" I greeted Tyriq.

We slapped hands as I placed my duffel bag down. I took a seat on the bench and exhaled heavily. I was not in the mood to workout; I wanted to take a fucking nap. Since it was the summer time, and Tyriq and I were being drafted, we only came to the practices to stay in shape. I didn't wanna be relaxing over the summer and be out of shape for my first season in the NBA.

"Nothing much, I think I chose a team though," he smiled and sat down on the bench with me.

"Word, who?"

"Charlotte Hornets."

I hadn't chosen a team yet, and damn had they been calling. I have some meetings coming up though, and I can't wait to see how much money they are offering. I also want to make sure I choose a place that is close to my home state, but that isn't looking too good. Why can't Maryland have a damn basketball team?

"That's dope man, I thought you would've chosen the 76'ers since you're from Philly," I said.

"Nah man, that's why I didn't choose that shit. I'm trying to be far away from my fucking home life."

"Even Tasha?"

"Especially fucking Tasha. I'm so tired of her ass, so any excuse I can get to be away from her, I'm using it. So Charlotte, here I come."

Tasha was Tyriq's baby mama, and he swore up and down that she trapped him. I didn't understand how she trapped him when he said he fucked raw. Niggas loved to say a bitch trapped them when they really meant, they just didn't want a baby with her in particular. I felt the same way about Rosalind when I thought she was having my baby, but to say she trapped me would've been a bit much. And shit, I never even raw dogged her ass. Tyriq's ass was just crazy as hell.

"Man, what about your shorty though?"

"I got him, I just ain't trying to deal with his fucking mama. What's up with yo' baby mama though, nigga?"

"I ain't got no damn baby mama, you know that."

"Nah, I know she lost it, but that don't mean she ain't your baby mama," he chuckled and I sucked my teeth.

"Man, that bitch was pregnant by someone else. Some bitch ass nigga named Pablo."

"Pablo? She got pregnant by a Mexican?" He bucked his eyes and we burst into laughter.

"Nah, homie was Black. I think that's his nickname or some shit. Anyway, that's her kid's father, not me. I can't say I'm not happy though. It feels good to know my kid didn't die," I said and he nodded.

I knew it sounded terrible to say, but it was a huge weight lifted off my shoulders knowing my cheating ways didn't kill a child of mine.

"I feel that. And Shannon's friends are still boo'd up?" He grinned.

"Yes, and by my damn cousins, so I ain't gon' help your ass out either."

"Oh yeah, one of them is fine as fuck, but she's real ghetto. She's light skinned, and be rocking them two long ass braids, shorts, and these little short ass tops that show her little sexy ass body. I usually like my women a bit thicker, but shorty's legs and stomach had my dick hard; and she's ghetto as fuck. I saw her dancing in her seat at a game once, popping her gum and shit. I like that. She was moving her body to "679" by Fetty Wap, and now every time I hear it I think of her. What's her name?"

"Why nigga?" I furrowed my brows.

"I just wanna know her fucking name shorty. She bad as fuck and I wanna put a name to her face."

"Willow man, and she's married to my cousin."

This nigga Tyriq was trying get served a two-piece and a biscuit from Kendrin. That nigga played no games when it came to Willow. It was hilarious that he tried to reprimand her for going ape shit on these hoes, when he was the exact same. If that nigga caught Tyriq eyeing her he would knock his ass out for sure. I could only imagine what he'd do if he knew this nigga was asking about her. Tyriq is lucky I fuck with him, and don't wanna see him sleep in the back of a club like Christian, because otherwise I'd tell.

"Oh alright, I was just asking. You ain't got to tell me that she married my nigga."

"Yeah I do, you'll get fucked up trying to fuck with Lo. You know my cousin ain't right in the head."

"Oh Kendrin? That is her nigga huh?"

"Yep," I nodded.

"His mama bad too," he cheesed. "I'll be that nigga's step daddy with no problems," he added and I couldn't help but join him in laughter.

"Nigga come on and let's shoot with yo' thirsty ass. Looking at my fucking aunt and shit," I said as we both continued to crack up.

"Aye nigga, yo' mama could get it, too. You know I like them feisty, *and* she speak Spanish. Next time I call the house I'm gon' spit some game."

I jumped at his crazy ass, and he flinched before we chuckled in unison.

After the workout I was tired as fuck. I was still kind of on edge every time I left practice because of what happened to Kaleeini. Hopefully, it would get better now that I knew Christian's ass was a goner.

I was tired of seeing his mom begging for help with finding his ass though. Sometimes I wanted to comment on the little posts and say, *That nigga dead, stfu.* Maybe if she paid that much attention to him before, he wouldn't have been all in my girl's grill and ending up dead with his bitch ass. Hoe ass nigga.

I made it home about fifteen minutes later, and Shannon came running out from the den with a smile on her face.

"What's up beautiful?" I pulled her close using one arm, and kissed her slowly and passionately.

"I told your parents I was gonna help you study tonight," she grinned.

"Studying this dick huh?" I whispered into her ear, and she nodded while biting her lip.

"Lets get started then," I said as I led her up the stairs.

I didn't have a game for three days, so I planned to fuck the shit out of her tonight. I just hoped my parents didn't walk in.

As soon as we made it to my room, I quietly closed the door behind us. We immediately began tearing one another's clothes off. I couldn't get her naked fast enough it seemed. Once we were both in our birthday suits, she pushed me down flat onto the bed.

"I like when you get aggressive," I nibbled on my bottom lip.

She just gave me a seductive smile, and then straddled me. Her expression turned serious when she reached the tip of my dick, and then she slowly moved down my rod. Being inside her was one of the greatest feelings next to winning my games.

"Kenzie," she purred as she moved her hips as if she was from the Caribbean.

Shannon was so sexy, from her smooth brown skin, sexy ass body, and full lips, to her long ass dark hair. My bitch was beyond bad.

"Fuck, shorty."

I reached up to squeeze her breasts, before sitting up to suck on them. She continued to bounce in my lap, as I sucked her nipples hungrily. Pinning her arms behind her back, I began kissing and licking her collarbone.

"Mmm uuuuh aaah," she whimpered. She stopped bouncing once she came, and began to roll her hips on me.

I unpinned her arms from being behind her, and then flipped her onto her back. Placing her legs onto my shoulders, I began ramming her, making her scream out.

"Fuuuuck!" I called out and released into her.

We both began panting heavily, and then I clenched my teeth together at how loud we were. She giggled and then cupped my face for a kiss.

"Pussy is too good to keep quiet," I grinned before sliding my tongue back into her mouth.

ONE WEEK LATER...

"Champagne ladies?" Eleanor, the associate at the dress shop offered my friends and I.

We weren't old enough to drink, but as much money as Kendrin was dropping, our age was the least of their worries.

"I can't because I'm breastfeeding," Gianna smiled and pointed to K-three.

He was so freaking cute, and had the fattest cheeks ever. It was so hard not to just kiss him constantly.

"Me either," Aysia rubbed her stomach.

"Can you just bring apple cider for everyone?" I asked and she nodded before sauntering away. She returned fairly quickly and then filled our glasses up.

"I will go get the reception dress Mrs. King, and be right back," she told me and I smiled.

"Oooh how does it feel to be called that?" Gianna asked. I knew her ass couldn't wait to be KJ's wife.

"It feels bomb as fuck. There was a time where I never thought I'd hear that shit," I sighed.

"What do you mean?" Shannon cocked her head.

"Y'all know that nigga was on some bullshit for the first half of the relationship; cheating, lying, doing dumb shit," I reminded them. I hated to think about it, but thank God it was a while ago.

"Yes, I remember your ass used to stay fucking crying over some new stuff. Kendrin stayed doing dirt, and then turning his phone off. I'm happy he changed for you though," Gianna nodded.

"You and me both. I used to want you to leave so bad, but I'm happy you didn't. I think you guys are perfect for each other," Aysia grinned.

Kendrin King was a piece of fucking work at the beginning, and I never thought he would become who he is today. I'd only caught him cheating once, but I knew there were plenty of other times just by the shit that he would do. There were multiple occasions where he told me he would be at home or doing something with his family when he really wasn't. Or, I would see girls texting his phone saying all kinds of shit, and sometimes I would just hear things. He swears he only cheated that one time when we first got together, but I beg to differ. All that shit was in the past though, and damn was it blissful now.

"Okay Mrs. King, it's ready for you."

Standing up, I set my glass of apple cider down. I went behind the little divider to put the dress on, and when I tried to zip it, it wouldn't go so easily.

"The fuck," I frowned. *I hoped this bitch didn't fuck up.*

Yeah, it was only my reception dress, but still it had to be right! I pulled it closed and then tried to zip it again. I finally got it to zip, but it was tight as hell. I couldn't dance in this shit! Rushing out, I pulled Eleanor to the side.

"It's really tight Eleanor."

"It's the same dress Mrs. King, I swear I didn't change anything honey," she responded as I walked to the mirror.

"It's so pretty Lo," Shannon beamed.

"Somebody has been eating their rice and cabbage though. You're getting thick," Gianna laughed along with Shannon and Aysia.

I wasn't in a laughing mood, because I needed this fucking dress to fit. I was confused as hell, because the last time I came it didn't fit like this.

"Eleanor, this is too tight I can't wear this," I huffed.

"Okay honey, let me just redo the measurements and we will adjust it."

I wanted to scream. Why had I gained so fucking much? I just wanted to cry right now. If this didn't fit, then neither would my wedding dress. That fifty thousand dollar wedding dress may not fit. I was gonna have to fast or some shit, or Kendrin would murder me.

"How long is it gonna take?" I asked as tears started to fall.

"What's wrong Lo?" Gianna walked over to me holding her baby.

"I'm fat."

"You are not fat Willow. You're too small to be fat if that makes sense. I'm fat!" Aysia chimed in.

"I wanna go home."

I turned on my heels and went behind the divider to change out of this snug ass dress. Once I was done, Eleanor took my measurements, and I had indeed gotten a bit bigger. It wasn't by much, but I was still very upset about it. My mood was all over the place, and I just wanted to ball up and cry myself to sleep.

I didn't feel like going to dinner with my friends, so I just dropped them off at home and then went to the house I shared with Kendrin. When I laid down, I saw my mother was calling. I knew she'd be asking about the fitting, and I didn't wanna talk. I didn't feel like repeating that I'd grown out of my dress somehow.

I laid there in the bed wondering why this was fucking happening to me. I wasn't eating anything that I hadn't been eating before, so how did I gain so much? I even stopped eating after eight just so I wouldn't gain weight, but somehow that must've hindered me.

As I pondered, Kendrin walked in with his beautiful ass. He smiled at me and then walked to the bed with his hands in his hoodie pocket. I sat up so that he could sit next to me and make me feel better. Kendrin always kept my self esteem high with his words. His actions in the past negated his kind words, but I still liked to hear them.

Leaning on his shoulder, I let out a huge sigh.

"What's wrong baby?" he asked.

"I'm fat Kendrin."

"What?" he chuckled. "Baby how are you fat?"

"I couldn't fit my reception dress anymore," I started to cry. "I zipped it up and it was so tight around my midsection that I couldn't bend over."

"So what Lo, that doesn't mean that you're fat. Your body looks the same to me baby. It's always been sexy and slim," he smiled and began to pull me into his lap.

"Excuse me," I pushed him away and rushed off to the bathroom.

I quickly lifted the toilet top and puked everything inside of me out. Once I was done damn near dying, I looked up at Kendrin who was standing in the doorway. We made eye contact, and he exhaled heavily. I breathed hard as my eyes began to tear up even more.

"Please tell me I'm just sick Kendrin," I cried and sniffled.

"I don't think so shorty," he squatted down to the floor to look into my eyes.

"We have to get married before I get bigger," I sobbed into his chest.

"It's only a month away Lo. You're not gonna change that much by then right?"

"I'm already gaining weight Kendrin!"

I stood up, still crying, and began to brush my teeth. Before I could even get a good brush in, I was puking again. Kendrin brought the trashcan up just in time for me to blow chunks.

After a couple minutes, I was able to brush my teeth, and then Kendrin ran me a bubble bath.

"Do you wanna get in?" I asked him.

"Nah shorty, I have to make some calls. But relax yourself."

I nodded my head and then he helped me undress. He left once I was naked, but made sure to kiss me beforehand. I slipped down into the tub, and just stared at the pretty porcelain walls of the shower.

I didn't know how to feel about being pregnant. I did not want to walk down the aisle with a huge stomach. I cringed at the thought of me looking like Shamu as I walked towards the alter.

I calmed myself down and then got clean, before entering back into the bedroom. Walking over to Kendrin, a smile spread across my face. He hugged my midsection and then kissed it a couple times.

"You're gonna be a daddy," I whispered.

"I know shorty," he nodded and then hugged my waist tightly.

I wished this happened *after* I walked down the aisle, but I was happy to have a baby with the man that I loved. I rubbed his head as he continued to hug me.

Summer was here and school was no longer in session. It was the middle of June, so the weather was really nice out. It wasn't too hot and it definitely wasn't cold; it was just right.

I was gonna go to the nail shop with my friends later, but, I wanted to get some Starbucks first. I'd been obsessed with their damn frappuccinos lately, so I'd been indulging more than usual. I knew they weren't good for me, but it was summertime and I just wanted to enjoy myself after such a trying semester.

As I stood in line, someone came behind me and began talking loudly. It wasn't really loud, just too loud for this quiet ass cafe. I looked to my left so that I could get a glimpse of who it was, and my eyes almost bulged out of my head when I saw it was thirsty ass Rosalind. Couldn't this bitch just fucking disappear?

"Look who it is," she smirked when she saw me. I turned back around to ignore her, because we had nothing to say to one another. "Oh you don't know me now?" she questioned. The girl standing with her was eyeing me as well.

"I never knew you," I said.

"Oh I think you did. Don't play dumb Shannon. You killed my

baby remember?" I blinked repeatedly to calm myself, and moved up in the line as it continued to get shorter. This bitch was trying me and she didn't want it with me right now. "Hello bitch are de-"

WHAM!

I punched her and she fell backwards, sliding across one of the unstable wooden tables inside Starbucks. Her friend punched me in the nose as repayment, and then she and I started going at it like two bitches on Jerry Springer.

As I was fucking her friend up, Rosalind jumped on my back and started beating me in the head and pulling my bun down. I tried to keep up my pace with her friend, but the constant blows that Rosalind delivered were taking me down. I ran backwards into a wall, causing Rosalind to groan in pain. I kept ramming the wall until she fell off of my back and slid to the floor.

Before I could recoup, her friend came for me again and took off on me. I heard sirens in the distance as I swung and punched on whomever came into view. Whenever I would swing on Rosalind, her friend would fight me from behind and vice versa. Even if I lost, I wanted someone to come out looking fucked up. You can't brag about jumping me if your homegirl is busted the fuck up.

"Break it up!" I heard a man yell, as Rosalind and I fought like wild banshees.

He yanked her friend from beating me in the head and back from behind, and then I was yanked as well.

"You stupid bitch!" Rosalind hollered as blood spilled from her nose.

Her hair was in complete disarray, and so were her clothes. Thank God I had on jeans and a t-shirt, because Rosalind and her friend's titties were all out. I even think I saw her homegirl's vagina.

The police officers pinned the three of us against the wall once we got outside. I was so fucking embarrassed right now. I hoped someone didn't record that shit.

"Who started the fight?" one officer asked the Starbucks barista.

"Her," she pointed directly to me.

He turned me around and slapped some cuffs on me before walking me to the car. Tears spilled from my eyes as my head throbbed and back ached. I could taste blood in my mouth, so I knew my lip was busted.

Rosalind's friend stuck her tongue out and flicked me off as I sat in the backseat of the police car. I just wanted to hop out and fight again, but I was in enough fucking trouble. How did I go from an innocent Starbucks trip, to being in the back of a fucking police car?

The police took me down to the station, where I was held for hours. I was only let go when my father came to get me. He was pissed that he had to get my car towed home from Starbucks, and that I was fighting in public. My whole fucking day was ruined, and to top it off I cracked my phone screen.

On the way home my dad and I said nothing, but when we got into the house he decided to speak up.

"Fighting over Kenzie, Shannon?" he frowned as we sat opposite of one another on the couches.

"No, I fought because she was disrespecting me," I wiped the loan tear traveling down my cheek.

"Shannon, baby I love you, but I just don't think this relationship with Kenzie is worth all the stuff you're going through. He's put you through a lot."

"No he has not!" I screamed through tears.

"Yeah, he has. First the baby with another girl, then you had to deal with the guilt of killing her child, and now this. Fighting in public and-"

"Goodnight Dad."

I didn't want to hear anymore, because a part of me felt like he was right. Lately, I'd been having to deal with so much shit because of Kenzie, and I was tired of it. I wanted to go back to the days where we didn't have drama every damn week; the days where I was sure about us.

I powered my phone off because it was getting blown up by my friends. I'm sure they were wondering why I missed the nail appointment, and frankly I didn't feel like explaining. I needed to rest my sore ass body, and think if being with Kenzie was even what I wanted anymore.

"DID I tell you how beautiful you are? And how fucking sexy your body is to me baby?" I asked Gianna as I planted kisses all over her naked body.

My son had done her some good, and I couldn't get enough of it. My shorty already had me addicted, but now, it was on some next level shit. I just may have been obsessed. It was okay though, because she was mine and that pussy had my name on it, and I'm not speaking figuratively.

"Yes, but I like hearing it," she smiled. I kissed between her legs and she let out a soft moan. "I think I'm too sore for another round KJ," she whispered and caressed my head.

I licked between the slit, and then leaned up a bit to kiss the tattoo of my name on the side of her pussy. I loved seeing my name there, especially when I was deep inside of her. I began kissing up her stomach until I made it to her full lips. I sucked them for a bit, and then rolled off of the bed. I wanted to fuck again, but I'd done so three times back to back, and she said she was sore. I wanted her to enjoy the shit and not just do it because I wanted it.

"Where are you going?" she quizzed.

"I have to go handle some business baby. Leave the covers off of you so I can look at you while I get my stuff together."

"What time will you be back? I want us to eat together," she said as she removed the covers from her body.

She bent one of her legs so that her foot was flat on the bed, giving me a good view of her center. She smirked when she saw me looking.

"I shouldn't be gone long at all," I smiled.

"I'm serious KJ, it's already 8pm."

"Gianna, I will be home by ten, is that okay? Huh? Huh?" I got in her face and she giggled before kissing my lips.

"Yes that's fine."

"Good. Daddy loves you shorty," I tucked my bottom lip in for a second before kissing her hungrily. She caressed the side of my face as we made love with our mouths.

"I love you too," she responded once I pulled away.

I took a quick little shower, brushed my teeth, and then got dressed. I text my brother, Lenny, and Kaleeini, so that they could meet me at the warehouse for a quick little roundtable.

Kendrin gave me that info on them niggas Pablo and Chef, so tonight the four of us were gonna rob the trap. I wanted to get the rest of my product back, but I also wanted to kidnap their workers and get more information. I didn't know where them niggas Pablo and Chef were hiding, but they were hiding out good. They were smart enough not to come and rob us again either, but dumb enough to actually wanna have a war with us.

I made it to the warehouse about thirty minutes later, and when I climbed out of my car I saw Lenny, Kendrin, and Kaleeini waiting. We greeted one another, and then walked inside. The four of us sat down at the huge table, and then I pulled out some blank pieces of paper and a marker.

"Aight look, we gon' pull up and park across the street, but a little ways down. Kendrin, you and me are gonna run up through the back, while Kaleeini, you come through the front. Lenny stay in the car because as soon as we come out we're gonna need you to drive off," I explained. "How many niggas did Swiss say worked there at this time?"

"Two," Kendrin responded.

"Aight cool. So Kendrin and Kaleeini, sack and clock them niggas while I grab up all the money and product. Let's try not to kill them before we can get them back here and pump them for information aight?" I said and everyone nodded saying they understood.

We walked out and all got into the black Chevy Suburban that I told Lenny to bring. On the way to the trap, we made sure we had everything we needed, ready and loaded. Lenny parked across the street and down a little ways as I'd directed him.

"Keep some heat in your lap Len," I said and he nodded while showing me he already had it out.

The three of us climbed up out of the car, and once we neared the trap, we realized them niggas were sitting in the living room with the door wide open. *Amateur ass muthafuckas*, I thought. I couldn't really blame them though. With Pablo and Chef as their bosses, it was a case of the blind leading the stupid.

I pointed towards the front for Kaleeini, and then my brother and I ran down around the back. We jimmied open the backdoor, and walked in as if we had a damn key. Once Kendrin got into the living room, Kaleeini walked in and shut the front door. Upon hearing the door slam, both dudes woke up and shot up off the couch, still a little dazed from their slumber.

Kaleeini and Kendrin immediately sacked and clocked them, then began carrying them out. That was like taking candy from a fucking baby.

"Where the fuck is this shit?" I asked myself as I searched around.

The heater looked a little funny, so I yanked on it until it fell forward. I smiled when I spotted all the days earnings, and some product which I assumed was mine. I snatched all that shit out, and then dipped and booked it across the street. The ride to the warehouse was quiet, and once we made it, we dragged them niggas up out. Lenny and Kendrin doused them with water a couple times, and finally they came to.

"KJ," one whispered.

"Oh you know me?" I asked and he nodded.

"You work for Pablo and Chef?" Kendrin double-checked and they both nodded.

"Where these niggas be at?" I questioned.

"I don't know man. They always meet us at different locations to supply us."

"So you don't know shit?" Kaleeini frowned.

"All I know is that they don't fuck with y'all because of some bitch named Rosalind. Her baby daddy was Pablo, and the baby died because of y'all cousin," the other one explained. I was so confused right now.

"Wait what? What the fuck are you talking about?" I grimaced. What kind of game were these niggas playing?

"That's the nigga I must've seen with Rosalind that day," Kendrin scoffed.

"So you've seen his ass before?" I grinned and Kendrin nodded.

"Well at least we got a face. But since y'all can't supply shit, deuces."

POP! POP!

AFTER EATING DINNER WITH GIANNA, I watched her put our son to sleep. Once he was out like a light, she handed him to me so I could put him in his crib. I never saw myself being a damn daddy at this age, but I wouldn't trade that shit for anything. I turned on the little crib mobile, and watched it light up and spin over him as he slept. Taking Gianna's hand in mine, we walked to our bedroom.

She turned the lights down low, and then removed her long silk robe to expose her naked body. I lit up a blunt as I watched her walk to me, looking like an angel or some shit. She straddled my lap, and I smiled before turning my face to blow the smoke out.

"Even in the dark I can see how beautiful you are shorty," I said as I ran my pointing finger over her body.

"And even in the dark I can see how fine you are."

I took another pull, and then ashed the blunt as I blew out the smoke. I turned on the miniature fan I had next to my side of the bed, and moved it around in between Gianna and I, to blow the smoke away. Once I'd cleared it out, I cut it off.

"You just like looking at me," she smiled and threw her long hair to the other side.

"I do. I always have. Your body is so amazing me to me, inside and out. To think you've just given me a baby, and you already look the same as you did before, just with a few additions that only complement you, is crazy."

"I'm glad you like what you see."

"I'm in love with what I see shorty," I spoke honestly.

She half smiled and pushed her long hair to the other side while blushing. I leaned up to kiss between her small breasts, and then sat back to continue to admire her nakedness.

"How did your parents meet?"

"What?" I chuckled and gripped her waist to kiss on her neck.

"How did your mom and dad meet? I wanna compare to ours," she nudged me back.

I leaned back against the headboard, but kept my hands on her small waist. I saw she'd gotten her belly ring re-done, so I moved it around a little bit before speaking.

"I'm pretty sure it was like a party or something," I squinted my eyes as I tried to remember. "Oh, yeah it was a party. It was my mom's *current* boyfriend's birthday party," I said and we both chuckled.

"Really? I knew this would be juicy."

"Yeah, and she was leaving the party because she was mad at her boyfriend about something. And as she was walking out, my dad saw her and pulled her arm. Five months later I was conceived," I smiled.

"Dang five months? Now I don't feel so bad about us getting pregnant fast."

"You shouldn't feel bad about it regardless. So what, we weren't together that long before you got pregnant. We were in love long before we got together, that counts for something. But babies are what come about when two people who love each other as much as we do, spend a lot of time together."

"Like your parents."

"Exactly."

"You're so smart Kendrick," she whispered as we intertwined our fingers. "I love you."

"I love you too, Gianna."

I was sitting down on the couch when my phone rang. I looked down at it to see it was KJ calling from a Montana number, so I immediately answered. I was hoping it had something to do with us robbing that fucking trap. I was tired of them niggas and I was anxious to get rid of them. It was bothering the fuck out of me that they were still breathing. This shit was not a good look.

"What's up?" I answered.

"Aye I'm outside your crib, come take a ride with me."

"Do I need heat?"

"When don't you need heat?" he countered before disconnecting.

I stood up and then jogged upstairs to put on my shoes. Aysia was sleeping in the bed, since I guess she'd finally found a comfortable spot. These days it was hard for her to find a good spot to sleep in, so I was happy to see her enjoying a tranquil slumber. I kissed her forehead and then her belly before leaving the room.

It was around 9pm, and I was really wondering what the hell KJ had up his sleeve at this time of night. He was so damn unpredictable, so you really never knew what the fuck this nigga was on. I didn't put shit past his crazy ass.

I went down to my basement and grabbed a gun, some gloves,

and towels just in case, before walking outside. I spotted KJ's Cutlass and smirked before jogging to it. We were about to kill somebody, because he always drove this car when we went on murdering sprees.

"What's good?" I dapped him up once I got into the car.

"So the nigga Chef is over at the trap right now talking big shit. He's hot that we got the product and killed his boys, so he's been barking and running his mouth for the last forty minutes. So why not go over there and answer any questions he may have," he flashed an evil grin.

"Fasho, but how do you know this?" I asked.

"Swiss told Kendrin that the nigga was over there threatening our lives and shit, so I wanna see what's up with him. Willow is sick as fuck tonight, and he was scared to leave her if you're wondering why he's not here."

"Nah, I knew it must've been a legit reason for him not wanting in on this right here."

"Yep, you ready?"

I nodded as he pulled from the curb, and headed towards the trap that we'd just robbed last night. Once we made it, KJ parked in the same spot that Lenny had parked in the night before. We could see from where we were, that someone was pacing on the porch and shit. What was this nigga's purpose for standing on the porch bumping his gums?

"I know this nigga is strapped, so how are we gonna do this?" I quizzed.

I didn't wanna run up on him and get shot, and then we couldn't just kill him because we needed him to disclose the whereabouts of this Pablo nigga, and anyone else he was working with. Getting shot again was not in the plans for me. I had a bulletproof vest, but my head was still an open target.

"I know. I'm wondering if he knows what we look like," KJ said as he stared out the window at him.

"Probably you for sure, but maybe not me."

"Yeah right, nigga. If they know me, they know yo' ass," he chuck-led. "Aye stop him," KJ pointed to a nigga stumbling by.

I rolled down the window and waved him over. He looked around for a couple seconds even though I was right in front of his ass. Finally, he approached the car, and smiled showing the three teeth he had left in his mouth. He smelled like he'd just climbed out of a sewer, and it was taking everything inside of me not to throw up on his ass. I leaned my seat back as far as it would go, and let KJ converse with his funky ass.

"Aye man, you need a hit?" KJ asked him.

"Yeah, mhm, yeah, yeah," he nodded repeatedly, and then scratched his scruffy beard.

"Aight, I just need you to go over there and talk to that nigga on the porch for a bit. You know, keep him occupied. You do that and I got you."

"Cool," the addict nodded.

Once he backed away, I inhaled sharply, causing KJ to laugh.

"Nigga were you holding your breath?"

"Hell yeah I was. Funky ass nigga," I frowned and rolled the window up.

We watched the addict near the trap, and then soon after, he and Chef started talking. KJ waved for me to come on, so we both exited the car and ran across the street. We made sure to stay close to the houses so that we wouldn't be illuminated by the streetlights. Moving quietly and quickly, we finally got close to the trap.

"Aye man, get yo' ass out of here! I don' told you I ain't got shit! I ain't got shit because niggas wanna fuck with me!" Chef hollered out loud into the streets, punching his chest like a fool.

I guess he wanted people to think he was some monster. He just looked like a fucking buffoon to me. I don't even know where he and this nigga came from. It's like they robbed our trap, and then all of sudden they so called had beef with us that we never fucking knew about. And over Rosalind? These niggas were reaching like a muthafucka. I refused to let them ride the wave using our name. There was no beef; they were just some hating ass niggas.

PHEW!

KJ shot Chef in the leg, and then he and I blended into the darkness of the neighboring house. Chef dropped to the floor shouting, and the addict got the fuck out of there quickly as hell. I laughed to myself at how fast that nigga dipped, completely forgetting about the drugs KJ promised him.

Chef got to his feet using the banister, and then fired in our direction. But since he couldn't see us, his ass missed something terrible. As he looked around with his gun at his side, groaning in pain every now and then, KJ popped his ass again. It was so funny how he had no idea who was hitting his stupid ass. KJ and I snickered lightly even though we didn't want to.

"Ahhhhhh!" he hollered. The gun was silenced, so nothing was heard but his wails and screams.

As porch lights started to come on, KJ and I booked it around the back of the house, and came in through the already broken back door. He and I discreetly pulled Chef into the house as he screamed like a bitch. He'd dropped his heat on the porch while trying to apply pressure to his wounds, so it was perfect.

"Y'all got me fucked up!" Chef yelled.

WHAM!

KJ bitch slapped his ass with his gun, busting his lip and nose.

"I'm tired of hearing your voice nigga, it's my turn to fucking talk. If you scream or howl one more got damn time, I'm gon' shoot your fucking balls off bitch," KJ gritted.

"Where is ya' boy Pablo?" I asked.

"Man fuck y'all! I ain't giving up my boy," he looked us up and down like we were fucking nuts. KJ suddenly started whooping his ass, making him holler loudly. "I ain't giving up my boy," he cried hysterically.

KJ stood over him panting angrily as fuck.

"I can't even be mad at you for showing loyalty to your homie. You still a bitch though," KJ said before he blew his head open.

We rushed back out the backdoor, and made sure no one was outside before we rushed across the street to the Cutlass. Once inside, we removed our gloves and cloth shoe covers.

It's crazy how people heard Chef screaming, but no one called the police or anything. I swear I loved my city, because snitching was rare. You'd have a better chance at winning the lottery than getting someone to snitch.

"So what the fuck we gon' do?" I asked KJ as we drove back to my crib.

"Hopefully we're getting closer. Robbing the trap got us closer than we were, because we were able to off one of them niggas."

"True. Maybe since we killed his boy, he will come out and try to retaliate."

"That's what I'm hoping. I just don't know who else they're conspiring with."

"Oscar ain't got shit?"

"He told me it's just them two, but something is telling me that ain't true. Since when do muthafuckas only rock as a duo?" He raised a brow as he pulled onto my street. "But hey if it is just two, I won't complain."

"You right. But I ain't tripping, we gon' get them niggas."

"Oh, I know we are. When was the last time a King man took a loss?"

A COUPLE DAYS LATER...

SHIT WAS NOT GOING as planned at all. I spent months planning all of this shit out, and building a fucking team, just for all of the shit to fall through. All of the little niggas I put on to work for me, chickened the fuck out when they found out the King boys were looking to kill any and every muthafucka working for Chef and me. And the only guys who had balls big enough to stick by us, got murdered recently when the Kings robbed our damn trap.

After stealing their product from the trap in Park Heights, Chef and I were doing pretty good. We were making a nice amount of bread, despite the streets still being dominated by the Kings. What worked in our favor was that no one knew where the hell our trap was, because they never saw Chef and me visiting it. And to protect ourselves, we never let the niggas under us know where we laid our heads at or nothing. I was happy about that because I'm sure the niggas who recently got caught would've told.

Anyway, everything was running smoothly until somehow them niggas found out the location of the only damn trap we had. They took their shit back and now there was no way for me to get money. I tried finding a connect, but I have no damn history in the game, so no one is willing to take a chance on me. It's almost like trying to get that first job, but every damn interviewer wants you to have experience. How the hell am I gonna get some fucking experience if I can't get that first chance?

I thought when I initiated the beef between the King boys and me, that would get me some sort of boost, but they were taking me out before I could even get to that point. They hadn't given me a chance to make my name ring bells, and that shit was pissing me off. The only niggas who knew me, were the little niggas in certain areas. I wasn't hood famous like the Kings. Shit fuck hood famous, everyone in Maryland knew them.

As for Rosalind, I had to cut that bitch off after I gave her some bread, because I heard she was trying to get back into Kenzie's good graces. I knew as soon as he took that hoe back, she would be spilling all the information to him, so it was best I ceased contact now before I made any more moves. Snake ass bitch for ya' man.

"So what you got for me?" this dude name Buzz asked.

He was a young cat that I met while locked up. I don't know how we ended up in the same jail since he was from New Jersey, but we did. Anyway, he knew nothing of the legacy of the King brothers, so he was willing to partner up with me now that Chef was dead. It felt good to have someone who was unaware of what we were up against, because that meant they wouldn't run.

"We need a supplier," I shook my head.

"I know these cats who are coming down here soon. They're about to claim the whole city, and they offered for me to get on."

"Fuck that gotta do with me? And who are these niggas?"

"Duck and Lucky. They're twin brothers and they run shit up in Camden. I told them I knew someone who was planning to take down the Kings, and they said they were about to do the same thing, and that if we banded together it'd be a piece of cake."

"Do they have a supplier?" I inquired. These twins had definitely piqued my interest.

"Not anymore. They stopped fucking with the one they have, and are looking to get a new one."

"See that's where I'm at, so we're in the same fucking boat," I scoffed.

"That's where you're wrong. Duck and Lucky have made a name for themselves in the drug game. Them obtaining a connect is far easier than you obtaining one."

"That makes sense. I'm really liking the sound of this," I nodded with a smirk.

"I mean, you said the Kings are some bitches, and I know for a fact Duck and Lucky aren't anything to mess with. They could take the Kings out alone, so just imagine if we were to help them," he raised a brow.

"We'd have the city in our hands in no time. But do you think they'd share the wealth? Or we'd just be some pawns."

"Duck and Lucky would still reign supreme, but we would be working right beside them, calling a couple shots too."

See I didn't have a problem working for some niggas at all. I didn't need to be king. Being able to make a lot of money was my only concern. I would've gladly worked for KJ and his team, but that nigga acted like I wasn't good enough to rock with him. He made a big mistake though, because now he had all of us coming for him.

These Duck and Lucky guys sounded like they weren't anything nice, and with Buzz's and my help, the Kings would be dethroned in no time.

"When are they coming?" I asked Buzz as I cracked open a beer.

I was currently staying in a condo in Ellwood Park. It wasn't too nice, but it wasn't bad either. I hadn't left to do so much as get some food. I wasn't stupid, I knew them King niggas had muthafuckas itching to drop me.

"They wouldn't tell me. They wanna pop up on them Kings and catch them off guard. Duck said he would hit me when he got here."

"Cool. We need a fucking team. I can't recruit for shit."

"We can recruit on the strength of Duck and Lucky, the same

way we can get a supplier. Let's just explain to them that Duck and Lucky are the Camden version of the Kings."

"Just better."

"Exactly."

My mood had improved knowing that I was on my way to being back on top. I just wished my boy Chef was still here to see me conquer Baltimore. It's cool though, because them Kings would suffer greatly for killing my boy

I was ready to get my body back together, namely my little two pack, so I was going to the gym today. As much as my man complimented my body, I almost wasn't gonna go. But I missed my abs; I wasn't a simple flat stomach type of girl. I didn't want a six-pack or anything, just the two at the top to keep it feminine.

I wanted to go with Shannon, but she claimed she was too busy. I don't know what the hell she could be busy with since school wasn't in session, but I wasn't one to pressure someone into hanging out with me. She'd been busy like this for the past couple of days though. I would've been offended slightly, but she was telling Willow and Aysia the same thing. In my gut I felt something was going on, and wanted to have KJ ask Kenzie, but I knew he wouldn't do it. The guys hated when we pried into each other's personal lives. We couldn't help it though; we were best friends.

I put my shit up in the locker, and then plugged my headphones into my phone to listen to music. I decided to start with some cardio like I always did, so I climbed onto an elliptical. I hadn't been on this thing in forever, so after ten minutes I was already sweating. I refused to bow out now though.

As I was listening to music and getting my work out on, this guy came switching down and got on the one next to me. He was the gayest guy I'd ever seen. He was more feminine than me even. He had on long ass acrylic nails like me, and tight ass pants with a sports bra like me too. He looked over at me so I looked away and up at the TV, slightly embarrassed. I remembered my mom said when she moved here from Florence at nineteen, she was staring at a gay guy in a burger spot. And when he caught her, he cursed her out so bad that she just left. *My poor foreign mother*, I chuckled at the thought. Me and this boy would go at it if he tried me though.

I forgot all about him as I began really getting into my workout. It was kind of hard to pay attention and stay focused however, because I kept thinking about my baby. I knew he was home with KJ, but I missed him already. He was just so cute and always doing new things that I didn't wanna miss. I was for sure gonna look into some workout classes that I could bring him with me to. As I shook my head at myself, I felt someone tap me. I looked over and it was the gay guy.

"Yes?" I pulled one of my earphones out.

"I don't mean to bother you girl, but where did you get those shoes?"

"I got them online from the Nike website," I smiled.

"When? I went on there and they were sold the fuck out," he frowned and put his hand on his nonexistent hip.

"Oh, umm, I got them the first day they came out that's why. It was a couple weeks ago."

"I don't keep up with all that type of stuff girl, it's too time consuming."

"Well I'm really into fashion. I style people so it's kind of my job to stay up on the latest releases and stuff."

"Who do you style currently?" He stopped his machine. *Dude, I just wanna workout.*

"Well I do freelance. I don't have any set clients yet. People book me for their photoshoots, so right now I've mainly been helping indie artists and up and coming clothing lines."

"Oh really? My friend is looking for a stylist."

"Really?"

"Yes girl, and the job pays very well. I can give you the card and you could call about interviewing."

"Wow, umm, I don't know. I just had a baby and I can't get too busy ya know."

"Damn girl you got that snapback. Your body is tight. But umm, you not with the baby daddy?" he asked and put his acrylic between his teeth.

"Yes, I'm engaged to the father. But I just don't wanna leave my baby alone a lot ya' know?"

"Not really, maybe it's because I don't really have motherly instincts yet," he chuckled and so did I.

"Maybe so. But yes, I don't wanna leave my baby too much, so I have to choose a job carefully."

"Well still call, and say Sunshine recommended you. And hey, you never know, this could really get you where you wanna go. And like I said, the money is good. You'd be styling celebrity clients."

That piqued my interest, because I knew that would look good on my resume. Plus I would be making a nice amount of change. I was tired of bumming off of KJ, and I just wanted to have my own money. I mean I made a couple hundred bucks from styling jobs, but it wasn't anywhere near what I could be making.

"Thanks," I said once he handed me the card out of his sports bra.

"Welcome boo. Good luck."

I put my earphone back in and continued working out. Once I'd done an hour on the elliptical, I went to do some abs and leg workouts as well. I was done two hours later, and immediately rushed home to see my baby. I hoped KJ didn't have him on the floor or something, because I would strangle his sexy ass.

Once I got home, I ran up the stairs and looked in K-Three's crib. When I didn't see him, I rushed to the bedroom. No one was in there, so I frantically ran downstairs, through the foyer, and to the den. When I walked into the den, I smiled. KJ was knocked out on the couch, and K-Three was asleep in his lap. KJ was wearing a grey jogger suit, and K-Three had on a grey thermal material onesie, making them look like little twins. KJ's big tattooed hand was covering K-Three's little belly, holding him in place. He'd recently gotten my name tatted on the side of his hand.

I took my phone out to take some photos, and then took my baby out of KJ's lap. It was so cute to see his rugged ass on daddy duty. You would never know he did the shit that he did.

I took my baby upstairs, and put him in his crib before taking a shower. While washing off, my mind wandered to Sunshine from the gym. He really had me thinking about calling his friend. That would be a dream job styling celebrities, but I didn't want it taking time from me being a mom, because that was more important to me. I finished cleaning myself, and when I got into the bedroom, I grabbed the card off the dresser to make the call. I really wanted this and needed this.

I'D JUST DROPPED K-Three off at his paternal grandparent's home, and since I was alone and had nothing to do, I decided to bring some food to my baby down at Kingin'. I knew he'd be hungry around this time, so I chose to surprise him.

It was the middle of a weekday, around 4pm, so it wouldn't be crowded really. The only people who would be there at this time, were the people who just got off work and wanted to chill at the bar and drink. The strippers didn't come until 9pm, and the club portion was only open Thursdays to Sundays, so that's pretty much all they could do at 4pm on a Tuesday.

I parked my G-Wagon in the back parking lot, and then climbed out. I was wearing distressed jean shorts that showed my new slightly thicker thighs, an off the shoulder crop top exposing my flat stomach, and two-piece sandal stilettos revealing my fresh pedicure. My long brownish-red hair was hanging down, since I'd just gotten it done at KJ's mom's shop.

I strutted through the parking lot with my Chanel bag hanging from my forearm, and my engagement ring blinding everybody on the way. KJ's food dangled from my hand in a nice little paper bag, folded perfectly at the top. Ignoring the niggas trying to holla at me, I stopped at the entrance to wait for that same short and stout doorman from last time to let me by.

"Gigi," he nodded and moved out the way to let me in.

I walked straight to the back, and went up the stairs so that I could get to KJ's office. I made it up the stairs, and then sashayed down the hallway until I got to the door with his name on it. I knocked lightly, and then twisted the knob to enter. When I walked in, I saw that Diana girl sitting on the edge of KJ's desk laughing.

"Hello," I said with a *whole* bunch of attitude.

"Baby," KJ stood up. "You look good," he said and then came from around his desk. "Too good," he grinned and leaned down to kiss me.

I walked around him and then dropped my bag and his lunch onto the couch.

"Hi Gigi," Diana smiled. I folded my arms and chuckled at her fake ass after sitting down. She was saying hi to me as if she wouldn't fuck KJ behind my back if he wanted.

"Diana, I know you've fucked my man a long ass time ago, but sweetie don't make it so obvious that you still want to. It's not very becoming of you," I cocked my head.

"No, I don't wanna have sex with KJ, we were-"

"Save the Snow White innocent tone for someone who has time for it. This is like the third time that I've come here and seen you in his office. Ain't shit you need to talk to him about, especially not while sitting on the edge of his desk, laughing like a fuckin' hyena. I was pregnant those last times Diana, but I'm not anymore. Keep fucking with me. If I come here one more time and I see you around, by, or in this office, I'm gonna beat your ass." I then turned my attention to KJ. "And I will stab you."

Diana looked from me to KJ, and then stood to her feet to smooth her skirt down. She quickly rushed out, and KJ just closed the door behind her.

"I swear I haven't touched her Gigi. I haven't been with anybody else since the first time we had sex."

"I know, you're not crazy," I smiled and stood to my feet.

"But you are," he grinned and pulled me close.

"Just about you. And I'm serious KJ, I'm gonna whoop her ass."

I was hella fucking serious. That bitch was gonna get flung around this whole damn room if I caught her in here again. I don't know what the hell she was trying to do, but I was crazy about KJ and didn't mind proving it to a few.

"I know, I'm gonna make sure she doesn't come in here, even though I think today was the last time she'll try to."

"Good. I brought you some barbecue. I know you're hungry."

"I am, but for something else."

"KJ no," I giggled as he pushed me to the desk.

He quickly began unbuttoning my jean shorts, and then pulled them down along with my G-string. Spreading my legs open, he began feasting on my center. As I was getting some of the best head ever, I spotted Diana walking by. I could see her bun through the little rectangular window at the top of the door. When she heard me moaning, she stopped right in front of it.

"Kendrick, I love when you eat it," I whimpered extra loudly just for her eavesdropping ass.

After KJ made me cum super hard with his tongue, I cleaned myself in the bathroom within his office, as he brushed and rinsed his mouth. He then washed his face, while I washed my hands, before we both walked back out into his office.

"What time will you be home?" I asked as he sat at his desk and began to eat.

"Like nine."

"Don't make me wait too long," I winked and he cheesed with his cute self. I jogged back over to him and kissed his lips before leaving.

I saw Diana collecting some empty glasses from one of the tables, so I walked over to her.

WHAM!

After tapping her on the shoulder, I punched the shit out of her. She stumbled back, and then fell on her ass.

"I said to not even come around his office," I gritted as I towered over her, before heading towards the exit. The short stout bouncer stared at me with his mouth open, as I gave him a finger wave.

Halfway home, my phone buzzed with a text message from KJ.

Daddy: *You wild shorty. I love you.*

I just smiled and locked my phone. I wasn't fucking around with *that* bitch, or any other bitch.

I WANTED to make a nice little dinner for Kaleeini, because lately I'd been too tired to cook. I was so fat and I just felt like a fucking whale. I didn't even like having sex anymore, because I just felt huge the whole time. I just wanted to put the covers over my top half and let him do his thing with the bottom. Kaleeini claimed he didn't care, but I did, a lot. I couldn't wait to get this baby out of me and go back to getting dicked down every single fucking night. The spooning position was getting old, and I felt like Kaleeini had to do all the work while I just laid there getting off.

I walked down the aisle looking for rice, and when I spotted it I rolled my eyes. It was on the lowest fucking shelf it could be on. I took a deep breath and just stared at it, wondering what the hell I was gonna do. There was no way I was squatting down to this fucking floor, because I was sure I wouldn't be able to get back up. I saw a girl who worked there rushing by, but when I called out for her she'd already passed me.

"Fuck!" I grunted.

I felt tears coming up, so I threw my head back to hopefully stop them. For the past month, everything had been making me cry. Mostly when shit didn't go my way.

"Did you need help with something?" a guy asked me.

"Umm, no not really."

"You sure?" he smiled.

He had an innocent aura, and seemed like a nice guy, so I decided to get his help. It seemed genuine and not like he was trying to get at me. And yes, plenty of men still tried to get my number even though my belly was big as hell. Especially when they were looking at me from behind, because they couldn't tell I was pregnant that way. You should see their faces when I turn around though.

"If you don't mind, could you get me two bags of rice from down there," I pointed.

"Uh, yeah sure."

He squatted down, pointed to one of the brands to make sure it was the one I wanted, and once I gave him the okay, he picked up two of them. He placed them into the basket, and then smiled at me.

"Thank you." I started to push my basket but he stopped me.

"Tamal."

"Nice to meet you Tamal, Aysia." I shook his hand.

"So are you originally from Baltimore?" he asked.

"Born and raised. I can tell you're not though."

"Oh yeah, how?" He folded his arms.

"Because you haven't called me shorty yet." We both laughed.

"Well you're right. I'm actually from Oklahoma."

He was in for a rude awakening here in Baltimore. I wondered why the hell he came all the way over here from Oklahoma.

"Wow, what are you doing over here?" I questioned.

"I found a really great job over here, so I decided to move. It's not like I had a family or anything to keep me there."

"I see."

"But since you're from here, maybe you could show me around or something, and help me get to know this beautiful place."

"Umm, no probably not. I'm not in the condition to do much showing around." I palmed my belly.

"Right, I somehow forgot about that."

"How? I'm so big!" I chuckled.

"Nah, you actually look nothing like the pregnant women on TV. You're way smaller and you look great, Aysia." He stared into my eyes and licked his lips.

"Well it was nice meeting you Tamal, I hope you enjoy Baltimore. It's a really nice place."

"Yeah ,I love the historical look of it. Hey maybe I can just get your number, and then if I need a quick answer to something about the town, I can hit you up."

"Tamal I have a boyfriend. I'm having his baby as you can see, so it's pretty serious."

"I didn't even mean it like that. I meant like as a friend you know? I wouldn't try to date someone who is pregnant anyway."

"I see."

"Not like that, but you know what I mean. I ain't gonna try nothing with you, I just want someone who can help me out and knows Baltimore."

"Yeah. Look, like I said, I have a boyfriend and I can't text other guys no matter what's it regarding."

"Oh, the controlling type."

"No, he's not the controlling type, he just doesn't play. And honestly I don't even wanna text you."

I didn't mean for it to come out that way, but it was true. I wasn't itching to text his ass, so why ruffle Kaleeini's feathers by doing so?

"Damn, well okay. Have a good day." He turned around and left the aisle.

I kind of felt bad because he appeared to have no malicious intent. But still, the fact remains that my boyfriend is a tall ass crazy nigga with dreads and muscles, who shoots guns on the regular with his sexy ass. I'm clearly getting off topic. However, in a way, I saved Tamal's life. Now that I think about it, his ass probably wasn't genuine.

I didn't know what the fuck he was thinking, like I was actually gonna fall for that tour guide shit. Negro please. Plus, why are you even interested in me when clearly I'm pregnant, talking about he forgot. Boy bye! Then again he looked so harmless. Yeah, these days I couldn't make up my mind for shit as you can see. This baby had changed me in more ways than one.

I finished my grocery shopping, and thankfully I didn't run into that nigga again. As soon as I got home I started preparing dinner for my love. I pulled out all of the stops, making chicken, rice, yams, greens, cornbread, and pie. He was gonna be so happy to see that my ass had finally gotten enough energy to cook for him.

I looked at the clock, which read 9pm, and I knew he'd be home soon, so I made the plates. I sat down at the table and waited, and waited, and waited. I got too hungry so I just began eating my own fucking food without him. When I finished he still wasn't here, so I text him. After waiting a whole fucking hour, I still got no response. I was pissed to say the least.

I snatched up our plates from the table, and then went to clean them before going to bed. It took so much for me not to cry. I was angry and sad, so a lot of tears were waiting to fall. Kaleeini always texted me back, so my mind was conjuring up all kinds of scenarios regarding his whereabouts. Was he fucking another girl? I bet he was, he was sick of me. I needed to get in the gym as soon as this baby was out. If he was out fucking another girl, I was gonna kill him.

I heard him walk in the house, even though it was huge, and when I looked at the clock it read 2am. I threw the covers off of me and stood to my feet, waiting for him to enter the bedroom. *I should've brought my knife to bed with me.*

"Baby what are you doing up?" he asked once he entered the bedroom.

"I cooked for you."

"Oh word. Where is it?"

"I threw it out." I began to tear up.

"Aysia, why are you crying?"

"Where have you been?"

"I've been working, like always. Where else would I be? With another female?" He raised a brow and then sat down.

"You probably were!"

"Is that what you honestly think?"

"No."

"Then stop talking out of your ass. When I come home late it's because I'm working and you know that. Stop sitting at home making shit up in your fucking head Aysia."

"You need to at least text me back Kaleeini." I climbed back into the bed. Once he finished undressing he joined me.

"I'm sorry I didn't text you back. I forgot how sensitive you are right now."

"No, I'm not sensitive. Stop saying that."

"Then why are you pouting and crying and shit for no reason?"

"Because I didn't know what you were doing."

"Don't worry about what I'm doing Aysia, just know that I ain't doing it to nobody else but you." He kissed my shoulder.

"You swear on your dick?"

"On my dick?" he jerked his neck back.

"Yeah, so if you're lying it will fall off."

"Shorty why you always thinking of all this crazy shit?" he grinned and rubbed my stomach.

"Answer the question."

"I swear. That's where I'm gonna end that sentence. I love you shorty. I only have eyes for you."

A smile appeared on my face, so I cupped his to kiss his lips.

"You always know what to say Kaleeini."

"No, I'm just being honest."

THE NEXT MORNING...

Swiss said that he needed to talk to me, and usually that always meant he had more information to give. I was hoping that whatever he dropped on me today, would be exactly what I needed in order for us to dead this nigga Pablo.

He was hiding out like the bitch that he was, and I knew he possibly couldn't be going anywhere. Wherever he was, he was staying put and not getting any fresh air. If he had gotten any, he would've been dead by now. You would think he would at least come out to avenge the murder of his partner, but pussy niggas like him didn't care about anybody but themselves. And to think his homie didn't even give him up, even though he had a pistol in his face. People needed to learn that not everybody you fucked with deserved that amount of loyalty. Too bad that Chef cat had to die to find that out.

I parked a little ways down from Swiss' spot, and then secured my heat in my waist. Even though I knew Swiss was no fool, and would never try and come at me with some bullshit, I didn't trust anybody that didn't have the last name King around these parts; and even then only, the ones directly related to me.

I made sure my vest was secure under my crew neck, and then I exited the car. Saying what's up to a couple niggas walking by, I finally made it to my destination. I banged on his rickety screen door, and he immediately answered wearing a smile. Hopefully, that smile meant that he had come through with some real good information.

"Ken, what's up?" He grinned and opened the door.

I peeped the scene a bit before walking in, just in case he had some shit going on. I saw a girl sitting there, with hair the same color and length as Beyoncé's. She had on some tight ass jeans, a little ass top that was barely covering her breasts, and some heels. She was thick as fuck and bad as fuck, too. She had a big ass poppy tatted on her stomach, and two belly button piercings. Shorty was nothing short of perfection.

"Yo, what the fuck is this?" I frowned and turned my attention towards Swiss.

"This is Bailey," he smiled and gestured towards her as she stood up. She licked her lips at me and then neared me. Why have I never seen her sexy ass before?

"Damn, the rumors are true."

"What rumors?" I looked down into her pretty face as she licked her teeth seductively.

"That your whole damn family is fine. But, I think you're on the higher end of the spectrum."

"Swiss you got five minutes to tell me what the fuck is going on," I grimaced.

I didn't know what the hell was going on right now, but my trigger finger was itching to pull on something.

"No need daddy, I can tell you," Bailey responded.

She turned on her heels to go sit back down, and I unfortunately watched her ass the whole damn way. It was perfectly big, not them fake grandma asses bitches liked to rock these days.

"See the little guys that work for Pablo are catching on to Swiss, so I think it's best that I step in and help. They will never expect a woman to be spying for you. Also I'm a great distraction, conversation piece, and pawn. I'm sure you would agree."

I sat down and stared at her to listen some more, as Swiss smiled widely.

"Do you know where Pablo is?" I asked.

"No not yet, but I'm sure I can find out. Once they see that a bitch as bad as me is looking for him, I'm sure he will come out."

"How can you be so sure?"

"Look at me Kendrin. If I was looking for you, wouldn't you come running?" *If I was single, hell yeah.*

"No bitch makes me run. I don't run to anything but the money."

"Excuse me sexy. Well you're one of a kind, so I guess it wouldn't work for you. But this nigga is a sucker, and once he sees that I'm checking for him, he will be out and about. Or ,if your people have another plan that you'd like to use me for, I'm down."

"Otherwise *you're* gonna get the word out, meet him somewhere, and get us the address of the meeting right?" Swiss inquired.

"That's exactly the plan. Or, I can go to his crib and get the address for you, discreetly of course." She reached for her beer and sipped it. The way her lips wrapped around the tip had my dick twitching.

"Why?" I leaned back on the couch.

"Why what?" She cocked her head.

"Why the fuck are you so willing to help me?"

"Because who wouldn't wanna be down with the King family."

"So you're looking for something permanent with us?" I raised a brow.

"I'm looking for something permanent with you," she giggled, making her caramel complexion beam. "You are just so fucking bomb."

"You know I'm in a relationship I'm sure." *No, you're married Kendrin.* "I'm married actually."

"I'm not surprised, look at you. There is no way bitches would let someone as fine as you stay single. And to be honest Kendrin, I don't care about you being married. As long as you can keep me happy too, I have no problem being the side. I will be just fine and very faithful." She sipped her beer again, and Swiss bucked his eyes while grinning.

"I don't want a side. Now we're gonna have to do some background research on you, and you better not be on any bullshit."

"I swear I'm not. I'm not stupid enough to play you, and frankly I wouldn't want to," she giggled.

She was bad as fuck, but Willow was badder and she had my heart. There was nothing Bailey could do for me except lead me to Pablo. Once she did, she was gon' take her ass on. And if she didn't wanna do that, I had no problems murking her.

"Well that's good to know. Swiss, I still need you to work. I want you to keep an ear out for these niggas coming from Camden named Duck and Lucky. Let me know something as soon as you hear it. And I hope both of you know, that I will murder you with no problem, and in an instant if you try to fuck me over. You choose if that's how you wanna go out. I suggest you stick with the winning team because we always come out on top."

With that said, I quickly left Swiss' crib with a semi hard dick.

I wasn't playing around with either of them, but if they could help, and so far Swiss had, then shit I was happy to have them be a part of the team... temporarily.

SHANNON TOLD me what that bitch and some friend did, and boy was I hot. Rosalind had some nerve starting shit with Shannon, when I wasn't even her baby's father. In addition, not only was I not her baby's father, but she'd been cheating the whole got damn relationship! I didn't understand why her muthafucking ass was still on this shit! She had no reason to hate Shannon, because the same shit I did to her, she was doing to me. So today, I was going to check her stupid ass.

As soon as I got into my car, my phone rang. I saw it was from a weird ass number, so I knew it was KJ's ass. This nigga stayed calling you from weird ass random numbers. Sometimes they would even be from different states and shit too. He told us to always make sure it was him before we got to talking though, as if we didn't know his fucking voice by now.

"Who is this?" I answered already knowing who it was.

"Nigga who else!" he barked.

"Muthafucka you're the one that said to always check and make sure it's you," I laughed.

"I know, but you know it's me nigga. Now anyway, what you doing?"

"I'm about to go holla at Rosalind, why?"

"Why you going to holla at shorty?" he countered.

"Because she and her homegirl decided to jump Shannon. She got her arrested and everything."

"Wow, what the hell? Umm, I need you to do something for me since you're already headed over there."

"What?"

"Pump her little ass for more information on her baby daddy."

"What why?"

"Because that nigga is the one behind robbing our trap in Park Heights. He was selling our shit until we robbed his one little trap and took it back. I'm wondering if Rosalind knows where the fuck he's hiding at."

"I thought y'all caught his accomplice?"

"We did, but unlike the Pablo cat, he wasn't no bitch, so he refused to tell on his boy. I swear when you need niggas to sing, they're tight lipped."

"Damn."

"I don't wanna have to involve you, but I feel like you can get more from shorty since she love you. Well shit she acts like she loves you. You get more flies with honey than vinegar, and if I approach her she gon' have a pistol to her dome."

"Nah, I get you. She definitely don't love me because that pussy was for everybody. But I'm gon' see what I can do."

"She's the definition of a thot. But thank you. And don't call me when you get the information, I'm gon' call you. I'll check back in like an hour because we about to go take some family pictures."

"Nigga what?" I burst into laughter.

"Family pictures homie. My fucking mom showed Gigi all the ones we took after each of us were born, so now she wants to do the same thing. I'm gon' be looking just as miserable in these as my Pops looked in ours," he replied and we cackled together. "But yeah, I will hit you when I'm done with that shit."

"Aight fasho, I'll be waiting."

We disconnected and then I sped off out of my parents' driveway. I made it to Rosalind's crib in Coppin Heights, and parked my car right in front of her shit. I ran up her little porch steps, and beat on her door like I was the fucking Feds. After a few moments, the door flew open. She rolled her eyes and smiled before stepping away to let me in.

"I'm guessing you're here because your bitch got her ass whooped," she chuckled and closed her front door.

"From the looks of it so did you," I said, referring to her black eye and partially swollen lip.

"What do you want Kenzie?"

"No what do you want shorty? Fuck you coming at my girl for? Worry about your baby daddy and leave me alone. Worry about all the other niggas that you spread your legs for while with me."

"*You're* my baby daddy, and I'm *very* worried about you."

"No, the nigga you had up in here the last time I saw you was your fucking baby daddy. Don't play games with me Rosalind!"

"I lied Kenzie! It was yours."

I twisted my face and started to near her. In fear, she backed away from me until her back hit the wall. I was two seconds away from whooping her ass Ike Turner style. I was tired of these fucking games that she was playing. I towered over her contracting my fists to calm myself down.

"Rosalind, I don't know what kind of fucking games you're playing, but you're about to make me catch a fucking case. Whose baby was that in your stomach? You better be honest, because if I even think you're lying, I'm gon' crack your face shorty." Staring up at me, her lips trembled and shook. "Answer me!" I hollered down into her face making her jump. She hit her head lightly against the wall.

"I don't know Kenzie!" she cried.

"Damn, that many niggas huh? Yo, you're disgusting as fuck Ros."

Lord, was I glad that I had never fucked her raw or ate that vile ass pussy. That shit was getting beat the fuck up by every nigga in the DMV. I would've had no choice but to kill that bitch if I had have found out that I sucked on her pussy after she just fucked another nigga. The NBA would've lost a great player that day to the prison system.

"No, I don't remember his name. I met him in D.C. when my sister and I went to a party."

"Whatever, I don't even care. Any beef that you have with Shannon, end it now. If you do one more thing to her, it's a wrap."

"You wouldn't dare kill me, you don't wanna lose that little NBA contract," she sniffled and folded her arms.

"You're right, but my cousins will dead you with no problem." Her face changed immediately, causing an evil smile to cover my face. "Did you forget about them Ros?" She shook her head no, and wiped the two tears that fell from each eye.

"Good. Now where is this Pablo cat?"

"I don't know."

"Rosalind."

"I don't know Kenzie! Once he got the product and started making money, he broke me off like he promised, and we haven't talked since."

"You ain't got his number or nothing?" I frowned at her useless ass.

"I did but it's been disconnected. It's almost like he vanished. I don't ever see him out or anything like I used to."

"You know it's a wrap for you right?"

"Why? I didn't do anything Kenzie! All I did was help start the beef! I didn't help them rob your cousins or anything!"

"Yeah, but you knew about it!"

"No I didn't! Pablo told me he was gonna use me to initiate some beef and that's it! He didn't tell me how he was gonna make the money really. All he said is that once his name started to ring bells, he would be able to build a team and get product."

"Why should I fucking believe you? You ain't nothing but a lying ass hoe."

"I don't have anything to show you in order to convince you

Kenzie, but I'm begging you not to tell your cousins on me. I know I've done you dirty just like you've done me, but do I really deserve to die? The only reason I helped Pablo was because I loved you and I was hurt. I promise I don't fuck with him, just let me live."

"I don't know, you fighting Shannon has me wanting to fuck you up. She won't even let me see her."

Rosalind just looked away, and then went and sat down on the couch.

"Kenzie I can't say that I'm sad that she is mad at you. I still love you and I can't root for your relationship with her."

"How do you love me when you've been cheating the entire duration of our relationship Rosalind? How can the word love even roll off of that ball tickling tongue of yours?"

"I was lonely Kenzie! That is all! You were never available, and when we did spend time, you would just fuck me and leave! I never met your family, went to your games, or anything."

"And now you know why."

"You hurt me so much Kenzie. I was never like this before you."

"Well you better figure out some way to cope because I'm not taking anymore shit from you Rosalind, and that's on some real shit. Peace. Oh and if I find out you're lying about knowing where Pablo is, I'm gonna make sure my cousins take real good care of you."

I pulled open her front door and then left abruptly. I tried calling Shannon once I got into the car, but she didn't answer.

I was getting annoyed with her ass, because she was acting as if I was the cause of her getting jumped. I mean, yeah I was the reason she and Rosalind had beef, but she shouldn't be shutting me out over the fight. Rosalind is her own fucking person, and does what the hell she wants. You can't blame me for her hoe ass having free will.

After calling Shannon five times, I sped home to wait for KJ to hit my line. I knew he'd be just as disappointed as I was to find out Rosalind was just an incompetent hoe.

A COUPLE DAYS LATER...

"Is this one too much Kendrin?" I turned to him so he could look at the dress I was wearing.

"Why the fuck are you acting like you ain't never met my parents before?" he scoffed and continued texting on his phone. *Better not be no bitch*, I thought.

"I know, but we're telling them something big and I wanna look right."

"I highly doubt either of them will care about how the hell you look. You're my wife now, so it really doesn't even matter shorty. Ain't much they can say at this point. Plus, they like you Lo."

"Fine."

I made sure my two French braids looked right, and then I slipped into my heels. I don't know why I was so frantic. I was more nervous than the first time he introduced me to his parents and brought me to dinner. Then again, I hadn't had one on one time with them since I acted like a big damn fool at Kenzie's scholarship party. Yes, Nic came and helped out with my wedding tasting, and came to the court to see Kendrin and I get married, but other people were around and we were in public. Tonight would be just the four of us, and we would be in her home where she could get in my ass. I didn't even wanna think about what Mr. King would say to me. Like his sons, he was never one to hold his tongue. Matter fact, all of Mr. King's kids were like him, not just his sons, because Kendria never held back.

"Okay, ready," I told Kendrin. He stood up and slipped one of his phones into his pocket before nearing me. He was so handsome it was ridiculous.

"Chill out Lo, this is gonna be a cool little thing, watch," he smiled and I nodded.

We left our home and drove straight to his parent's house, which was only about ten minutes away. As soon as we made it through the gate, my palms began to sweat profusely. Nothing was calming me down, and I didn't know why. *What's the worse that can happen Willow? It is not gonna be that bad, Nic and Kendrick are nice. Wait but they were nice before you beat up Kenzie's homegirls at the grand-parent's home.* My mind was jumbling all kinds of thoughts around.

"They hate me," I said aloud as Kendrin shut the engine off.

"Who hates you?"

"Your mom and dad."

"No they don't Lo, why the fuck would they hate you?"

"Because I acted like a ratchet that night!"

"Baby that was a long time ago aight? Chill, you know my parents aren't even like that," he started to rub my back.

"Kendrin don't rub me so hard, my stomach hurts and when you rock me I feel like throwing up."

"I'm sorry shorty, you throw up a lot you know."

"Isn't that normal?" I looked to him.

"How the fuck would I know?"

"Did your mom throw up a lot when she was pregnant?"

"Baby I was only three and four years old when my mom had

Drae and Kendria, so I don't really recall," he raised a brow. "Drink some water."

I took the bottle of water he extended to me, and then downed it. Once my stomach settled a bit, Kendrin got out and then came to open my door. I hesitated a bit, and then finally got out of the car.

"Relax," he whispered and then kissed my lips.

We walked to the huge beige wood doors, and Kendrin stuck his key in. These were the thickest damn doors ever. As many times as I had been here, the thickness of the wood doors always amazed me. I didn't even know doors came that thick. If someone rammed you into the door, you would die, no ifs, ands, or buts about it.

Kendrin pushed the door open to allow me in, and as much as I wanted to hide behind him I didn't. My stomach began to flip and do all kinds of shit as I anticipated his parents coming into the foyer.

"Hey Lo," Kendria walked by and up the winding staircase.

"Hey boo," I smiled and waved.

Kendrin took my hand into his, and led me to the dining room since that was where we'd be having dinner.

"Be right back, sit down," he said.

I sat down in the chair, and then waited nervously. After about five minutes, I heard the voices of Kendrin and his parents. They entered the dining room, all carrying dishes with food on it. Nic was carrying a pitcher of something with strawberries, juice, and bubbles. It looked tasty, and the food smelled so good. I was starving. Nic cooked salmon, rice, seasoned squash, and for dessert it was black-berry pie. The drink she made was a Strawberry Sparkler she said. I was happy that she'd cooked a fish I could eat, even without knowing I was having a baby. I was famished as hell and couldn't wait to dig in to everything.

After standing up and greeting his parents, we all sat down and prayed over the meal. So far so good, I thought since they were acting normally.

"How are you Willow?" Mr. King asked as he covered his lap with the cloth napkin.

"I'm doing okay, thank you. How are you?" I smiled.

"Perfect," he grinned back.

Kendrin and KJ looked just like him. So did Kendrae, but he didn't have much facial hair yet so it wasn't as mind-blowing. When he did get some though, I'm sure people would think they were all triplets. And although Mr. King was in his early forties, he could definitely pass for being in his early to mid thirties. Bitches my age still checked for him and his brothers, I heard it all the time.

"Good. And you Mrs. King?"

"I'm doing just fine Willow, but I'm anxious to know what you two had to tell us," she responded before putting some food into her mouth.

"Well ma, I'm just gonna get right to it. Willow is pregnant," Kendrin smiled.

"Really?" Nic's face lit up, surprising me. I thought she would be a little bothered by me having his baby.

"Yeah really," Kendrin smirked and squeezed my leg.

"Congrats son," Mr. King nodded slowly. "When did you find out?"

"Just a couple weeks ago, and I'm already growing out of my clothes," I sighed.

"Already?" Nic squinted her eyes in confusion.

"Yes, I can still get the zipper up on things, but it's squishing me and uncomfortable. I'm always sick too."

"Wow sweetie, I do not miss those days," she replied, making the table crack up.

"It was worth it though for me, huh ma?" Kendrin grinned with his cute self. His deep dimples were showing, and his green eyes were lightning in color, signaling his happy mood.

"Yes baby, you were the only one who didn't make me cry from being so sick," she chuckled.

"For real?" Kendrin raised both brows.

"No, I was miserable all four times at the beginning," she replied, causing us all to roar with laughter.

"She's serious. I can't tell you how many times she would be sitting in the bathroom, crying after throwing up, and saying she was about to die. She was so dramatic," Mr. King chimed in. "Kendrick, I'm not gonna make it," he imitated her as we laughed, and she playfully hit his arm.

We talked and ate some more, until Nic passed out dessert. It was so good. I didn't even know that I liked blackberries, but it was definitely my new favorite dessert.

"Willow come with me so I can talk to you for a second," Nic said as she collected the empty dessert plates. *No, fuck why me? I didn't wanna do this! I knew this was gonna happen.*

"Okay," I chuckled nervously and then followed her to the kitchen.

Once we made it, she pulled on the accordion like divider to give us some privacy. I sat at the island as she began cleaning off the plates, waiting to see what was to come. The longer she took, the more nervous I became. Once she was done, she placed the dishes into the dishwasher, and then dried her hands off. She pumped some lotion into her hands, and then turned to me wearing a smile. Nic was so beautiful, and she looked just like the chick who played Santana on the show Glee. Even though that girl was younger than Nic, it didn't look like it.

"So you're having a baby, are you excited?" she asked.

"Yes I'm excited. I'm very sick but I'm excited."

"That's good honey. I wanted to talk to you alone because I kind of want you to understand something." I just stared at her, fidgeting. "Now, I know you love my son very much, and it's very hard to witness women show interest in him and not say anything. But right now you have to think about the life inside of you. It's gonna be hard not to pop a girl in the mouth who's smiling too hard at him, but you have to think, is she worth me harming my baby?"

"I get it. It is hard to ignore it. I just get so angry, and I feel disrespected, so I wanna fight."

"Trust me honey I know. Women seem to be very fond of King

men, and it's difficult to keep them at bay. Because sometimes no matter how many times he tells her no, she will keep going and keep going, so I understand that it gets irking. These women seem to be willing to die over them."

"Have you ever fought over Mr. King?"

She laughed and then shook her head at herself.

"Plenty of times. Sometimes I regretted it because I felt like there was no need for me to do it. I knew what it was between him and me, so beating the girl up really was a waste at times. But like you, I felt disrespected, and I felt the need to show them that they couldn't do that to me. I wanted to show them that they couldn't blatantly show interest in my man and not have to deal with some repercussions. Some girls deserved it though, I will admit. But I never did anything while pregnant, because as much as I love Kendrick, I love my babies more. No woman was worth me losing my child."

"I don't even know this baby, but I have love for it already."

"That's how it works. And I know Willow, when a man is unfaithful, it seems that every woman who comes near him has had a piece. That adds fuel to the fire, but you just have to trust that person if you're gonna be with them." I dropped my head because I was embarrassed that she knew Kendrin had cheated on me and made me insecure. "Don't be embarrassed honey, it happens to the best of us. Look at Halle Berry," she said and we laughed in unison.

"You've been cheated on?" I brought my head back up and bucked my eyes.

"Unfortunately, but the key is not to haul off and beat the girl up Willow. I mean you can if you want, but it's not the most important action needing to take place."

"It's not?" I quizzed and she began to crack up.

"No sweetie. The most important action is letting your man know that being cheated on is not something you will stand for. Crying and fighting does nothing to stop him, and it only makes you feel better for a couple of minutes."

"So just tell him?"

"Yes tell him you won't stand for it. But, also tell him that you have no problem leaving. And if you do leave, make sure it's not with the intention that he will come chasing you. If you only leave for him to chase you, then you never really left. Because if he doesn't come running, eventually you will, defeating your purpose."

I nodded as my mind absorbed all of this information. She was right, I needed to focus more on putting my foot down with Kendrin, and not so much on putting my foot in the bitch's ass. I don't think Kendrin is stupid enough to cheat again, but still, if he did we were gonna have some problems.

"That makes sense. I hope I won't have to leave him, because I love him very much. I don't think I could live without him."

"Well I will say that my baby loves you very much as well, so there is no need for you to worry or wanna fight every girl who likes him. For him to wanna marry you and actually do it, says a lot coming from my son. I'm sure you know he's not usually the monogamous type."

"Yes, I know and I agree. Thank you for talking to me."

"No problem, anytime." She walked over to me and gave me a tight hug. "But just because you can't get physical, does not mean you can't get a little verbally abusive here and there."

We laughed in unison.

"Oh, please believe I will be exercising the French language very frequently," I giggled.

"Good, well do you wanna go back to the dining room?"

"Yes." As we walked through the house I said, "You know I thought you would be mad that I was pregnant by Kendrin."

"What? Girl I'm happy that my sons have enough sense to impregnate their girlfriends and not random women. I must admit I was worried about you carrying a baby because of your behavior, which is why I wanted to talk to you. But mad, not at all. As over-joyed as I was seeing you guys get married, you should've known I wouldn't have been angry Willow."

"True."

We walked back to the room, and Kendrin, Kendrae, and Mr. King were conversing.

"You didn't kill her," Mr. King joked as Nic slid into his lap. She patted his chest playfully as we all chuckled.

Shit, I was thinking the same damn thing...

KENZIE HADN'T STOPPED TRYING to get me to see him, but his efforts weren't working whatsoever. I didn't want him to see my face for one, and secondly I didn't wanna see his. He was the reason that this had even happened to me, and I just might whoop his ass if I see him. I never wanted to be that girl who had to constantly fight for her nigga. I mean it was okay for Willow, but it wasn't my thing. If our relationship is everything it should be, I shouldn't have to physically fight over you. That's the way that I see it.

I wanted Rosalind to just go the fuck away. The baby she was carrying wasn't even Kenzie's, so why was she still coming at me? I was over our fucking beef, and just wanted it to be over, but now that she jumped me, my hate towards her had only grown. I really wanted to get at her again, one on one, but that was just adding more drama to my life that I didn't need. Come to think of it, I wanted her friend's fade more than hers.

I paused the show I was watching on Hulu, and then padded to the kitchen to make me a snack. I was just chilling today, and since my face had healed a bit more, I was in a somewhat happy mood. I would be back to going out with my friends in no time, once all my injuries disappeared.

As I stood by the microwave, letting it warm my TV dinner, I heard a knock at the door. I opened the microwave door so that it would stop, and then slowly walked over to peep out of the hole. I saw it was Gianna, so I pulled it open. She was wearing black tights, a black hoodie, black Nike's, and her hair was up in a tight bun. She looked like she was possibly about to work out, or possibly about to do some matrix shit.

"Gigi, what are you doing here?" I quizzed as she barged into my apartment.

"Get dressed," she said before plopping down onto the couch.

After closing and locking the door I asked, "Dressed for what?"

"Because we're about to go beat that bitch's ass."

"What bitch?"

"That Rosalind hoe."

"How do you even know we fought?"

Gianna was crazy, which is why Italians and Blacks should never procreate. Then her mixed with crazy ass KJ, poor K-Three was gonna be a damn serial killer.

"Because KJ told me. Now hurry up, I can taste the ass whooping I'm about to deliver her."

Oh, how I wished she was pregnant still and couldn't fight. Now that she had dropped the baby, she was itching to fight any and every damn person, place, or thing.

"No Gigi, I just wanna relax today. I don't feel like dealing with any drama."

"Fine, I will beat her ass alone, just get me her address from Kenzie."

"I can't let you fight her alone Gigi! She may have that girl with her again."

"Well then get dressed Shan. Either way I'm tagging her ass."

I inhaled sharply and then went to get my phone to text Kenzie.

Me: *What is Rosalind's address?*

Kenzie: *Why?*

Me: *Just give it to me.*

Kenzie: *You've barely been texting me back and that's the first thing you hit me for?*

Me: *Please baby, can I just have it?*

I took the nice approach.

I waited for a few moments, and he finally sent it over. I locked my phone, and then quickly got dressed in some attire that was similar to what Gigi was wearing. Once I was done, I tied my hair up into a tight bun so that it couldn't be pulled, and then snatched up my phone and keys.

"Got the address," I said once I entered the living room. A wide ass smile spread across Gianna's face, and then we left out. "Where is K-Three?" I asked as Gianna dipped through the streets, headed to Rosalind's.

"At home with his damn daddy."

"KJ was okay with you coming out to fight?" I frowned.

"No, I told him I was gonna work out and grocery shop," she chuckled.

"Gigi, if he finds out what we're doing, you're gonna have another fight on your hands," I laughed and so did she.

"No, all he's gonna do is pout and curse me out. Once he does that, we're both gonna lie down in bed not talking to one another. I'm gonna pretend to be sleep, while pressing my ass against him. He's gonna try and resist at first, but then he's gonna start kissing the nape of my neck, and pulling my panties down. He's gonna apologize for cursing me out so he can get some pussy, and then we'll be good," she explained as I laughed the whole time. "Either that, or while he's going off, I will just start taking my bottoms off. By the time my panties get off, he'll only be worried about fucking."

"Damn bitch, he'd be mad if he knew you was playing his ass."

"I know, that's our little secret though. Power of the pussy," she said and I nodded in agreement.

Once we got onto Rosalind's street, we slowed down until Siri told us we'd arrived. Gianna parked the car a little ways down, and then we quickly got out. Rosalind was chilling on her porch with the same girl that she fought me with, which was fucking perfect.

"Who you want?" I asked as we got closer to her home.

"I don't know. We just gon' run up and whoever we get is who we get," Gianna replied.

Once they spotted us, they both stood up and came down the steps. The four of us immediately started throwing hands like crazy, choosing to skip the bickering. We were doing shit Kendrin King style; fuck the talking. People started coming out of their houses to watch, and other people were screaming and cheering. I was fucking Rosalind's homegirl up, and was happy about it since she was the one who had gotten the best of me last time.

Once I got her down onto the grass, I quickly glanced over to see if I needed to help Gianna. Gianna was wailing on poor Rosalind, so I went back to fucking up the friend. Gianna and I tirelessly kept going in, pulling hair and punching their faces constantly, until somebody yelled,

"Five oh!"

Gianna and I hopped off of the girls, and booked it to her car. We didn't even buckle up as we sped off of Rosalind's street, hoping to dodge the police. She darted straight to her home, and on the way my heart was beating fast.

"That was so much fun!" I laughed loudly as she made a right turn.

"I know huh!" she chuckled and pulled into the gate.

"I'm so happy you convinced me to do that shit. I feel so much better. Her homegirl had me losing sleep because of the way she was able to sneak me."

"I feel better too, that brought some fun to my day. I ain't fucked a bitch up in a long time, I needed that," Gianna said before we got out of her car.

When we got inside, we went upstairs so she could check on her baby. I rubbed his back as we looked at him sleeping peacefully. He was so cute with his toffee colored skin and fat cheeks. Every time he inhaled, his deep dimples would appear.

"He is so freaking cute Gigi," I whispered. I was getting baby fever with my young ass.

"Thank you. I love playing with him and spending time, which makes me wonder what I did with my time before him," she giggled.

"Umm, spent time making him," I half joked and we chortled.

As we descended the stairs, KJ was coming from the den. When he spotted Gianna, he yanked her closer and into the nearby room. *Aww damn, he knows.* It looked to be a laundry room that he'd pulled her into, because before he closed the door I saw a dryer.

"How did you get that scratch Gigi? Please tell me you were not one of the girls in that brawl on Presbury."

"Okay, I wasn't," I heard her respond.

"I told yo' ass not to try and fight them girls shorty!" he hollered.

I walked closer to the door, and stood on the wall part next to it so I could hear better.

It was quiet and then I heard Gianna say, "I'm sorry baby."

"Nah, that sorry ain't gon' cut it. I'm getting tired of yo' little disobedient ass."

Silence again. I waited and waited, and then all of a sudden I heard Gianna moaning. Is this bitch really? Are they really fucking while I'm out here waiting?

"Fuck shorty, you play too much," I heard KJ grumble as Gianna continued to whimper like a little puppy or something. Just that quick, that nigga was calm and had given in like she said he would.

I rushed off not wanting to hear anymore, and then made it to the kitchen to find some food. Whooping that hoe's ass had just made my day all the better.

I CUT OFF THE SHOWER, and then stepped out so I could dry off. I brushed my teeth, rinsed, and then exited the bathroom and got dressed. My father wanted to talk to me today, so I was going to see what he wanted before going to check up on Kendrin for some new information.

Once I was dressed, I headed down the stairs and into the kitchen. I walked in to see Gianna feeding K-Three, while stirring some shit, so I came behind her and kissed her neck. She smelled like some sort of cookies or pound cake like always.

"You scared me," she jumped a little.

She had this little blanket covering her, so that you couldn't see she was breastfeeding. I made sure to purchase that shit swiftly, because I'll be damned if she was out in public showing niggas my shit. Muthafuckas were perverts, and they didn't care if it was nasty to get turned on by that shit. There were some freaky people in this world, and they weren't about to be getting their rocks off to my woman and son.

"You smell like vanilla wafers shorty," I said before putting some candy into my mouth.

"I guess that's a compliment," she grinned up at me.

I planted a kiss on her soft lips, and then left the crib. Pulling into my dad's driveway, I shut off the engine, and climbed out. As soon as I entered, I saw my mom walking through the foyer.

"Hi, are you hungry sweetie?" she asked. Damn, she clearly thought that was the only reason that I came by.

"No, but when I'm done with Dad I will take a smoothie," I grinned and she nodded with a half smile.

I treaded through the foyer, and down the small hallway until I neared my father's big wooden office door. Knocking lightly with my knuckles, I waited for him give me the okay to come in.

"Come on KJ," he finally called out, already knowing it was me. I walked in and closed the door behind me, before sitting down across from his desk. "How are you?" he inquired as he turned from his computer to me.

"I'm good."

"So right now it seems that a lot of people are gunning for you."

"Nothing new."

"Right, and what's the problem right now?"

"Couple of niggas are coming down from Camden, and they're rumored to cause some problems, but we don't know yet. We have an ear out there right now who's gonna update us."

"That's it?"

Why was he asking me all of this shit? The only reason I was answering was because he was my father. If it were anybody else I would've told their ass to kick rocks.

"Some other dude that we're trying to catch up with, but it ain't nothing. We gon' get his ass soon."

"I'm asking this because your uncles and I were thinking about coming out of retirement."

"For what?" I frowned.

He couldn't be serious right now. This shit was beyond unnecessary and stupid. I didn't need any fucking help, and I wasn't about to accept any. I don't know if he was bored or what, but he'd better find some other shit to occupy his time. And shit, to my knowledge he had plenty of businesses to tend to, so why try and come this way?

"Why do you think? To be of some assistance to you," he clasped his hands under his chin, awaiting my response.

"I don't need any assistance Pop."

"You're so sure."

"I'm very sure."

"I don't know if you are KJ, which is why we wanna come back and get you guys back on track."

Okay now this nigga was getting me hot.

"I just said I don't need that. I got this shit under control. Your assistance wasn't needed before and it isn't needed now."

"And what if I decide to give my assistance anyway?" he raised a brow, as if his question was supposed to rattle me in some way.

"Then we're gonna have a big problem on our hands Pop."

"Oh what, you think you can survive a war against me?" he stood to his feet so I stood to mine.

He looked me up and down before lightly chuckling, but I saw nothing comical about this right here.

"I don't know, but I'm damn sure gonna try. I don't want your help, but ultimately I don't need it. I got shit handled, so there is no need for you to start prying and trying to burp us like some fucking babies."

"I don't have to listen to you."

"Then don't, but if you come out of retirement we will not be on the same team," I grimaced.

"Am I supposed to be scared?" he bucked his eyes and chuckled.

"I don't need you to be scared to mean what I say. It'll be y'all against us, and I do not mind dying for my pride. I will not take your help, plain and simple. If you wanna come back into the game to help somebody, help them moist ass niggas coming down from Camden. You ain't needed over this way."

He stared into my eyes angrily, and then all of a sudden a sneer appeared on his face. He was fucking with me. This muthafucka right here.

"That's the exact answer I wanted from you KJ. I was just making sure you were still on your game."

"When am I not on my game?"

"Never obviously, just like me. You got me so fucking proud over here," he grinned making me laugh. This nigga really had me hot just a minute ago, so I had to take a few seconds to adjust my tenor. He walked over to me and then pulled me into a hug. "Keep doing what you're doing KJ. Whether you win or lose, people will always respect you because you have heart. That's the way I raised you and how I want you to stay."

I nodded and then we hugged again.

After talking with him, I went and drank two smoothies, courtesy of my mother. Them shits hit the spot just like always. She needed to open a business or some shit, because those smoothies were like crack.

I left my parents home and went straight to Kendrin's. I was interested to hear what he had for us, because I was tired of looking for this Pablo nigga. He was a small fry trying to play games with the big dogs, and should've been taken care of already. I wanted to focus all of my attention on taking out Duck and Lucky, just in case they were actually as ruthless as Oscar had explained. By saying that, I had no time for little Shih Tzu poodle ass niggas like Pablo.

I parked in Kendrin's driveway, and then greeted Kaleeini as we approached Kendrin's door together.

"Follow me," Kendrin said once he answered.

We trailed him to his den, and then he pulled on the sliding door to give us three some privacy.

"Aight Swiss let me know that Duck and Lucky are here," Kendrin said.

"Damn, and we still haven't found that Pablo cat," Kaleeini sighed and dropped back against the couch's back pillows.

"Nope, but we need to look into this chick named Bailey, because she's willing to help us in any way. We need to make sure she doesn't have an ulterior motive though, before we entrust her."

"I wanna meet her," I said.

"No problem. But look, Duck and Lucky are gonna be at Fresh nightclub tomorrow night," Kendrin smirked.

"We should go and see what's up. Make sure they know they didn't just sneak into town," I suggested.

"Kill them right there?" Kaleeini frowned.

"Nah, not at all. We're just gonna make sure them niggas know that we're up on game about them getting here. Oscar said they planned to slither into town and come up silently. So when they realize we know they're here, it's gonna throw a major monkey wrench into their plans."

"I see," Kaleeini nodded. "Well looks like we gon' be hitting the club tomorrow."

"Aight I'll text Lenny," I smiled.

Kendrin's little homie Swiss was really coming through. I wanted to meet this new bitch though and look into her, because she may be just what I needed to catch Pablo's ass slipping.

THE NEXT NIGHT...

Tonight was the night we would finally meet them Duck and Lucky niggas. I couldn't wait to come face to face with the niggas who thought they were gonna come through Baltimore and take our shit. I tell you jealousy was a muthafucka, because these niggas had no reason to want to come here, other than bragging rights. They simply wanted to try and take out the niggas who'd been screaming undefeated for decades. It was cool though, if niggas wanted to seal their fate, I wasn't one to stop them.

"Before we go, I wanna meet Oscar at the warehouse, because he said he has something new for us," KJ explained as Bolo headed over that way.

"Fasho," Lenny responded for the rest of us.

After about thirty minutes, we made it to the warehouse and climbed out to go into the conference room.

"He's here," Blade let us know, before leaving to go get Oscar from outside. A few moments later, Blade was bringing him in.

"Alright what you got?" KJ asked Oscar as he sat down with his laptop.

"Okay so I will start with the small stuff first. Bailey checks out. She has no history with any previous hustlers, nor does she have a criminal history of any kind. She moved here from Los Angeles to get away from her boyfriend Brandon Lay. He's a hustler out there, and for some reason she felt the need to get away from him. Anyway, she heard about y'all and she just wants to be down with the best," Oscar explained. "She ain't trying to work for no suckas, and she wants to get paid."

"Smart choice," Lenny nodded.

"Now as far as Duck and Lucky, their real names are Tamal and Jamal Paine. They're twins from Camden, NJ, which you knew. They both have girlfriends and children, but the children are with exes."

"What are the current girlfriends names?" I asked.

"Cassandra or Cassi Wartz, and Valentina Martinez," Oscar replied.

"Any other family members?" KJ quizzed.

"Not that I know of."

"Oscar, stop coming to me with half assed shit! Not that you fucking know of, I need yes or no answers only muthafucka! You've been serving cake with no icing for a couple minutes now, and you need to fix that shit before I get rid of your fruitless ass! Is there anything else?" KJ barked.

I agreed with KJ. This nigga was always delivering puzzle pieces instead of the whole damn picture. But at least now we knew Bailey was A1.

"Nah, that's all I got," Oscar replied nervously to KJ.

"Blade get his ass up out of here. You better have some more shit for me within a week O!" KJ hollered as Blade escorted Oscar out.

"I know another chick who is real good with this shit KJ. She can probably do us way more good than him," Lenny chimed in.

"What's her name?" Kendrin asked.

"It's Xandra. I can have her checked out and then you two can meet if you want," Lenny responded.

"Yeah set that up after you look into her. Let's head to Fresh," KJ patted the table.

We all got up and then piled into the truck driven by Bolo. Pulling up to the front of Fresh, Blade hopped out and opened the back door for us. When we exited, all eyes were on us, and I was tempted to tell some of the females to put their tongues back into their mouths. It wasn't sexy at all to be drooling over niggas. Only us men could pant and shit over women, and even that was whack sometimes.

The bouncers didn't even question us. As soon as we got to the door, they removed the velvet rope to let us in. Bolo moved to the front of us, talked to the bouncer a little, and then waved for the four of us to follow him. Blade stayed behind us to make sure no mutha-fuckas played stupid from behind.

We trailed Bolo all the way up, until we reached a VIP table that was freshly prepared for us. The seats were a black velvet color, and there were bottles of expensive ass liquor lined up. We didn't even pay anything, so it was wild that they were just letting us have this. We all sat down and started pouring ourselves a glass of the liquor of our choice, and then Bolo whispered something to KJ, before walking back over to join Blade in securing our VIP area.

"So them niggas are gonna be seated over there when they come," KJ pointed to the right of us, divulging what Bolo had just said.

"How much was this table?" I inquired and sipped my drink.

"Hell if I know, but I ain't paying shit though. I think they let us in free because if people know we're here, they're gonna wanna pay to come in," he replied. "Especially the women, because usually they never wanna pay shit unless it's a nigga inside that they wanna get their hands on."

"Makes sense," Kendrin nodded.

We began drinking and unintentionally having fun, until we saw like eight shorties begging for us to tell Bolo and Blade to let them by. We tried to ignore them because it was no point in entertaining some shit we couldn't touch.

"I'm single!" Lenny yelled making us laugh.

He got up and began allowing only the cutest ones to come in. His ass was crazy as hell. Out of the eight girls, only three walked in, and I must admit they were sexy as fuck. Too bad they were thirsty as fuck also.

One chick in particular walked up and sat down to the right of me, since KJ was on my left.

"Hey," she smiled.

"What's up?" I said dryly, while focusing my attention straight ahead. She looked like she was Puerto Rican or something. I don't really know, but she was bad as fuck.

"I'm Sicily," she introduced herself.

"Kaleeini."

"I already know you're taken, unless this is my lucky day," Sicily grinned and leaned up to look into my face.

I just shook my head and declined to respond. I was here on business, not to get some pussy. Sicily was tempting as hell, but not tempting enough.

"Diamond," some fine ass brown skinned chick rolled up on KJ. She was rocking a tight light purple dress that clung to her sexy body.

"I'm taken shorty," he shook his head repeatedly, as if he was saying, *Not today satan*; that shit made me titter a little.

"Why are all the fine niggas taken? What fine man is single?" She cocked her head making him laugh. "I knew you had a bitch. I'm bummed but still interested."

"Go on shorty," KJ cheesed up her, as she continued to stand over him.

"You still didn't answer me Kaleeini. Are you single?" Sicily asked me.

"Very taken," I responded and sipped my drink.

I spotted two niggas being escorted in by some big burly ass bodyguards, and I knew exactly who they were. I tapped KJ's chest, and the smile he was giving the Diamond chick quickly faded once he spotted Duck and Lucky taking their seats. They were dressed in expensive shit from head to toe, and it appeared to be from Brooks Brothers. So far, the rumors seemed too carry some validity. They were definitely getting money out in Camden.

"What about your twin?" the Diamond chick licked her lips at Kendrin. Kendrin just ignored her with his mean ass, and continued to type on his phone.

"That's not my twin shorty. But aye, go over to the next VIP, and tell them we sent you as a gift," KJ told Diamond.

"But I wanna be over here with y'all!" she whined.

"Look shorty," KJ pulled her into his lap, and licked his lips as he eyed her body. "Go over there and do what I said, and I promise I'll hit it hard tonight."

She swallowed the lump in her throat, and hopped up with the quickness.

We watched her saunter over there and start talking to the brothers. Suddenly they both looked over at the four of us with blank expressions. We held up our drinks while smiling, and you could see all in their faces that they weren't happy about us knowing they'd gotten here already.

"You gon' really fuck shorty tonight?" I quizzed KJ once we ended our stare off with Duck and Lucky.

"Nah, I'm more in the mood for some pussy that has my name on it, literally," he chuckled referring to Gianna.

I was happy to hear that he wasn't playing them games anymore. That nigga would lose his mind if Gianna chucked the deuces, and everybody knew it. And I wasn't about to be letting him cry on my shoulder because he wanted to be dumb.

TODAY I HAD to meet and interview with the manager that Sunshine from the gym had introduced me to. When I called him he seemed happy that I was interested, so we immediately scheduled a time for me to come down. His office building was located on Ostend Street, in an area where a lot of other business buildings were. His was right next door to the M.C. Dean building.

I parked my BMW right outside, and then hit the alarm before walking in and taking the elevator to the right floor. When I stepped off, I spotted a young lady sitting behind a huge bar like desk, so I approached it.

"Good morning, I'm Priscilla," she smiled.

"Good morning, I'm here to see Mr. Casey Morris," I responded. "I'm Gianna Daniels."

"Oh yes, I see you're here for an interview at 11:30am. I will call back there right now, just have a seat please."

"Great, thank you."

I went to sit down in one of the little chairs, and waited nervously. I really wanted this job, because it would give me more experience working in the field that I preferred, and because it would pay me a lot of money. Everything about it was perfect, and it almost seemed too good to be true. But as my mom said, sometimes blessings just fell out of the sky.

"Gianna, he's ready for you," the girl stood up so she could see me.

I stood to my feet and then followed her to the back, until we reached a door with Casey's name on it. She knocked lightly and then opened his door. Standing up was a man who appeared to be in his early thirties. I thought he would be older, but I guess I thought wrong. He had short curly hair, very little facial hair, and he was a bit skinny. He reminded me of a younger version of Michael Ealy.

"Welcome Gianna, I'm Casey Morris," he greeted me once the chick left.

"Nice to meet you, thank you for having me." I smoothed down my burgundy dress and then sat down across from him.

"Wow you look stunning," he licked his lips.

I tousled my hair to the other side and said, "I do?"

"Yeah you do."

"Thanks."

I really didn't know what else to say. It felt weird hearing him compliment me like that, but then again this was somewhat the fashion world, so maybe they did it all the time. I was happy that he liked my sense of style though, because he'd be less likely to hire me if I came in here displaying a minimal taste in fashion.

"Okay Gianna, tell me a bit about yourself," he clasped his hands together and leaned back in his big office chair.

"Alright, I've been into fashion for a very long time, for as long as I can remember actually. I first started-"

"No, let's start with some more personal details," he cut me off and eyed my body.

"Personal details?"

"Yes, history, parents, race, relationships."

"Well, I was born here in Baltimore. My mother is from Florence-"

"Italy?"

"Yes Italy, and my father is a Baltimore native like myself. They met when he traveled to Italy one summer. My grandparents bought him a ticket as a college graduation gift. So they met, fell in love, and then he finally brought her over."

"So your mother is new to Baltimore?"

How could she be new to Baltimore if I'm obviously grown and I was born here? I think because his attention was so focused on my legs, he couldn't listen well.

"No, she moved here with my father when she nineteen."

"Wow nice, so do you speak Italian?"

"Yes, I'm fluent. My mother spoke to me only in Italian until I was four, in order to make sure I knew the language before English. Then once I was able to hold conversations in Italian, my father kind of did a cram session with me to learn English before I started Kindergarten."

"Say something for me in Italian," he squinted his eyes. Maybe he's testing my honesty, I thought.

"Umm, alright. Voglio davvero questo lavoro."

"That sounds very sexy, what did you say?"

"I really want this job," I replied and he laughed.

"Wow funny, beautiful, *and* bilingual. That's very sexy. Now what about your relationships?"

"Shouldn't we talk more about my fashion experience?" I frowned. Why was he so interested in my personal life?

"We will get to that, but Gianna I need to feel like I know you first. In this world, being personable is everything."

"Right, umm, well I have a fiancé, and we just had a baby boy almost three months ago."

"Wow, just three months? Your body looks great."

"Thank you."

"Say it in Italian."

"Grazie."

"I bet your fiancé loves hearing you speak that way. I don't mean to be frank, but does he ask you to speak Italian in bed? I swear I'm not being a pervert, I've just always wondered that about bilingual people. Humor me Gianna."

Was he serious?

"He doesn't ask me to no, but it does slip out, and he enjoys it," I responded uncomfortably.

"Does he keep you happy?"

"Very happy Mr. Morris."

"Good. Well, let me tell you about the job Gianna." *Finally,* I thought. "What you will be doing is styling my music clients. As you know I'm a music manager, and I have three female musicians that I work with. I would need you to style them for any jobs that they book."

"Okay, I just had a baby though, so I can't be away from him too much. Maybe I wouldn't be good for something that extensive. Maybe one artist would be better."

"No it's fine Gianna, I will work around your schedule. And I have no problem with you bringing your baby to work."

"Really?" I cocked my head.

"Really. If you need to have him on your chest in one of those little carrier things while you style, that's fine."

"Wow, that sounds fabulous. I hate to ask but what is the pay?"

"The pay is five grand per girl, per job."

"So, if I style all three of them in one day, each for just one appearance, that's-"

"That'll be fifteen thousand dollars." My eyes almost popped out of my head at the sound of that. "And just think, if you do that four or five times a week, you'll be making sixty to seventy-five thousand dollars weekly Gianna."

"Wow," was all I could say. I really wanted and needed this job.

"Are you the provider in the home Gianna?"

"No, my fiancé is."

"Well, I'm sure you'll be the breadwinner if you work this job."

Was he trying to throw jabs? KJ could live Casey's life *and* his own at the same time, that's just how paid he was.

"Not quite, I live pretty well. But yes, I would love this job if you'll have me."

"I will have to give you a call after interviewing some other candidates."

"Mr. Morris, you don't need to interview them. I'm the best person for this. I know everything about fashion, from lingerie to even sportswear. You won't regret it."

He stared at me for a couple seconds and then said, "You're hired. Can you come back here in two days at 9am? I'm gonna email you photos of my clients, along with their sizes and events. I want you to bring in some pictures or ideas of what's you'd put them in."

"Not a problem sir," I answered giddily as I stood up to leave.

"Say it in Italian."

"Non c'è problema."

"Gianna tu bella," he smiled, speaking Ebonics.

I just chuckled very lightly before leaving. I needed to go celebrate my new job.

THE NEXT MORNING...

GIANNA and I were out to breakfast because she wanted to celebrate getting that new styling job for the music manager. I was happy for her because she's wanted to do this for a long ass time. Gianna had a great sense of style and she was really passionate about fashion, even the technical shit. I had no idea what color block was until I met her. She'd spent many days and nights just studying the fashion world, and reading all types of articles on the current events of it. She deserved such a great opportunity.

"So how much money is it again?"

"Girl, five thousand per girl, per event or appearance!"

"Damn bitch, I'm gonna need you to let me hold something."

"I might throw you some cash if you work for it," she giggled.

"I don't plan on working for shit, you just need to throw that shit my way thank you."

We chuckled in unison.

"So how are you feeling knowing the baby is almost here in a couple weeks? Get ready for the sleepless nights and sex session interruptions."

"Oh my gosh, I know! I'm excited but scared. I keep thinking about how much pain you were in when you had K-three, and now I'm just worried as fuck. I hate pain."

"Yeah I've never felt such horrific pain in my life," she shook her head.

"What does it feel like? Is it like menstrual cramps? A knife in your vagina? What?" I turned my lip up.

"I can't explain it, it's something you have to experience. Are you gonna get the medicine?"

"I want to but I'm not sure. What do you think? Kaleeini's mom said not to. My mom said she got it when she had me, but she wished she hadn't."

"KJ's mom and my mom told me not to get it, which is why I didn't. I don't know, though, I thought I was gonna die during, but when it's over it's over. Getting the medicine can cause you to have pelvic floor problems over a lifetime my mom said."

"Damn, well umm, never mind then. I guess I will be strong like you," I chuckled.

I was so scared to have this baby. Gianna sounded like she was dying in her delivery video, and then watching him come out of her was like watching a watermelon come out of a lemon. I just didn't know what the fuck to do. But I for damn sure didn't wanna deal with pain all of my fucking life, just because I couldn't take one day of it. I just needed to suck it the fuck up and go all natural.

As we waited for our meals to come, someone approached our table. Gianna and I looked up to see that Tamal guy. What are the fucking odds?

"What are the odds, Aysia?" He smirked, reading my mind. Just my luck this nigga would run into me.

"Oh hey. Gianna this is Tamal, Tamal this is my best friend, Gianna," I introduced them.

"Nice to meet you," Gianna shook his hand.

"Likewise. You know Aysia, I've been needing your services while out here. I got lost for an hour yesterday," he said and both Gianna and I laughed.

"How?"

"Well I had my GPS going, but my phone died. I made one wrong turn, and bam, I was lost for a cool hour and a half."

"Well if your phone was dead I couldn't have helped you anyways Tamal."

"Yes you could've because I wouldn't have needed my phone's GPS if you had have just texted me what I needed," he smiled. "You could've just said make two lefts then a right Tamal. Much easier than that GPS shit."

"Well, I apologize Tamal."

"I would prefer your number so that this wouldn't happen again."

"Tamal-"

"I know you're in a relationship and that's not what I'm trying to do. Honestly, it's lonely as hell out here. I'm from Oklahoma, a town where everyone speaks to each other and helps one another out. I'm not used to everyone being so cold," he explained and looked back and forth between Gianna and I. "You know the other day I spoke to a young lady in passing, and she rolled her eyes at me and said to fuck off. Is that how all of you are?" he quizzed.

"It's just not common for people to speak when they don't know you in B-more," Gianna chuckled.

"I see, well damn. I guess I have to get used to that. So I still can't get your number Aysia?"

I stared into his innocent eyes for a bit, and then finally obliged.

"Now that you have it, please do not text me after 8pm."

"I will make sure I'm in the house for good by 6:30pm so that I won't need you after that."

"Thank you, I don't want my boyfriend to come after you because that wouldn't be good."

"Oh yeah? Is he a thug or something?"

"He's just who he is, and like I told you before, he plays no games."

"Well, I for sure don't want any problems with him then. I'm just trying to work and meet new people," he palmed his chest.

"Then you know what to do," I smiled.

"Well thank you Aysia, and nice meeting you Gianna." He walked away and sat down at a table with another guy.

"He's kind of cute," Gianna shrugged. "I can't believe you gave him your number, though."

"Girl, I gave him my Google voice number," I waved her off.

"Oh my gosh. I couldn't even tell with how confidently you read it off. Shit all I do is tap your name, so I honestly don't know your number by heart."

"Same here. But you think he's trying to come for me?"

"I don't know. He seems a bit nerdy, so I hope not."

"Yeah, he looks like an early nutter," I joked as we burst into laughter.

Poor Tamal better not be trying to get at me. He was no match for Kaleeini, and I would hate for him to find that out. Good thing I gave him my Google number, though, because if he did get fresh with me, I could just remove the number so he couldn't contact me.

THIS EVENING I was taking Bailey to meet my brother. Since she checked out and appeared not to be on any bullshit, KJ wanted to meet her and possibly give her some directions on what he wanted from her. I prayed to God that she was the piece we needed to catch this nigga Pablo.

I pulled in front of the warehouse and text KJ to let him know I was there.

KJ: *Go on inside.*

I nodded my head towards my window so Bailey could get out of the car and follow me in. Once we got inside the conference room, I sat down to wait for KJ.

"I didn't expect a room so nice to be inside this raggedy ass warehouse," she chuckled and walked next to the table, gliding her finger across it.

"That's the point shorty. It needs to blend in. Every building over is raggedy as fuck. We can't have some glamorous ass shit sitting here, looking like a sore thumb. Plus we don't do glamorous things in here."

"You do dirty things?" she licked her lips and I just laughed.

"Watch your mouth shorty."

"Why? You don't like when I flirt with you Kendrin?"

"Not really."

"I don't even have to talk if you don't want me to. I can just sit on it for you," she smiled with her pretty ass.

"Nah, I told you I'm married."

"And I told you it doesn't bother me."

"I'm not telling you for that reason. I'm telling you so you can see that I'm not interested."

"You're not?" she pointed to my crotch, and my dick was hard as hell.

I couldn't help it. She had on a short ass dress that hugged every part of her body, with some low top air force. She didn't have on a bra, and I could see that her nipples were pierced under the dress. Her smooth caramel skin looked so soft, and her legs were so fucking sexy. She had her golden brown hair hanging down, with a baseball cap on.

"I'm a man," I tried to explain.

"A man who likes what he sees and should take it. You're rich, young, and fine, no reason why you can't have two bitches."

"I don't want two bitches. I want my wife."

"Every nigga wants multiple women Kendrin, it's just that they don't deal with the right girls who would allow it. Did you know humans are the only species who practice monogamy?"

"So if your husband wanted a girlfriend you wouldn't care?"

"Not unless he was you. I wouldn't wanna share you, but since you're married already, I would have to deal."

"So what makes you think my wife would wanna share me?"

"I know she wouldn't, she'd be a fool to want to. But that doesn't matter to me Ken," she licked her full lips and dropped to her knees. My dick grew even harder seeing her on the floor like that. "I could do it right here before your brother comes in."

"Why are you so thirsty? Or are you just a hoe?"

"I'm not a hoe, nor am I thirsty baby, I'm just not shy about what I want. Closed mouths don't get fed. I want you and I'm making it known," she raised a brow. *Damn.*

"Man get up off of your fucking knees."

Just then, my brother walked in, so Bailey hopped to her feet. My brother furrowed his brows and stared at me. I slowly shook my head no, so he could stop thinking whatever the fuck he was thinking.

"Bailey," she stuck her hand out to KJ.

"Nice to meet you shorty, have a seat," KJ said as he dapped me up. He gave me a look, so I knew he agreed with me on the fact that Bailey was nothing short of flawless.

Once we were all seated, KJ said, "So do you know anything about Pablo that we don't know?"

"I just know where his new workers hang out at. They've been complaining because he doesn't have any work for them to push. I also think he has a new partner, but I don't know who."

"So he needs a supplier," KJ smiled.

"I would assume so. All he had was what he stole from you guys, and since you took that they've been dry. Swiss went by the trap you guys robbed, and it was like a ghost house," Bailey explained.

"And you said you know where his people be at?" I asked to be sure and she nodded.

"Do they know you?" KJ asked her.

"No, I highly doubt it. I'm not from around here, and I usually don't go many places except to Swiss' spot."

"I need you to get your hair dyed just in case," KJ suggested.

"Uh-"

"Either you dye your hair or we can end this meeting right now," KJ stated sternly.

"I can dye it," she nodded and sighed.

"Good, once you get your hair dyed, I need to see you and make sure you look different. Where do they hang out at?"

"Mainly around West Fried Chicken on Edmundson Avenue, I think the street is called. They're always there just talking and shooting the shit."

"Alright, I need you and Kendrin to have a 'meeting' there. Talk as if you're a potential new connect that Kendrin is trying to acquire.

Make sure they overhear you. Word is gonna get back to Pablo, and since he's a snake, he's gonna try and steal you to be his connect. Once you set up a meeting time with Pablo, I need you to shoot me the details."

"How will they find me to tell me about Pablo?" Bailey asked.

"Hang around outside a little after Kendrin leaves, and I guarantee one of them will approach you. When they do, agree to meet their boss. Simple as that."

"Don't you wanna just capture and kill them?" she frowned.

"No, I want you to do what I just asked you to do. Dye your damn hair and have the meeting with my brother. I'm tired of capturing and killing corner boys; I want Pablo. I'll be expecting an invitation to you and Pablo's meeting very soon. Don't fuck this up, Bailey."

"I-I won't," she stammered slightly.

After discussing shit with KJ, we left the warehouse. I wanted to go home and run on the treadmill to clear my head. It was important that I be on my toes and ready for battle.

"Am I taking you back to Swiss' crib?" I asked Bailey. It was around 7pm at night, and already dark.

"Yeah, I have nowhere else to go."

"You don't like staying with Swiss?"

"I don't mind, he's nice enough to allow me to stay there for free, so I don't complain. I wish I had somewhere better, though."

"You fled with no money from Cali?" I asked as I made a left turn.

"How did you know that's where I came from?"

"Don't worry about that, just answer the question."

"Yeah I did. My boyfriend Brandon would've killed me if I hadn't."

"What you do to him?" I was hoping that she wasn't some little hoe. I don't why I cared but I did.

"I did nothing to him. I just wouldn't let him beat on me anymore," she exhaled. I glanced over at her and she was staring out the window.

"So you chose the farthest state possible huh?"

"I initially wanted to go to Maine, but I ran out of money."

We laughed in unison as I turned and made it to Swiss' crib. I pulled over and threw the car in park so that she could get out.

"Here," I handed her six hundred dollars.

"Kendrin it's fine-"

"Take the damn money shorty."

"Thank you," she whispered and slid it from my hands. "Can I hug you?"

"Come here," I waved her over.

She threw her arms around my neck and squeezed me. She smelled good as hell, and her body felt even better in my arms.

"I really wanna be with you and be down for you if you let me. I'm dead serious about being on the side. As long as you love me enough I'll be good," she whispered and rubbed the back of my head.

"Why?" I asked, still holding her.

"I'm just really feeling you. Your personality, your demeanor, and your sexy obviously. Those eyes and dimples did it for me."

I removed her from my embrace and said, "I'll catch you later shorty. Let me know when we're gonna have the fake meeting."

"Okay, and if you ever want someone to just chill with, text me," she said before getting out of the car.

I closed my eyes and took a deep breath before pulling from the curb. Shorty was persistent.

I FINISHED RUNNING on the treadmill for an hour, and then I climbed into the shower. When I walked out of the bathroom and into the bedroom, Willow was sitting in the bed watching TV. She had on a bikini type top and some panties. I noticed her stomach was starting to bulge, even though we'd just found out that she was pregnant. Regardless, she looked beautiful as ever.

"What you watching shorty?" I questioned as I rubbed deodorant under my pits. I still had the towel wrapped around my waist.

"This show called Gossip Girl, have you ever seen it?"

"I think you know the answer to that baby."

I walked over to the bed and removed the towel I was wearing. I then grabbed the remote from her hand and cut the TV off.

"Kendrin!" she whined and chuckled as I pulled her down to slip my tongue into her mouth.

I pulled her little bra top to the sides since I didn't know how to get it off and then began sucking her nipples as if I was getting barbecue sauce off of my fingertips. While doing that, I slipped my hand down between her legs and began to play with her clit while she moaned. She was dripping already. I stopped sucking her nipples and yanked down her panties with the quickness. Spreading her legs wide, I got down between them and rubbed my dick along the slit between her legs. I could see in her face that she was hoping I didn't make her uncomfortable.

"Uuuhh," she cooed as I began to push into her. It was so snug yet gushy, making it the perfect combination.

"Damn Lo," I whispered before sucking her soft full lips. Her long ass hair was covering the whole damn pillow because of how spread out it was. "You are so beautiful shorty," I said before gripping her face for a kiss.

"Uuuh aah uuuh," she called out and I felt her burst on my dick. "Kendri-" I forced my tongue into her mouth before she could finish, and kissed her hungrily.

I wound my hips into her, making sure to be very careful. Cupping one of her breast, I began to devour it again while speeding up my thrusts. Once I felt my dick get a little harder, and my pelvis tighten, I knew my peak was near. I lifted up as if I was doing a push up and then began to beat it up.

"Oh! Uhhh! Oh my gosh, Kendriiin!" Willow yelped before drenching my pole again.

"Shit!" I grumbled after slamming into her three good times and releasing. "Was that good?" I asked as I rubbed her hair back, still inside her.

"Perfect," she nodded before we began tonguing it up. Pregnant pussy was a game changer for sure.

"ARE YOU ALMOST READY PAPI?" My mother came into my room as I was fixing my tie. I was getting ready for a meeting that would change my life forever.

"I'm trying to get there, but this tie is irking my nerves."

"Are you still frustrated about Shannon?"

"Yeah, she hasn't said anything to me really. When we text it's dry because she only gives one word answers. Then she won't answer the phone or FaceTime calls, so it seems we're just coming a part at the seams," I sighed.

"I know you love her Kenzie, but you need to focus tonight," my mother finished fixing my tie and then rubbed it down. "You need to be in the right mind set for this dinner in order to make the right decision."

"I know ma, I'm gonna be good," I smiled down at her and she grinned.

"Good, I will be downstairs setting the table. Peter should be here in about half an hour."

"I'll be ready with bells on."

We both laughed at my sarcasm, and then she left out.

I plopped down on the bed after tucking my tie under the V-neck sweater I had on. Shannon ignoring me and being cold had me all in my fucking feelings. I honestly didn't understand why she was acting like this, all because of a damn fight she had with Rosalind. She's acting as if I sent the bitch in there to start something. Plus, I knew she and Gianna went over there to retaliate, so she should really be over it. *Get it together Kenzie,* I told myself.

I took a couple deep breaths and then went downstairs to see if my mom needed any help. After setting the table with her, the door-bell rang making me more nervous than ever. I had bigger shit to think about than Shannon's flip flopping ass.

"Have a seat son and chill," my father pointed to a chair at the table before he and my mother went to let in Peter Ayers, the college scout for the Brooklyn Nets.

My choices were between them and the 76'ers. Right now I was looking at money and years since closeness wasn't in the cards. I didn't care too much about the teams wins and losses, because once I joined everything would change.

"Kenzie!" Peter walked in with my parents. I stood up to greet him and we shook hands.

"How are you, Mr. Ayers?"

"Please, call me Peter."

"Everyone sit down so we can eat," my mother smiled as my father pulled her chair out.

We did as she asked and then prayed together over the meal. After everyone had filled their plates up, the conversation began.

"So are the Nets your first choice Kenzie?"

"They are," I lied. I didn't know who was my first choice between them and Philly, but I was gonna stroke his ego for him.

"Great, well I'm pretty much ready to talk to you about contracts, that's if Mr. and Mrs. King don't mind discussing business over the meal," Peter looked to my parents who shook their heads to say they didn't mind.

"I'm ready too," I nodded.

"We know you're a shooting guard, so that is the position we'd put you in Kenzie. But the big thing here is money I know. No need to sugarcoat things, I'm sure you're wondering how much we are looking to pay you. The answer to that is twenty-one million per year, and we wanna sign you for three years to the Nets," he paused, looked at my parents and then back to me.

"And after that three years?" I inquired. Twenty-one million sounded marvelous.

"Well, we have to play it by ear and see how well our relationship is working. If after three years we wanna keep you on, which I'm sure we will, then at that point we will draw up a new contract. Most likely it will be for a higher amount than what we're offering you now, just because you'll be a more seasoned NBA player. That's if you wanted to stay with us. I think you'll love being with the Nets, though, and I think you could take us to some championships for sure."

His offer was sounding a little better than Philly's, but Philly was closer.

"Would Kenzie have to live in Brooklyn?" my mother asked.

"Well he would be there a lot, so it would be best for him to have at least an apartment in New York," he responded.

"I think the Nets are a great choice for you Kenzie," my father nodded as he cut into his steak.

"All the way in New York huh?" my mom looked at me and half smiled.

"But he's a big boy, he'll be okay," Peter added and laughed heartily.

My mom just pursed her lips and nodded. I knew her usually tough ass was gon' cry when I left. We talked some more about the contract and what I would be dealing with out there. And hearing that I would be starting was like music to my ears. Philly said they would maybe have me as a part of the starting line up, but Peter was promising. I refused to go from the starting five to a bench warmer. Making sure I started was a big thing for me, because I've seen many players get into the NBA and never get out of their warm up gear. I was too good at what I did for that to happen to me, even in Philly, but I wanted to be on the court out the gate.

"Well the dinner was great Mrs. King, but I must be going now. Kenzie when you decide, give me a call and we can pull out the paperwork," Peter nodded.

"Thank you, sir," I shook his hand.

Once Peter left, I said goodnight to my parents and ran upstairs. I was exhausted as hell, so as soon as I changed out of my clothes and showered, I knocked the fuck out.

1am the next morning…

"Oooh fuck, baby."

"Whose pussy is it Jess?" my dad grunted and I almost threw up.

"Yours Kendon," my mother whimpered, almost sounding like she was about to cry.

"What the fuck!" I shouted. I hated when I woke up in the middle of the night to them fucking. And why did they have to talk so nastily to one another?

I snatched my phone and shoved some headphones in it so that I could listen to some music and drown out my pornstar parents. When it lit up I saw I had a text message from this chick named Imani. She was a cute little Asian and Black chick that went to Morgan State with me. We used to flirt a lot before I got with Shannon, and while I was with Rosalind, but shit started getting serious with Shannon so I stopped replying to her messages.

Imani: *I miss talking to you.*

I clicked her contact information, scrolled down, and tapped the phone icon. I waited as the line trilled, and then finally she picked up.

"Kenzie, I missed you."

"Oh yeah? What you doing texting me at booty call hours?" I asked as I stared at my dark ceiling.

"I don't know. I just texted you when you popped into my mind. I've been seeing you on TV. I watched your last game against Alabama when school was in, good job!"

"Thanks, shorty, I appreciate the support. You've been good?"

"Yes, my grades are popping and that's the only thing that matters right now. Does Shannon know you're calling my phone at 1am?" she chuckled.

"Does she know that you texted me at 1am?"

"No," she laughed.

"Aight then shorty."

"When can I see you Kenzie? I need a hug or something. I missed how cool we used to be, and how close."

I was at the doctor today, because I wanted to check on my baby and hopefully get something for the morning sickness. I was vomiting so much it was ridiculous. Almost everything I ate was coming up, and I knew that wasn't right. I was eating for two, so throwing everything up couldn't be healthy for either of us. I felt miserable overall, and I could barely handle the things I needed to for my wedding. Speaking of my wedding, I had shit to do later on today, so I hoped my doctor could make me feel better so my business could be handled.

Kendrin leaned over and kissed my cheek, making a smile form on my face. He'd been so helpful to me, and he didn't seem to mind us only doing missionary every night. For some reason, doggystyle was too painful, and getting on top made me nauseous. He said he didn't care because I felt good either way. Yeah right, as freaky as he liked to get, I knew he was lying.

"Hopefully, she can give me something so I can start satisfying you again," I squeezed his hand. He kissed the back of mine and then stared into my eyes with his green ones.

"You always satisfy me, Lo."

"Even though it's always missionary?"

"Yeah, I get to see your beautiful face, kiss you, and then these," he squeezed my one of my breasts.

"Kendrin that hurt," I whined and chuckled.

"I'm sorry shorty," he placed a kiss on my lips.

Ten minutes later we were called to the back where I was to get my first ultrasound. I laid back on the little examination table, and then Kendrin sat in the chair and held my hand.

"Can I say something? But you have to promise not to get mad," he said as he touched me.

"What?" I was scared of what the hell he was about to say. You never knew when it came to Kendrin.

"I know we just found out that you're pregnant babe, but your stomach is already sticking out a little."

"Kendrin!" I yelped. I was about to cry at the fact that he was calling me fat. I didn't have time for complaints right now.

"It's not huge shorty, your stomach just isn't flat anymore down here," he touched the bottom part of my stomach.

I admit it was weird. I'd just found out I was pregnant a couple weeks ago when I threw up, but my stomach was already looking bigger than it should've. It wasn't protruding crazily or anything, but the bulge down by my pelvis area was small yet pronounced.

"You think something is wrong?" I looked into his eyes and he shrugged.

"Don't worry yourself, just chill and wait to see what she says."

I nodded my head and gripped his hand, as my palms began to sweat. Something wasn't right, but I was scared to find out. I didn't want my first pregnancy to be filled with drama and complications, all the while trying to get married. Something had to go smoothly for me, shit I already didn't fit into my damn dress!

"Good morning Mrs. King!" the doctor floated in and closed the door behind her.

"Good morning," I smiled.

"And good morning to you Mr. King." she looked at Kendrin and he nodded. "Now how are we feeling?" She diverted her attention back to me.

"Terrible. I'm throwing up a lot every morning. I even asked my best friend who just had a baby if it was normal, and she said it was more than what she puked. Also, my stomach is already showing," I lifted my shirt to show her my small bulge.

"Wow okay, yeah that definitely looks like four months there. Well, let's find out what's going on Mrs. King. When did you realize you were pregnant?" She began cleaning her hands.

"A couple weeks ago?" I looked to Kendrin.

"Yeah like three weeks ago," he nodded.

"And how did you come to that conclusion?" she asked as she pulled some gloves on.

"I threw up, but I took a test the next morning and it showed positive as soon as my pee hit it."

"Hmm, okay. So the symptoms are what informed you of your pregnancy, and the test confirmed it," she stated to be clear.

"Yes," Kendrin and I replied together.

"Okay, and before throwing up, you experienced nothing strange going on with your body?" she quizzed and I shook my head no.

"Well, she was complaining about pain when we had sex," Kendrin admitted.

"Kendrin!" I bucked my eyes at him. Did he really tell her that? What the fuck was wrong with his blunt ass?

"No, it's fine. Actually, that is a common symptom of pregnancy. Certain positions aren't as comfortable or pleasurable. Alright let's see what's going on Mrs. King," she replied. She place the vaginal cameria inside of me, and then began to move it around alittle, causing some discomfort. "Alrighty," she said and continued to move it around.

"I know something's wrong," I sniffled and Kendrin rubbed my hand.

"Well Mrs. King, you've absolutely been pregnant longer than a couple weeks. You're almost eleven weeks pregnant, and with twins."

My mouth dropped open as I stared at her, waiting for her to say she was joking with me.

"Twins? You sure?" Kendrin quizzed.

"Yes, that explains why you're showing way more than someone else who is almost three months."

"So two babies?"

"Yes, and your pregnancy is perfectly healthy Mrs. King. But you're vomiting more because it's two of them in there," she giggled.

I wanted to faint, but at the same time, I wanted to celebrate the fact that my babies were okay. We discussed some more things and other signs I needed to look out for when carrying twins, and then she got me some prenatal pills before we left.

I was still in disbelief that I was having two kids. I'd just coped with the fact that I was having one, and now it was two?

"How are you feeling about us having twins?" I asked Kendrin as we walked to the car.

"I'm happy that you're not ill or anything, and that they're healthy. I don't know how to feel about it being two, though."

"Me either, but the bright side is that I'll be done having kids after them."

"No, you won't, I want four like my parents."

"Well, hopefully we can have two sets of twins," I nudged him.

"That could work," he said before kissing my lips and opening the passenger side door for me.

I didn't know what to think, but I was gonna embrace it. Two babies were definitely gonna put my ass through the ringer.

After sitting down and eating lunch, we decided to tell Kendrin's parents and then my mom what was happening. I knew they were gonna be just as floored as we were.

"What bomb are you dropping now?" Nic asked as she leaned back on the couch.

Mr. King, Kendria, and Kendrae were in the den as well, because we wanted to tell everybody at once.

"We're having twins," I replied and clenched my teeth.

"Oh my gosh, I'm gonna have three grandkids," Nic chuckled. "The both of us," she kissed Mr. King on the cheek as he nodded while chuckling.

"Dang bro, goodluck," Kendrae dapped Kendrin up and then hugged me.

"Y'all gon' be real stressed. My friend from school has twins, and now her hair is falling out, she never has time for homework, she even-"

"Kendria, baby girl, this is supposed to be a happy thing," Mr. King stopped his daughter from scaring the shit out of me.

"Right, congrats guys," she grinned.

FRIDAY EVENING...

I SAT at my vanity listening and swaying to Migos. I was going to a party tonight with my cousin Kendlie, and I couldn't wait. Kendlie was my uncle Kendon's daughter and my best friend. I loved that she was my cousin too because it was easier for us to hang out all the time.

We weren't supposed to go to a party tonight, though, I was supposedly spending the night with my friend Victoria from school. My dad called her mom to make sure, and of course, she covered for me. Victoria's mom was more like her sister, but my daddy didn't know that. If he did, he would never allow me to hang with her. I mean Kendlie and I *were* spending the night with Victoria, just after the damn party.

My dad and brothers did not want to let me do my thing. They watched my every move, and when *they* weren't doing it, they had someone else watching me. I was almost sixteen years old, and I'd never had a boyfriend, nor have I seen a dick in person. Well I accidently saw KJ's when I burst into his room a couple of years ago, and boy was I traumatized. But other than my fucking brother, I hadn't seen one. I was about the only girl in school who was still a damn virgin, other than Kendlie. People knew Kendlie and I were family, though, so she didn't count to me.

I wanted to have sex sometimes, but then when I thought about how disappointed my daddy would be, I changed my mind. I loved to make him happy, so I was gonna wait until I was married like he wanted. He'd even given me a beautiful diamond ring band that symbolized my promise to him, and I just couldn't break it.

I stood up and walked to the mirror so that I could check myself out. I was wearing some tight skinny jeans that hugged my ankles and my slim thick body just right. I was gonna wear a tube top, but I wore an oversized button up on top to trick my daddy. My mom never fell for the clothes trick, but she wasn't as strict about my attire as my dad was. He hated for me to wear anything that showed my skin.

I slipped into some moccasins and then stuffed these new heels I bought into my duffle bag under all of my shit. I left my long hair down so it could sweep my tailbone just the way that I liked it to. Once I had my phone, keys, and purse, I was ready for the night.

I walked out of my room and down the stairs so that I could find my daddy. I knew he was in the den around this time, watching sports.

"Daddy, can you tell Dice I'm ready," I smiled as I walked into the den.

Dice was one of my dad's men that always drove me around and watched me like a fucking hawk. Tonight he wouldn't be watching me because he thought I was simply sleeping over Victoria's. The thought alone had me laughing giddily on the inside.

"Come all the way in and let me see what you got on," he waved me in. I rolled my eyes but not to where he could see, and then stood in front of him.

"You look beautiful," he smiled as he took in my skinny jeans, oversized button up, and moccasins. Little did he know, I was gonna be dressed like a little thottie tonight. "You need some money?" he asked.

"Yes of course. We may go to the mall and breakfast in the morning."

"I'll have Dice take you guys."

"Daddy no! Victoria's mom can take us to eat and stuff!" I whined.

"No, Dice is gonna take you," he stated sternly. I inhaled sharply, taking in the bomb ass smell of his cologne. "How much do you need baby?"

"Like a grand," I grinned making him laugh. "I want three hundred and in twenties dad, please no big bills."

He smacked his lips at me, and then typed a code into his little drawer next to him. He counted out the money in twenties as I'd requested, and then handed it over.

"Have a good time," he said as I kissed his face.

I rushed out and through the foyer, and spotted my mom so I kissed her before slipping out of the door. Kendrae was walking up as I was leaving.

"Fuck you going all in a hurry?" he looked me up and down with his matching green eyes, looking like a teenage version of my father.

"To Victoria's."

"Yeah right, you're going to that fucking house party on Beehler ain't you?" he grinned, obviously peeping game.

"How did you know about the party?"

"Dria, I know everything about every party that cracks in Baltimore." I hated and loved him at the same time. He was clever as fuck already, just like my Daddy, KJ, and Kendrin.

"Don't tell daddy!" I begged.

"Ain't nobody a snitch aight? But Dad may find out anyways."

"No, he won't, thanks!" I kissed his cheek and then darted off.

"Aye did ma cook?" he called after me.

"Yeah!" I shouted back, as Dice opened the backseat door for me. I climbed in, and squealed with excitement before Dice got into the driver's seat.

VICTORIA, Kendlie, and I walked into the house on Beehler, and this shit was poppin' already. I had on my same tight jeans, but with a red tube top, and red stilettos to match. My long ass hair was parted down the middle, and hanging down. I even had some red lipstick on that I'd recently purchased on my last mall trip.

"Damn bitch, when did you get that watch?" Victoria asked me.

Victoria was a baddie, too. She had smooth dark skin, thick shoulder length curly hair, and a slim frame like myself. Other than Kendlie, she was my best friend.

"Dad bought it for me for Valentine's Day earlier this year," I replied as we continued walking through the party.

"I wish I had your Daddy, but for other uses," she chuckled as Kendlie and I pretended to throw up.

"Please stop crushing on my father, he's old."

"He don't look like it. Your daddy is fine as fuck bitch. Even my mama agreed. You know when he be calling she be softening her voice and tryna prolong the conversation."

"Girl, you better tell your mama to chill, because my mother don't play that shit," I chuckled even though I was dead serious.

"She's right Victoria, our moms used to kick ass together over our dads," Kendlie backed me up.

Kendlie looked just like my aunt Jessica. She had smooth caramel skin, bra strap length brown hair, and a slim thick frame. We both looked just like our moms, but we had green eyes. Our friendship was so perfect.

"Damn," Victoria laughed.

We continued sauntering through the party, slowly dancing to the music. "Back Up" by Dej Loaf came on, and we really started dancing. As I was moving my body to the beat, I felt someone come behind me and grab my waist. I looked at Kendlie who was in front of me, and she gave me a thumbs up, letting me know he was cute. I checked over my shoulder quickly, and he shot me a cute smile. Once I saw how bomb he was, I really started popping my ass. I moved my long hair over my shoulder so he could get a better view of my small round ass, and continued to wind and twerk my hips. I was having so much fun grinding all on this nigga. I felt his dick get hard, which only motivated me to keep going to the Dej Loaf track. When we made eye contact, I mouthed the part where she says *If I fuck and make you cum, you gotta promise not to stress me.* He just chuckled at me. I continued to dance on him until the song was over.

As soon as the song switched, he hugged my body tightly from behind. He then turned me to face him. He had deep caramel skin, full lips, perfect teeth, and short curly hair. He was so fucking bomb. I'd never seen him around Baltimore though, so I wondered where he'd been. He was way taller than me too, even though I was only 5'4, and had a lean muscular build, with a few tattoos.

"What's your name?" he asked me.

"Kendria," I replied and waited for him to scurry off in fear.

"That's a unique and pretty ass name. Mine is Marcel." I was shocked that he was still standing here in front of me after hearing my name.

"Nice to meet you Marcel," I giggled.

"Likewise Kendria," he licked his lips as he gazed into my eyes lustfully. "Let me get your number."

I'd never been asked that before. Well, I had been, but as soon as they were about to store it, they would ask for my name, which changed their mind. Was I really about to successfully give my number out?

"Okay." I read it off to him as he typed it into his phone.

He shot me a text right away, and then I pulled my iPhone out to store him as well. I got warm all over at the thought of texting a boy.

"How old are you?" he questioned as he pulled me to a table in the dark ass house, which was only lit up with blue and purple strobe lights.

"I'm almost sixteen," I nibbled on my lip. I didn't like saying I was fifteen. "How old are you?"

"I'm nineteen. Is that cool?"

"Yeah, I like older men."

We both chuckled in unison.

"Good, because I'm about to change your life," he said as his eyes wandered all over my body.

Oh shit, I think I found me a man. I just hoped the men in my family didn't run him off. My brothers weren't the only ones who tripped, Kaleeini, Kenzie, and Kendrew Jr. were just as protective. I was willing to risk it for his fine ass, though. I just hoped he felt the same way about me.

THE NEXT DAY...

I woke up and was still tired from that party last night. That shit was so much fun, and I even met me a little something to get into. She was off top the prettiest little bitch I'd ever seen. She had a cute little frame, a small round ass, long ass dark hair, full lips, perfect teeth, a little bunny nose, and some pretty ass dark green eyes. Little mama was young as fuck but I wasn't tripping. I wondered if she was a virgin. Either way, I was smashing, but if she'd never been touched that meant I could claim the pussy as mine. Plus the way she was moving her little body had my dick hard as a damn brick.

I looked at the clock next to me and saw it was already ten in the damn morning. I needed to get up and see what I could get into today; hopefully, I could get into Kendria. I picked my phone up off the nightstand and went into my texts.

Me: *Good morning beautiful.*

After about fifteen minutes she finally replied.

Kendria: *Good morning. You're just waking up?*

Me: *Yeah I am. What you doing?*

Kendria: *At IHOP with my friends.*

_Me:_ _I wanna see you today, you should come to my hotel._
Kendria: _I can't._
_Me:_ _Why?_

Fuck the texting, I decided to call her ass. I really wanted to get her over here. I wanted to fuck her all day if I could.

"Hello?" she answered and I could tell she was in the bathroom of the restaurant.

"What's up baby, why can't you come see me?"

"Because I just can't. I would need a ride over there."

"I can pick you up. That's no problem, I got a car."

"You can't pick me up, Marcel. Look, next Friday you can pick me up. I have to pull some strings in order to see you."

Who the fuck was she? Some king's daughter? She was acting like she was undercover or something.

"Damn baby, that's a little less than a week from now. I really wanted to chill with you," I sighed hoping to convince her.

BOOM! BOOM! BOOM!

I heard someone beating on the door.

"I know Marcel, but next Friday okay? Bye," she quickly hung up.

BOOM! BOOM! BOOM!

"Aight! Shit!" I hollered and got out of the hotel bed. I snatched the door open, and my brothers walked in smiling. "Fuck y'all beating on the door like the police for."

"Who was you in here on the phone with little nigga?" my brother Duck asked me.

"Man don't worry about who the fuck I was on the phone with. What do y'all nigga's want?"

My brother Lucky darted and snatched my phone up from the dresser. These niggas were so childish some fucking times. I hated having twins as my brothers. They were always conspiring shit together, and just expecting me to go along with it. Hence, why I had to leave the comfort of my home in New Jersey to come down to Maryland.

"Kendria," Lucky chuckled and nodded as he looked into my phone.

"Give me my shit," I hollered and snatched my phone.

"Wait, Kendria. I've heard that name before," Duck squinted his eyes and folded his arms. "Oh shit, Kendria King," he grinned and looked at Lucky who began to laugh.

"Aye bro, keep talking to that little bitch. We may need to kidnap her ass or something."

"Man, nah! I ain't about to be a part of that shit! I'm trying to get me something," I frowned.

"You can fuck her all you want bro, but when we need you to bring her our way, you need to comply. You know we're rivaling them King boys, and taking their little sister or cousin would do wonders for us," Duck nodded.

I did not wanna be a part of their little feud with the King boys. I was just trying to get in where I fit in, namely inside Kendria. But my loyalty was to my brothers, so if they needed me to sacrifice her ass so they could win, I would do it in a heartbeat.

"Alright man," I sighed.

"Cool, so keep a cool relationship with her until we need her. And try to keep that shit on the low so her brothers and shit don't find out," Duck gripped my shoulder.

"I got you."

"Damn she's sexy as fuck, but young. You may have to pass that shit one of these nights," Lucky grinned, making Duck and I laugh loudly.

I FELT someone shaking me in my bed, and when I looked up I saw it was my father. I rubbed my hand over my face and looked around my room trying to gain some of my composure. I wanted to curse him out for waking me, but I was too tired to do so.

"Shannon, Kenzie is here. Do you want me to send him back here or tell him to go home?" he asked.

"Umm, you can send him back here," I sighed and then slammed my face back into the pillow.

I hated taking midday naps because I always felt really groggy whenever I woke up. I sat up and then grabbed my skirt to put on before Kenzie came back here. I then checked my breath, and although it was fine because I'd only taken a nap, I sprayed some breath spray.

I heard a light knock at the door, so I yelled "Come in!"

My dad peeked in, and I could see Kenzie's tall ass standing behind him. He looked so good, and I missed him. My clit began to throb a bit as I began to think about us fucking.

"I'm gonna run to the store, do you want anything?" my father questioned.

"No, I'm good thank you."

He nodded and walked away, allowing Kenzie to come into my room. After closing my bedroom door, he neared me and then pulled me into a tight hug.

"I missed you," he said as he cupped my face for a kiss.

I said nothing as we began to kiss hungrily and heavily. His lips felt so good, and I missed them, just not the drama that came along with him. He backed me into the bed, and I fell back on it. Rushing between my legs, he began to yank on my panties until he just changed his mind and moved them to the side. We kept kissing as he played with my clit, causing me to moan loudly. Thank God my father had stepped out. A few short moments later, I felt him pushing himself inside me. Kenzie was very well endowed, and damn was I grateful.

"Shit," he whispered as he began to hump me slowly.

He felt so good that I began pressing him into me. I hadn't fucked him in forever it seemed, so I was cumming already after only a few long strokes. He gripped my headboard, spread my legs wider, and then began pounding my center with every muscle in his body. I loved that he knew just how to fuck me, and when to fuck me a certain way. He knew when I wanted it slow and sensual, and when I wanted it rough and nasty.

"Oooh uuuh fuck! Kenzie!" I called out as he demolished my pussy.

I was cumming so hard that I was wetting my comforter. I was convinced he had the best dick, even though it was the only one I'd tried. I swear I could hear my pussy crying as he slammed into it.

"Ugghhhhh!" he grunted and released inside of me.

We laid there kissing for a bit, and once I came down from that orgasm, I nudged him off of me. I shouldn't have let him fuck, but my body was missing him.

"What?" He frowned.

"Move, I need to pee." I pushed him some more.

I felt bad for letting him fuck me when I was supposed to be mad at him. He sucked his teeth and moved from in between my legs.

Rushing off to the bathroom, I grabbed a face towel and wet it with warm water and soap, before cleaning my vagina. I then grabbed another one and brought it to Kenzie.

"Thanks babe," he sighed and then began cleaning his dick. Once he was finished, I took it to the bathroom and dropped it into the hamper. "What's wrong Shan?" he groaned and fell back onto my bed when I returned.

"Kenzie I can't be with you anymore." Before the words even came out of my mouth, he sat back up.

"What? Why?"

"It's too much drama. Our relationship used to be fun and now-"

"Wait, because we hit a rough patch you wanna break up?"

"A rough patch? This isn't a patch Kenzie! A patch is supposed to end quickly, we're still dealing with the shit!"

"So that's why you've been ignoring my calls and shit. I'm over here blowing up your fucking phone to tell you my good news, and yo' ass couldn't even answer. I see why now."

"What good news?" I walked closer to him.

"Don't even matter Shannon."

"It does baby, I wanna know. Just because I wanna break up doesn't mean I don't care about the things that happen in your life."

"Well I don't need you to care," he shook his head as he stared at the wall angrily.

His side profile was just as handsome as his front. His caramel complexion had a red undertone, signaling his anger.

I wasn't sure if I'd made a mistake or not, but I knew in this moment I didn't feel like dealing with the shit that came with our relationship right now. I needed some peace.

"Kenzie maybe we should just go on a break and figure out if we really wanna be together."

"I don't need to figure out shit Shannon. But if you wanna break up, cool. I'm gone." He stood to his feet and so did I. Was this really what I wanted? Maybe I reacted too soon.

"Kenzie wait I-"

"You need to figure your shit out Shan! There are always gonna be women who are after me, and you said you didn't care. I admit that I fucked up with the whole Rosalind shit, but I promised you it wouldn't happen again! And you forgave me, so why are we back at square one? If you loved me you wouldn't even be trying to leave me over some bullshit like this. But maybe you don't."

"Kenzie, you know I love you."

"Do you? Because it sure and the fuck doesn't seem like it."

He left my room and booked it through the apartment. I had to run after him because he was covering way more ground with his long ass legs.

"Kenzie-"

"I'm done with yo' indecisive ass! It's a wrap!" he hollered down into my face, and slammed the front door behind himself, making me jump.

I began to tear up before going into my bedroom and slamming the door myself. Sometimes the best things for us hurt the most. I just hoped that I didn't make a stupid decision.

My plan worked just the way I'd wanted it to, and I must say that I was over fucking joyed. Bailey met with my brother and pretended to be this connect just liked I'd asked. And just like I knew, Pablo's little flunkies approached her to get her contact information in order to meet up with him and become his supplier. This shit was so easy that it had me wondering if it was a set up. I was starting to get insulted that such dumb niggas like Pablo and TJ thought they could win against me. I was the King, and a part of me felt like these niggas should be jailed for committing treason.

Anyway, to Pablo's knowledge, Bailey was a chick named Alexia who had connects to a man named Gabriel out in Columbia. She could get him the best cocaine straight from Columbia, for him to push through the streets. She made it clear to him that she could only work with us or him, so you know he was doing the most to get her. He told her that all he needed was the product and that he could make her millions. That shit was hilarious. It was hilarious because he thought he could actually sell on our streets and not be met with any repercussions. I thought he was smarter than that but I should've known he wasn't. Any nigga that tried to come for me can't be smart.

"So where are they now?" I asked Kendrin as we passed a blunt back and forth.

We found out Pablo had a new partner named Buzz, and Bailey made sure they were both at this meeting tonight so we could dead both of their asses.

"She's on her way to his house. He told her that he couldn't meet outside because we were looking for him."

"That nigga is a for real bitch. Why start all this then retreat?" I scoffed as I cranked up my car.

"Okay, I plugged in the address," Kendrin informed me, so I pulled off in the Cutlass.

We made it to Pablo's crib in Sandtown, and it was pretty beat the fuck up. The condo styled home looked to be pretty spacious from the outside, but it definitely needed some improvement as far as the outer aesthetics. Kendrin and I locked our heat in our waists and waited until Bailey texted to confirm that she was inside his crib.

"Let's go," I said before the both of us climbed out of the car.

We walked up to the house calmly, as if we were just there to visit old friends. There was no need to sneak because Bailey was gonna let us in. I wasn't sure how, but she said she'd answer the door for us. I knocked on the door and smiled at my brother when I heard Bailey say that she would get it.

This nigga didn't even protest. That told me right there how dumb he was. It wouldn't alarm you that a complete stranger is willing to answer your door? Maybe he was too scared to answer his own door. I hoped not, because if so, he was for real a waste of my time then. Bailey slowly opened the door, and Kendrin and I walked in as if we had nothing to hide.

"Aye what the fuck! You stupid ass bitch!" Pablo hopped up and tried to run towards his back door.

PHEW!

I put my silencer on and capped his leg, causing him to collapse to the ground. His homeboy Buzz tried to scramble out, but Kendrin shot his ass in the back of the head with one try, causing him to fall face forward. We walked over by Pablo, as Bailey locked the door, and I kicked him so he could turn onto his back.

"You know, because it took so long for me to find you, I'm angry as fuck," I gritted as I looked down at him. "The more days that went by, the angrier I became."

He just stared up at me while holding his leg to his chest.

"I-I made a mistake man come on. This shit wasn't even my idea, it was Chef's," he pleaded making me chuckle to myself.

"Damn, Chef didn't even rat you out before he took his last breath, and you over here singing like a fucking canary," I shook my head.

PHEW!

Kendrin shot him in his other leg for being a snitch, and he howled to the damn moon.

"Fuck! What the fuck y'all gon' do to me man?" he sobbed like a bitch.

"Anybody else on your team?" I questioned.

"No, nobody else," he whimpered. "But aye, look, I was supposed to hook up with them Paine brothers coming down from Camden, but if you keep me alive-"

"What? You gon' cease contact with them?" I burst into laughter. "And if I killed you, you wouldn't?" I frowned down at his dumb ass.

No deals could be made while a gun was to your head. He just stared at me and cried hard like a bitch, realizing his logic was hella illogical.

"Kill him," I told Kendrin and then placed my gun back into my waist. Kendrin popped him and then the three of us left after setting up the cleanup.

One down, two more bitch boys to go.

We drove over to Swiss' place, and the three of us went inside to chop it up for a few minutes or so.

"Bailey, thanks for umm helping out," I told her and she smiled.

"No problem, any time you guys need help just let me know."

I nodded and turned to leave, but Kendrin was still standing there. He peeled off some cash for her, and gave her a hug, before we both walked out to the car. She stood in the doorway watching Kendrin until we pulled off. He and shorty definitely had something going on.

"You smashed?" I asked as I lit another blunt.

"Nah, she wants me to, though."

"That's obvious."

"Yeah, telling me she'll play her role and all this other wild stuff. She's bad but I ain't interested."

"You must be a little fond of her if you're breaking her off."

"I'm breaking her off because I feel bad for shorty, not because I'm taking her up on her offer."

"Right," I chuckled. "She does look good, though."

"Don't I know it."

Hanging around Bailey could be bad news for my little brother. Nothing good could come from being around a bitch as bad as her. She seemed to have a cool personality too, which was a double whammy. I hoped he could control himself.

I dropped Kendrin off at home, and then went to my own. I showered as soon as I got there, and when I was done, I went in search of Gianna. I found her in K-Three's room tidying up. I slowly crept behind her and gripped her little body before kissing her neck.

"Stop scaring me KJ," she giggled.

I picked her up from behind and carried her to our bedroom. I was horny as fuck and ready to beat something up. I put her down once we got into the bedroom, and then immediately pulled her gown over her head. I then yanked her thong down and dropped to the floor. I began licking from her pussy to her ass, as she stood there moaning and whimpering.

"KJ, I love how freaky you are," she cried out as I sucked the life out of her clit from behind. "Mmm uh uuuh shit. Ti amo tanto (I love you so much)," she called out and exploded. I didn't know what that last part meant, but it sounded sexy as hell.

I pushed her down onto the bed so that she was lying flat on her stomach, and then I stepped out of my boxers that I'd just put on. Climbing onto the bed, I spread her legs open with my knees. I lowered myself closer to her, and then pushed the head of my dick into her snug wet opening.

"Fuck," I grumbled.

I humped slowly until my whole dick was inside of her. I then wrapped her hair around my fist and began slamming into her from behind. The shit felt so fucking good, and the sight was wonderful, too.

"Ohh oooh uuuh Kendrick," she screamed as I rammed into her. Watching her little ass take this dick had me on one.

"Don't run," I told her.

I lifted her body up, placed one hand between her legs to toy with her clit, and then gripped one of her breasts with the other. I kept doing that as I wound my hips into her from behind. She looked so sexy, the way she was moaning and twisting her face up. Her body began sweating as I continued to let one hand play with her button, and the other grope her constantly. I made her turn her head to the side so I could suck her lips, while fucking her from behind.

"Kendrick, I'm about to cum," she whimpered right before gushing on my rod.

I wrapped my arm around her neck and then sat her up to continue working her. Her golden complexion began to turn red as I continued to fuck the shit out of her, bouncing her in my lap and sucking her neck.

"I'm about to nut, fuck. Tell me what I wanna hear Gigi," I growled.

"It's your pussy Kendrick, and nobody else's," she sniveled as I rubbed all over her little frame.

I sucked and bit the nape of her neck, and then finally I exploded. While trying to catch my breath, I rubbed all over her, and then bent her over so I could slide out. I turned her over so that she could face me, and then fell between her legs.

"You are a beast daddy," she panted as I kissed all over her stomach. I said nothing as I lifted my head and dipped my tongue into her mouth.

"WHAT EXACTLY DID he say about them, brothers?" I asked KJ as he, Kendrin, Lenny and I sipped beers at the warehouse.

"The nigga said he was supposed to link up with them, Paine brothers. So I'm thinking they were depending on Bailey to come through as connect for them as well. They were doing some alliance shit," KJ answered.

"Swiss, just hit me and said to come through, he got some pertinent information for us," Kendrin said after checking his work phone.

"Let's go," KJ instantly hopped up.

We piled into Lenny's Chevy Suburban and then headed over to see what Swiss was talking about. That nigga had really been down for the team and earning his stripes like a muthafucka.

"Aye we need to put homie on official payroll," I said as we pulled up and parked on Swiss' street.

"I was just thinking that. He's been helpful as fuck. Swiss is way more helpful than that nigga Oscar, and he ain't even got the laptop or tools," Kendrin agreed.

"Aye, the girl I was telling you about is ready to meet you whenever KJ," Lenny chimed in.

"Alright I'm gon' let you know when I have some time to get up with her," he replied before we all got out of the truck.

As we strolled up the walkway, Swiss came out and opened the door for us to come inside his house. Once we all got comfortable and situated, he pulled a stool up to sit on. I rubbed my hands together, ready to catch all that he was spilling.

"So them Paine brothers are about to start distributing, and they got two traps set up so far over in Park Heights," Swiss explained.

"Who is their supplier?" I frowned.

"I have no idea, you may wanna have your tech guy look into that," he shrugged. "All I know is, this is where the traps are." He slid a sheet of paper with the addresses onto the table.

"Would you guys like something to drink?" the chick Bailey asked once she entered the living room.

I'm assuming she was talking to all of us, but her eyes were locked on Kendrin as they smiled at one another.

"Nah, we good shorty," KJ responded as he looked over the paper Swiss had just handed over.

"Okay," Bailey replied and then came and sat next to Kendrin. He playfully squeezed her thick thigh while biting his lip, and she giggled before kissing his cheek.

This nigga was hella cozy with this girl, when he had a whole wife at home, and a wedding approaching in a damn week. On top of that, he had twins coming. I have no idea what he was thinking.

Bailey was beautiful as hell, and you'd need a magnifying glass to find a flaw on her, but Willow was the one for that nigga. Bailey also seemed too sweet to handle Kendrin's unhinged ass. She would be pulling her fucking hair out dealing with his wild ass.

"Let's go demolish this shit," KJ smiled.

"Tonight?" Kendrin frowned.

He then leaned up to look at the paper in KJ's hand, and Bailey placed her chin on his shoulder to look as well. I chuckled to myself because I knew Willow would murk this nigga if she walked in.

"Yeah, tonight. We gon' fuck that shit up and get this fucking war on the road," KJ chuckled.

"I'm with it," Lenny nodded.

"Let's go. Thanks, Swiss. I'm gon' be back tomorrow because I wanna talk about making shit permanent with our relationship. Maybe you too," KJ pointed to Bailey and she grinned.

We all started out, and as we were getting into the car, Bailey asked Kendrin, "You coming back after?"

"I'm going home shorty, what you talking about?" he cheesed.

"Text me if you change your mind," she looked up at him and then reached her hands out for a hug.

They embraced, and then he went and climbed into the car with us.

"He swear he's not smashing," KJ said as soon as Kendrin got into the car.

"You hit," I laughed and shook my head.

"Yo, I swear I have not fucked shorty. She's just cool and that's it, I promise."

"This nigga gave her money," KJ blabbed some more.

"Shorty is trying to get on her feet, and I helped her out. I'm not cheating on my wife. Y'all need to chill out with that shit before rumors start spreading," he sucked his teeth.

"Yeah, cause you know Willow would kill the both of y'all," Lenny chimed in and I nodded in agreement.

"She may not. She told me if she catches me doing anything again, she's leaving me. Talking about she ain't about to lose our babies over me," Kendrin smiled.

"Ma must've gotten ahold of her," KJ chimed in as Lenny continued to drive.

"Oh, I know she did. But I ain't worried because I'm being good to her. She can keep her little threats to herself," Kendrin replied.

We just laughed and continued to fuck with him until we got on the street of the first trap. We exited the vehicle together and then grabbed some gasoline and matches. We quickly ran onto the porch after double-checking the address and began pouring gasoline everywhere. Once we'd felt we'd covered enough ground, Lenny lit a match and then dropped it as we all booked it back to the car. The house went up in flames quicker than I thought it would have, and we sped off to the next one. We repeated the same steps at trap number two and then went back to the warehouse to chill for a bit.

"Them niggas gon' be hot!" Lenny laughed and so did we.

"Y'all better get ready. These niggas supposedly ain't shit to mess with," KJ sipped his beer.

"And neither are we," I chimed in and he nodded in agreement.

"The good thing about winning over these niggas, is that I think it may be the last time we need to prove ourselves," Kendrin said.

"Man I'm feeling like that, too. I know they gon' give us a run for our money, but in the end, we're gonna be seen as the ultimate in the game," Lenny said.

We all raised our beers in agreement, and then continued chilling and knocking them back. This was the calm before the storm.

***

"Babyyyyy," I stripped out of my clothes and climbed lazily into the bed with a sleeping Aysia.

"Kaleeini are you drunk?" she frowned as I kissed on her neck and rubbed her belly.

"Nope!" I chuckled.

I wasn't drunk, just a little buzzed. Those beers we were knocking back soon turned into Hennessy. The Hennessy was then used for a game of beer pong, despite it not being beer. If it weren't for Bolo, the four of us wouldn't have gotten home.

"Yes you are Kaleeini, mo- are you naked?" she bucked her eyes up at me. I was towering over her, but in between her legs.

I just nodded to answer question and pulled her panties down. Once I got them off, she pushed me onto my back, and then straddled me. She began bouncing on my dick slowly, and because I was drunk, I could barely contain myself.

"Fuck!" I called out as I nutted extra fucking quickly.

Next thing I knew, I was passed the fuck out. I'd had a great ass night.

A WEEK AND A HALF LATER...

I sat down on the toilet top at my new job, and let the tears fall from my eyes. I didn't feel like stopping them as I stared down at the positive pregnancy test. I'd just gotten a good career, and my first baby wasn't even six months, but here I was pregnant again. In addition to that, KJ and I weren't even married.

I'd taken three tests so far because I didn't wanna believe it. I took one last night, one this morning, and then just now. They all read the same fucking thing, and it took everything in me not to sob violently and loudly. I loved K-Three with all of my heart, but I just didn't need another baby right now. I'd just gotten my damn body back.

I was so confused. I made sure to be strict with my birth control this time because last time I wasn't as careful. This go round I made sure to take it everyday at the same time, but something still went wrong. I was starting to think it was because KJ and I had sex too much.

BAM! BAM! BAM!

"Gianna, are you coming out soon?" Casey yelled and beat on the bathroom door like an imbecile.

"Yes, um I'm just finishing up!" I responded and quickly wiped my face.

I pulled a Ziploc bag from my purse and then dropped the test into it before sealing it and putting it back. I washed my hands, and when I walked out of the bathroom, Casey was right in my face.

"Come into my office Gianna," he said and then strolled away. I went to drop my purse off in my workroom and then headed to his office.

I hoped I wasn't in trouble for being in the bathroom for so long. I was done picking out the outfits for the girls, and I was also finished placing the orders for the items that needed to be purchased online, so technically I was done for the day. That's the only reason I even left my area to take a pregnancy test.

As I sat down in Casey's office, he closed the door. I waited with bated breath, hoping this wasn't going to be a bad conversation.

"How are you liking the job so far Gianna?" he sat down next to me instead of behind his desk.

"I like it a lot, and I appreciate the opportunity very much," I smiled.

"Good, you look really pretty today," he smirked and then rubbed my bare leg.

"Casey, stop," I moved his hand away. He dropped his head down and began kissing my thighs. "Casey what are you doing!" I stood to my feet to get away from him. He hopped up and locked the door of his office. "Casey, what are you doing?" I asked again as I backed away.

"Gianna I just wanna get to know you in a more personal way," he licked his lips and moved closer to me.

Tears started to run down my cheeks as I looked for away to get out. He gripped my waist in his big hands, and then slammed me up against the wall to kiss on my neck. I was beyond disgusted by his touch.

"Move! I'm gonna scream!" I shouted as I pushed him away. He finally stopped and moved back.

"I'm sorry Gianna, I thought- I guess I got the wrong impression from you."

"How? I told you I had a fiancé," I sniffled.

"Yeah, but I thought you- I don't know." He looked down at the ground.

"It's okay Casey, umm I'm finished for the day so I'm gonna go home. I'm not feeling well."

"Okay, have a good night Gianna and feel better," he smiled.

"Thanks," I said in the lowest tone possible.

I walked to the door, but as soon as I got there he hugged me tightly from behind. He began rubbing up my leg while pressing his dick against my ass.

"Did you think I was gonna let you go that easy?" he whispered as his hand traveled further up my leg.

"Help!" I shouted and squirmed to get him off of me.

"Walls are sound proof Gianna la bella."

I tried to push him off of me, but he was too strong. I even slammed my stiletto heel into his foot, but nothing fazed him. We were wrestling damn near, and then he pinned me against the wall, smashing the side of my face into it.

"Please Casey!" I cried as I listened to him unbuckle his pants with his free hand. "I'm pregnant please!" I sobbed hysterically. This day was turning out to be horrible.

He shoved me into the wall, and stared at me with a disgusted expression.

"Get out!" he shouted.

I quickly fixed my dress, and then rushed out of his office. I grabbed my purse from the room I worked in and then booked it to the elevator. I couldn't get to my car fast enough, and when I did, I sped home like a bat out of hell.

Upon arriving, I ran straight up to my bedroom. When I entered, I spotted KJ watching TV, and K-Three lying on his stomach, sleeping with his baby pillow surrounding him to keep him from rolling.

"Hey baby, how was work?" KJ smiled.

I just dropped my purse on the recliner, and ran to the bathroom. I cut the shower on and stripped down out of my clothes and shoes, because I felt disgusting. The way Casey touched me and kissed on my neck made me feel like I was covered in mud.

As soon as I got in the shower, I began weeping. This was my dream job and it was ruined. I felt so stupid for taking that job knowing that Casey was interested in me. I didn't even think he would go that far, I just assumed he would be all talk. If I hadn't have been pregnant, he would've raped me right there.

I was so scared while in his office, and at the moment I was still shaken up. I knew people would blame me for his actions because I ignored his flirting in the interview. I just wanted the job so badly, that I went against my better judgment. The field I loved was so hard to break into, and I had become desperate to accomplish my goals. I felt so stupid and incompetent right now.

Once I'd gotten all my tears out, I felt a presence. I jumped when KJ touched me, so he turned me to face him. He was naked in the shower with me, looking just as gorgeous as always.

"You didn't hear me talking to you when you came into the bedroom?" he asked as he held my face, looking down at me.

"No," I whispered.

He gently pressed his lips against mine, making me feel somewhat better.

"Why are you crying shorty?"

"I-I messed up at work today, a-and it was just a really bad mistake on my part," I lied.

"Explain," he said as he took my loofah to put soap on it.

I turned my back to him to let him wash my body, as I told him about my day, excluding the very end.

"Kaleeini! Kaleeini wake up!" I rocked him back and forth hoping he got up.

My water had broken and the sheets were drenched, I'm surprised he didn't wake up on his own.

"What baby?" he frowned, and then looked down and around to see why he was wet.

"My water broke Kaleeini," I whimpered a little. I was starting to have little shocks of pain, and I was also getting scared as fuck.

"Oh shit, okay. Where is the bag we made?" he hopped up frantically.

"By the door, hurry up Kaleeini!" I shouted and stood up.

Water was dripping from between my legs and I had no idea what the hell was gonna happen next. Kaleeini quickly slipped on some sweats, a t-shirt, a hoodie, socks, and some Jordans, before he grabbed the bag and carried me down to the car bridal style.

"You sure you don't wanna change baby?" he asked me once he got in on the driver's side.

"No, just drive Kaleeini," I exhaled heavily. "And I'm cold, turn on the heat," I added as he peeled off.

He cut the heat on like I'd asked and blasted it the whole way to the hospital. We finally made it there about ten minutes later and he threw the car into park, right up front. Hopping out quickly, he retrieved the bag and then ran inside for help. A few moments later, he returned with some nurses and a wheel chair, in which the former helped me out of the car and wheeled me in. Lord, give me the strength.

Four hours had passed, and I was in so much pain it was ridiculous. I was regretting everything in my life as I rocked back and forth. I was silently begging God to forgive me for all of my sins, hoping that would make this unbearable pain go away. It made me cherish the moments where I was living my life pain free. It's crazy what you will think about when you're not feeling well.

"Get the baby out!" I cried as Kaleeini held my hand.

"Aysia relax baby, the doctor said if you do too much you can split yourself," my mother chimed in making things worse. Now I was scared of splitting myself in half. Thanks, mom.

"Please call the doctor, I think it's time," I sobbed and sweated. My whole body was wet and covered in sweat, as I continued to rock back and forth. "God, I'm sorry for complaining about having menstrual cramps and anything else!"

"Okay, let me have the doctor come check," the nurse said before leaving.

She soon returned with the doctor and I waited as he checked me.

"Yeah, the baby is ready," he nodded.

I wanted to sing praises of worship at the sound of those words. I was ready to get my daughter or son out of me. At this point, I didn't care what the gender was. It could be a damn alien for all I cared; I just wanted it out.

"Okay, Ms. Terrence, give me one good push," the doctor instructed me once he got situated. I pushed and tightened my grip on Kaleeini's hand. "Another," the doctor stated calmly. I gave him another, but then began to cry.

"It's too hard!" I shouted.

"Ms. Terrence that first one was perfect, just two more like that," the doctor said.

"You can do it shorty," Kaleeini encouraged.

I pushed two more times, and finally the sound of a baby wailing could be heard throughout the room. I collapsed against the pillow as if I had fainted, and began to pant heavily.

"We have a boy here!" the nurse called out as she waved Kaleeini over to come cut the umbilical cord.

I saw how happy he was that he had a son, and like I said, right now I didn't care. I was just happy that he was out. I didn't even care what they named him in this moment.

They took my son away to clean him, while another nurse cleaned me up. I waited and waited, and finally the nurse returned with him. He was so little and cute, and I was in love already.

"How can something so little cause so much pain," I said and everyone chuckled.

"Do you have a name for him?" the nurse asked and I looked at Kaleeini.

"Keeilan Drake King," he responded.

"That's so cute," I smiled and took him from the nurse.

I kissed his forehead and he opened his eyes a little. I could see the green color, and I was surprised that he had them.

"He has green eyes," I whispered.

"It's a hereditary condition that runs in the family shorty," Kaleeini chuckled.

"A condition?" I frowned.

"In a way. The lack of pigmentation in the eyes runs in my family, that's why most of us have green ones. Blue eyes are little to no pigment, and green eyes are blue eyes with a hint of pigment," he explained. "People who have a lot of pigment have brown eyes."

"I didn't know that," I nodded and so did my mother.

"Me either until I asked my dad if he thought our baby would have green eyes. He told me then that it was a 90% chance."

"So your eyes lack melanin?" my mother laughed.

"Pretty much," Kaleeini responded.

"You're so smart Kaleeini. I love you," I whispered and then kissed my baby.

"I love you too, baby," he turned me to face him and pecked my lips. I then handed Keeilan to him so he could hold him.

By the time noon came, Kaleeini's parents had arrived, and so did my friends. Everyone took turns holding him and I noticed I was already attached to his cute little self. I wanted to tell them to give him back, but I had to be nice.

"Was it as painful as you thought?" Gianna smiled.

"It was. I didn't think I was gonna make it at all."

"That is the exact same thing I thought," she chuckled. "Poor Willow has to push out two," Gianna rubbed Willow's back.

"Please do not remind me," she rolled her eyes.

"I am gonna spoil you. You are the cutest thing!" Morgan spoke in a baby voice as she held Keeilan.

"I told Kaleeini I was gonna kiss Keeilan's cheeks a lot, but he said not to. I told him you kissed his and he turned out fine, but he claims you didn't," I blabbed to Morgan.

"Boy quit telling lies. I tore them cheeks up and he loved it," she replied, making everyone laugh except Kaleeini.

Everyone cleared out around 9pm, and left the room to just Kaleeini and I.

"You did good today baby, even though you cried most of the time," he said as he walked over to make the pull out bed.

"You'd cry too if you felt that pain."

"I'm sure I would." He came back over to me, and then kissed my lips gently. "I love you more than anything shorty."

I was officially a mommy.

IT'D BEEN three weeks since I'd met Marcel, and we'd been texting pretty heavily since then. I'd promised him I would see him a week after we met, but I wasn't able to pull it off because of my father and brothers watching me. However, today I was finally gonna spend some time with my boo.

I told my parents that I was just going to hang out with Victoria, and of course my Dad called to check with her mother who confirmed. In actuality, Marcel was gonna pick me up from Victoria's once Dice dropped me off. Then, once he and I were done hanging out, I would have him take me back so that Dice could pick me up and take me home.

"Thanks D, see you later!" I said to Dice as he opened the door so I could get out of the black Escalade.

He nodded in response, and then jogged to the driver's side. He sat in the car and watched until he saw Victoria let me in the house.

"Bitch I know you're excited!" Victoria beamed as she closed the door behind me.

"Yeah, I can't wait to see him," I responded as we headed back to her room so that I could change into the dress I stuffed into my purse.

"I got a condom for you."

"For what?" I frowned as I pulled my shirt over my head.

"What you think? Ain't y'all gonna fuck?"

"No! I don't even know him, and you know I'm waiting until I get married," I scoffed and flashed her the promise ring from my Dad.

"Kendria, girl, you're gonna be alone forever if you don't start dropping your panties," she sighed and laid down.

"That's not true," I stated nonchalantly as I put on my earrings.

"Yes it is. Name one girl from around here who found love without spreading her legs Dria. Was your Mama even married to your Dad before she gave it up?"

"I don't know, maybe."

"Please Kendria, everyone knows your mama got gamed up and pregnant by a hustler in less than six months at seventeen."

"Watch your fucking mouth talking about my mama Victoria. Worry about yourself and why you've been spreading your legs for over a year and still don't have a man. At least my mother got married to the man that gamed her up. You just get gamed up, fucked, and dropped!"

She stared at me and just shook her head.

"I'm just trying to help you Kendria. You said you wanted a boyfriend, and I'm telling you that these niggas are not gonna put a ring on it for some pussy. They're gonna leave and get it from someone else. You want the ring you gotta give it up. Look at Gigi and Lo, they wouldn't have gotten rings from your brothers had they not been fucking and sucking."

"I'm gonna wait in the living room until Marcel gets here," I responded before snatching my purse up and leaving her bedroom.

I didn't feel like listening to Victoria anymore. I knew some of what she was saying was true, but I wasn't ready to have sex. I wanted to do it when I was ready and with someone who I knew loved me.

On top of that, I made a promise to my Daddy that I wouldn't lose my virginity before I walked down the aisle. No man was worth disappointing my father because I knew he was telling me what was best for me.

As I sat there pondering, my phone chimed. I looked down at the screen, and saw it was Marcel telling me he was outside. I ran to the back to tell Victoria I was leaving.

"Good luck, and you sure you don't want the condom Dria?"

"I won't need it."

I rushed out of her house and looked around. I heard a honking noise, and looked to my right to see a black Infiniti truck. I ran towards it, and a driver hopped out to open the backseat door for me. When he did, I spotted sexy Marcel sitting in the backseat.

"You have a driver?" I asked as I buckled in.

"Yeah, for umm, purposes like this where I would prefer to get to know my date than drive," he bit his lip. He then pulled me closer and hugged me tightly.

The driver pulled off, and I took a deep breath as I saw the sun was starting to set. It was getting close to being dark out, and I had no idea where Marcel and I were going. After about fifteen minutes, we pulled up in front of a hotel, and the driver cut the engine off. The hotel was right across the street from a big ass park. The driver cracked the windows a bit so he could get some fresh air while he waited I guess.

"Come on," Marcel smiled.

"No, umm let's just stay in the car," I suggested. I was too scared to go up to his room, because I knew he would want sex.

"Why baby? You scared?"

"No, I just-"

"It's cool," he smiled and then scooted closer to me.

He lifted my chin and began sucking my lips. Suddenly I felt his tongue go into my mouth, and then his large hand squeeze my small breast.

"Marcel, relax for a second," I nudged him.

"Relax? Baby I've been trying to see you for weeks. Quit fucking around," he bit his lip and then kissed me roughly.

I didn't like the kiss, and then on top of that he started to grope my body in this already tight dress I'd changed into. The driver acted like he wasn't even around.

"Marcel-"

"Chill the fuck out!" he shook me hard as fuck.

"Take me home!" I shouted and tried to push him away.

He began rubbing his hands up my dress, and trying to maneuver himself on top of me. I was pushing his face away, but he was still touching me all over.

POP!

"Ahhh!" I screamed at the sound of a gunshot.

Both Marcel and I stopped wrestling to see that the driver's head had been blown open. The backdoor on Marcel's side was yanked open, and a masked man pulled him from the truck and clocked him with his gun.

"Aahhh!" I hollered again as I watched blood leak from Marcel's head.

I quickly pulled the lever on my door, grabbed my purse, and hopped out of the truck to run. As soon as I got a good pace, I saw one of the masked men chasing me. I ran onto the park grass, and he was hot on my fucking heels. I was two seconds from pissing and shitting on myself. This was the one time I wished I hadn't worn sandals. I tried to dip around the tree, but he grabbed me from behind.

"Ahhh!" I shouted at the top of my lungs, so he covered my mouth as he carried me towards another black truck.

I squirmed and flailed my arms, hitting him as best as I could. He was strong and holding me from behind, so it was hard to fight him. I balled my fist up and swung back, punching him in the nuts as I bit the shit out of his gloved hand that was covering my mouth. I was trying to break the glove and skin on that shit.

"Fuck!" he hollered and dropped me.

I tried to book it back into the park, but his accomplice snatched my ass up and threw me into their black truck as if I weighed nothing. The one that I'd gotten away from limped to the truck and climbed into the driver's seat, while the second one who threw me into the truck got into the backseat with me. As soon as he closed the door, the other one drove off.

"Let me go!" I screamed and cried as I began to take off on the one in the backseat with me. I spotted Marcel in the trunk with a huge bullet hole wound in the back of his head, and began hollering and crying as I wailed on my assailant.

"Calm yo' monkey ass down!" the assailant in the backseat barked and grabbed my wrists.

He shoved me backward lightly, obviously not trying to hurt me. Then it dawned on me that I recognized the voice. I paused for a second, and he snatched off his ski mask.

"KJ!" I yelped, completely floored.

He fell back against the seat, and began to breathe heavily before saying, "Yes, shorty."

I looked at the person driving, but couldn't tell who he was, because he still had the ski mask on, just pushed up past his eyes a little. I sat up and stuck my head between the seats to see Kendrin.

"Thanks for the punch in the nuts Dria," he scoffed and shook his head. I sat back in the seat and folded my arms. I was so fucking angry.

"Kendria, damn do you know how to put up a fucking fight," KJ exhaled sharply and looked over at me as Kendrin continued to drive.

"Take me home, I hate you guys," I began to tear up.

"Shorty we're just trying to protect you," Kendrin looked into his rearview mirror at me.

I just shook my head and let the tears spill out of my eyes. I was completely fucking traumatized right now. KJ pulled me over to him. I tried to resist but he was too strong. He hugged me tightly against his chest, and I just broke down crying as he rubbed my back gently. I have never been so scared in my life.

FOUR DAYS LATER...

SWISS INFORMED me of some shit today and I needed to tell my brother immediately. I knew if shit hadn't hit the fan prior, it was definitely about to now. I wasn't tripping though, I just wanted the team to be up on their game.

I had KJ call a meeting at the warehouse because they had to know that shit was about to get way more real than it already had been. KJ hit my line and let me know that everyone was already in the conference room, so when I got to the warehouse, I wasted no time hopping out. I met Bolo at the conference room door, and he opened it for me. Greeting everybody when I walked in, I instantly took a seat so I could get down to business.

In the room was KJ, Kaleeini, Lenny, and Drew. These were the only people needed when there was shit this big needing to be dealt with. Everybody else could be informed later, unless it directly affected them. I knew that at this time, only us five would be targeted heavily, so there was no need to bring in the whole team.

"Aight look, a couple days ago, KJ and I snatched up and murdered some little nigga who was tryna get fresh with our little sister. It just so happens that he was the little brother of them Duck and Lucky niggas. Now, we had no idea that he was their little brother, thanks to substandard ass Oscar, but either way he would've gotten killed for coming on to Kendria too strongly. So right now Duck and Lucky are combing the streets for his ass, and I'm sure once they find out what we did, shit is really gon' hit the fan," I explained.

"So, that little nigga was a Paine huh?" KJ shook his head.

"He was." I nodded my head. "We're gonna need to really have Swiss keep his ear to the streets. Once them niggas get word that we were the ones who murked their little brother, they gon' be out for blood only," I added. "I don't even think the drug shit will be a factor at that point."

"Well I'm ready. We just need to off their asses, too. The only thing is, is that they've beefed up their security and shit, making it hard to get to them. Just like some bitches," Lenny said.

Everyone in our line of work needed some type of protection, but these niggas took it overboard. Their bodyguards were always right with them, and walking with them. The only time Bolo and Blade walked with us was when we went to the club. Anywhere else, we make sure they stay close by but not right with us. The reason for that is because one, we want some damn privacy, and two, it drew in too much attention. When people see you at a grocery store with two big ass bodyguards at your side, they're gonna wonder who you are. And if they've never seen you on TV or some shit, they're gonna start looking into you; it's just gonna bring about too much awareness. Attention was the last thing we wanted, because attention eventually meant the FEDS.

"We'll figure some shit out," KJ replied.

"Maybe we should purposely let them know we killed their little brother," Lenny suggested.

"I have a feeling they would send goons to handle that for them. I'm gon' find a way to touch them, you just watch," KJ smirked. "Until then, everybody on the team needs to keep a lookout for them, even Bolo and Blade."

We chopped it up for a bit more and then we went our separate ways. On my way home, my phone rang. I saw it was from Bailey, so I answered it on the car phone, allowing her voice come through the car speakers.

"What's up shorty?"

"Kendrin are you busy?" she sniffled.

"Nah, what's good?"

"I need you to come pick me up from Knights Inn."

"Aight, be there in a little bit."

I usually would've brushed her off, but she sounded a little bothered and for some reason I cared about shorty. I pulled up to the motel about twenty minutes later, and I saw her sitting outside with her purse. When she spotted my Porsche, she hopped up and power walked to me. She was wearing a casual little dress that clung to her body in all the right places. She looked so much prettier with her new dark hair against her caramel complexion. Shorty was way too bad for me to be chilling with. When she got into my car, I noticed her nose was bleeding a little.

"Fuck happened to you?"

"Nothing Kendrin, can you just take me to Swiss' crib?" she said and wiped the tears that fell.

"Tell me what happened."

"My ex saw me at the store, and made me come with him. He took me here, and when I wouldn't fuck him he smacked me and put me out."

"I thought he was in Los Angeles."

"Me too, but he found me," she sniffled.

I threw the car in park and asked "Which room?"

"Kendrin, no it's okay. You don't have to do this," she teared up and shook her head.

"What room?"

"That one with the pink curtain stain," she pointed to a room on the first floor.

I got out, booked it over there, and beat on the door as hard as I could. After waiting for a little bit, some big nigga answered the door.

"Yes?" he looked me up and down.

"I heard you got a problem with keeping your hands to yourself homie."

"Man what?" he frowned up even more.

WHAM!

I punched his ass and he flew back into the room. I walked in as well, and closed the door behind me using one of the folded towels by the door. He got up after finally getting his balance, and touched his nose to feel for blood, which there was plenty of.

WHAM! WHAM! WHAM!

I took off on him, landing hit after hit, until he dropped to the floor and cowered like the bitch that he was.

"Oh, now you wanna ball up like a bitch huh?" I grinned down at his ugly ass mug.

I was gonna leave, but I remembered what Christian did to Kaleeini, so I silenced my gun, placed it to his dome, and popped him. I took the same towel that I closed the door with, and then opened the door back up to leave.

"What did you do?" Bailey asked once I'd gotten back into my truck.

"Don't trip," was all I said as I sped off.

During the drive, Bailey rubbed my hand as it sat on the gearshift. I moved it from under her and turned down the radio.

"Where am I taking you?"

"I kind of want to be alone, so I'm gonna book a hotel."

I nodded and then drove to Swiss' so she could get some clothes, before taking her to the Marriott.

"Kendrin, no I meant a *motel*. I don't wanna spend this much," she said once I parked.

"Now you don' wasted my fucking gas," I grimaced. She stared into my face, and you could tell she was scared. "I'm fucking with you shorty, relax. I'm gonna pay for the room."

She chuckled and nudged me lightly, before we both exited the car. As we walked towards the entrance of the hotel, she slipped her small hand into mine. She intertwined our fingers, and then brought my hand up to look at the tattoo on the back of it.

"Why did you get a monster tattooed?" she giggled.

"Because I thought the artwork was dope and because I like monsters."

"You like monsters? Who the hell likes monsters Ken?" she laughed.

"Me. I wasn't that kid who was scared of monsters being under their bed. I actually used to wait until my family went to sleep and then I would take a flashlight and try to find the monster under my bed."

"Did you ever find it?"

"Yeah, the night my mom caught me and whooped my ass," I replied and we both cracked up.

I pulled my hand away slowly so that she would stop holding it, and then opened the door of the hotel for her. We checked her in, and then I walked her up to the room.

"Thank you for helping me Kendrin. That was sexy how you handled my ex."

"You don't even know what I did shorty."

"I can guess. That nigga came out to Baltimore just to get killed in less than a week," she grinned and took her shoes off. She laid across the bed, and moved her hair from one side to the other.

"You're so pretty," I half smiled as I admired her.

"Thank you baby. You're so fine," she chuckled.

"Well I'll check you later shorty, let me know if you need something, aight?" I looked at her and she nodded.

She then got up and walked closer to me for a hug. I gripped her body tightly as she hugged my neck. She kissed my cheek and then I let her go and left. I was proud of myself, because back in the day I would've fucked, no questions asked. But I loved Willow, and I wanted to be good to her.

I made it home about a half an hour later, and went straight to the bedroom. I saw Willow laid out on the chaise lounge, wearing a short nightgown, and a short silk robe. Her two braids were out, letting her long hair lie messily. Her chest and stomach moved up and down slowly, as she breathed while sleeping. I walked closer to her and stepped out of my sneakers before getting on the ground in front of her. I touched her face and she stirred a little bit. Her smooth vanilla complexion had a glow to it for some reason, making her look more beautiful than usual; something I didn't even know was possible. Her eyes opened slowly, and she smiled when she saw me.

"Watching me sleep?" she asked in a low tone.

"Yeah, I couldn't help myself. You look very alluring right now."

"Ooh alluring, I like that," she cheesed, showing her perfect teeth.

I leaned up to peck her full lips, which were getting fuller due to being pregnant. Every time I kissed Willow, that shit made me feel some type of way. She messed with my chin hairs, as we continued to peck sensually.

"What did you do today?" she inquired.

"Handle business as usual. You?"

"Just relaxed. I wasn't feeling too good, so I wanted to just lay down all day, and give my body some rest."

I put my hand under her gown, and caressed the bulge in her stomach that seemed to grow every week. I then lifted the gown to kiss it.

"I love you Willow. I love you, especially, because you've always loved a nigga even when I wasn't treating you right."

She just looked at me so I pressed my lips against hers. I loved Willow more than anything, and seeing my baby, well babies inside her just intensified that. As attracted as I was to Bailey, there was nothing she could do for me.

"Somebody needs to figure out where the fuck my little brother is!" I barked over the whole room.

Currently I was holding a meeting in the basement of this throwaway house that I'd purchased. Everybody that worked for me was in this room. It was a mixture of the niggas who agreed to come down from Camden with me, and some Baltimore natives that Buzz and Pablo recruited before they got killed.

"We're on it boss. Jake is out there right now trying to get information," one of my workers Jeremy said.

"I don't need anybody to fucking try! I need someone to actually fucking do it!" I hollered.

"Man we already fucking know what happened to Marcel, and who did it, we just need proof," my twin Lucky chimed in and everyone in the room nodded.

A couple of days ago my little brother Marcel disappeared. In my heart I knew he was gone, but I didn't wanna believe that shit. His driver's brains were blown out, so it was obvious what had been done to Marcel as well, we just didn't have a body. That was my little brother, though man, he couldn't be dead. I felt bad for getting him in this shit, and convincing him to use that little King bitch as a pawn for us. Now he was possibly dead because of it. And what makes it even worse, is that I don't even know how they found him so quickly and so easily.

I hated the Kings with a fucking passion, and I was beyond determined to bleed them dry, literally and monetarily. This all started because they somehow got wind they we were coming down to Baltimore to claim their territory, which was very true. I wasn't sure how they found out, but they did.

There were three reasons why Lucky and I chose to come down and take their shit. One was because they were making major bread out here and we knew it was because of the location. They had phenomenal product from a supplier I couldn't find, but their main benefit was the area. Yeah, Lucky and I made a lot of money up in Jersey, but we weren't making nearly as much as them niggas.

I'd visited Maryland once, and everyone knew their names. They were the Kings of the city, and it was like fate that King was their last name. Anyway, I'd peeped game long ago on how they were getting it out here, and when I went home, Lucky and I decided to come down some time later and snatch the shit up.

Second reason for wanting their territory was bragging rights. Like them, Lucky and I have encountered many enemies who tried to take our shit, or downright take us out, yet we always came out on top. In Camden, the Paine brothers were king, and like them we were undefeated. I knew we would come head to head one day, and I also knew we would win. I didn't care about how many people told me that the Kings weren't anything nice. Well shit, neither was I.

Lucky, Marcel and I were born and raised in Camden. We grew up in a two-parent household with a loving mother named Elaine, and strict but great father named Martin or simply Marty. When Lucky and I were born, my mother was nineteen and my father was thirty-seven years old. My Dad was the biggest drug lord in all of Camden and he ran shit up there just like I do now. Somehow my father and KJ's grandfather Kairio got into some type of war, and one day when my dad cranked his car, it burst into flames. The death of my dad really took a toll on my family, and I've hated the Kings since then. KJ's father and I are eleven years apart, so while he reigned Baltimore, I didn't feel that I was capable at the time to take on him and his brothers. However, his little bitch ass son was a different story.

"Jake is here boss," my bodyguard Raymond let me know as he escorted him down to the basement with the rest of us.

"You got something for me?" I frowned.

"The newest trap we put together was engulfed in flames and this was sitting out on the walkway," Jake replied and stuck the black duffle bag in his hand out to me.

I snatched it from his ass and sucked my teeth. I swear every time I got a fucking trap together, these niggas were burning it down before I could even get the shit popping. Someone was either snitching, or stupidly giving out information to the wrong people.

"Ah! The fuck!" I opened the bag and saw my brother's head in it, so I dropped it to the floor. Lucky came and looked in, along with the rest of team, and everyone groaned. "I'm tired of these niggas!!!! This shit is un-fucking-acceptable! This is my fucking brother!!!" I hollered as tears began to stream my cheeks. I flipped a table over, and kicked over a box of shit on the floor. "I don't wanna hear about anybody sleeping! Work all fucking day, until you get me some locations on these niggas! And when I find out which one of you are running your mouth, it's gonna be hell to pay!" I cleared another table of all the shit that was on it and stormed up out of the basement.

Them King niggas are gonna wished they never fucked with a nigga of my caliber. Since they wanted to go hard in the paint by blasting my brother, I was gonna go hard too. I couldn't get Kendria King, but I knew that little Aysia chick was just as important to them. I wasn't sure if I was gonna rape her and then kill her, or rape her, get her pregnant, and then keep her hostage until she was too far along for an abortion. Damn, I couldn't imagine having to deal with the fact that the woman I loved had my enemy's baby, so maybe I'd go with the latter. Shit, even if I did die, they would never forget me because my seed would be planted inside of sexy Aysia. Poor Kaleeini King.

"You okay daddy?" my girlfriend Cassi walked up to me in the bedroom of the little throwaway house.

"I need you to sit on it," I replied before sitting down and releasing my dick.

She lifted her skirt, pushed her panties down, and then straddled me. Shit wasn't about to get real; it was about to get deadly.

Slipping into my Jordan Retro 12's, a smile spread across my face because of tonight. I was no longer gonna wait on Shannon to come around. If she wanted to break up, then so be it. I had too much on my plate to always be worried about my relationship and if my girl wants to be with me or not. Granted I did fuck things up, but if she was gonna be all wishy-washy now because of that, then it was best we stay a part. With all the shit going on in my life, my relationship is the one thing that needs to be stable. I needed my focus to be on basketball, not petty drama within my relationship. Plus, this was a time for celebration and nothing else.

After dressing, I grabbed my keys and phone before leaving. Twenty minutes later, I pulled up to Imani's house and climbed out, hitting the alarm on my way. I rang her doorbell once I neared it, and her mother answered the door happily.

"Kenzie!" she beamed.

"Hello Mrs. Pham," I smiled as we embraced.

Imani's mother was a short and slim Black lady. This was the first time I'd seen a Black woman and an Asian man have a baby. It's usually the other way around, but whatever works.

"Imani will be out in just a second. Have a seat Kenzie." She pointed to the couch and I did as she asked. "So have you chosen a team yet?"

"Yeah, my mind is pretty much made up. I don't really wanna say who though yet. I'm gonna let the sports news announce it you know."

"Oh, of course, I can't wait to hear who you chose to go with. I hope it's close to Baltimore."

"Well, it's as close as I could get for the amount of money I wanted."

"I see, a nice fat salary is never a bad thing," she replied as we laughed in unison. "I'm so happy that you and Imani are finally going out. She's been crushing on you for the longest, so when she told me about tonight I was elated for her."

"Yeah Imani is cool," I nodded and pursed my lips.

Imani was a sexy and dope chick, but I wasn't looking for anything serious just yet, especially since I would be moving soon. We could be cool for now, and if it turned into something, then so be it. I wasn't quite ready to jump right into anything just yet, though.

"Didn't you have a girlfriend though Kenzie?" Mrs. Pham leaned back onto the couch.

"Yeah I did, but we decided to separate."

"May I ask why?"

Was she serious right now? Why did she need to know so much about my personal life? This was one damn date, not a fucking marriage proposal. If this was how it was gonna be every time I came by to get Imani, my ass would be honking from the curb.

"We just weren't happy together anymore," I half lied.

I was happy as hell with Shannon, but I guess she wasn't happy with me anymore. That shit bothered the fuck out of me, but whatever.

"Oh, I see. Time to move on to better things then, like Imani." *She sees dollar signs*, I thought.

Whenever I dated a girl, her parents always liked me and I knew it was because of where I was headed in life. I was the only freshman in high school that was on the Varsity basketball team and starting as well. Ever since then, parents have never been a problem, because they wanted me to choose their daughter and let them benefit from my success. The only parent who has ever given me a little problem was Mr. Breaux, which was all the more reason why I had it bad for Shannon. She saw me as simply Kenzie King, and not 'Kenzie King, first round draft pick'

"Mom, please leave Kenzie alone," Imani walked out from the back wearing a tight orange dress.

She was small because of her Asian ancestry, but she was fine as fuck. I didn't care about her being 5'3, as long as she can take the dick, we're good. I stood to my feet but not all the way, so that I could hug her. Her heels made her a little taller, but she was still way shorter than me. Her sexy golden legs and plump little ass had my dick hard as hell before we'd even gotten out of the door; those were her Black genes.

Saying goodbye to Mrs. Pham, Imani and I left out and headed to The Capital Grille. Because I hated to wait, I'd made a reservation prior, so we were seated about two minutes after getting there.

"Your server will be with you shortly," the hostess informed us. "Aren't you Kenzie King?" he questioned with a big smile.

"I am," I nodded.

" man, let me get your autograph." He patted his pockets for a paper and pen.

"Mine? I'm not even in the NBA yet," I chuckled.

"But you're about to be, you know that. Everyone is just waiting for the announcement. I wanna get it now because I may never see you again," he said as he set a pen and paper down. I shrugged and then scribbled my signature on the paper before handing it over. "Thanks man, appreciate it." He skated off happily, and back to the hostess stand to greet some new people who had walked in.

"That was crazy," Imani giggled.

"It was. I didn't expect that to start now."

"You've chosen a team?"

"Yeah I have, and you'll find out with everyone else," I bit my lip and smiled, making her blush.

"You are so fine, Kenzie. Shannon was a fool to let you slip through her fingers. But I cupped my hands right under hers," she said making us laugh in unison.

"I don't wanna think about her at all tonight, because this is about you and me." I took her hands into mine. Bringing up Shannon was not benefitting her at all.

"I like that idea."

"So why are you single Imani? You're beautiful and hella dope."

"Because no one is Kenzie King."

"What?" I frowned as someone came and set two glasses of water down, before walking off.

"No guy could compare to you, so when I went out with them I wasn't feeling it," she shrugged.

"So you waited for me?"

"Not intentionally. I tried dating guys, but none of them ever did it for me."

"Damn, so no action for you for the past what? A year and some change?"

"Not since that little run in we had."

While with Rosalind, and only in the talking stages with Shannon, I let Imani suck my dick. I don't know why I didn't fuck. I think it was because I had to meet Rosalind later. Damn, I was really the worst nigga.

"I don't believe you've just been high and dry, come on now," I grinned.

"I mean I got my pussy ate a couple times, but no penetration. You can end that drought, though," she licked her lips.

We stared into each other's eyes until I heard, "Kenzie."

I looked up to see Gianna standing by my table, and almost jumped out of my skin. She was staring at Imani and me with an evil glare. I scanned the room for KJ, and when I spotted him he shrugged, basically saying he couldn't stop Gianna from coming over.

"Gigi, what's up?" I smiled but she was stone-faced. "Umm, this is Imani, my date. And Imani, this is my cousin's girlfriend Gigi," I introduced them.

"Nice to meet you," Imani smiled but Gianna just sauntered back to the table with KJ. "Did I say something wrong?" Imani frowned.

"No, that's one of Shannon's best friends."

"Ohhh, okay."

I knew some shit was about to pop off, but I didn't care. Shannon said she wanted to break up, so that's what the fuck we did. She had no right to try and reprimand me for being out with another girl. Either we were gonna be together or we weren't, no gray areas.

ONE WEEK LATER...

Tonight my friends and I were chilling in my room at Hotel Monaco Baltimore because I was getting married in their wedding chapel in the morning. I was so excited to have my wedding because I think the fact that I was already Kendrin's wife hadn't settled in yet. I needed those ceremony pictures, and to experience walking down the aisle to really have it hit me. Oh, how I couldn't wait to wake up tomorrow and get ready for my wedding.

"I have champagne if anyone wants some. I think the only person who can drink it is Shannon," I offered.

"Yeah we're both breast feeding," Aysia playfully rolled her eyes and pointed to Gianna and herself.

"I don't want any right now, I will take cider," Shannon said.

Gianna and Aysia both had their babies in the room, and I didn't mind at all. Keeilan and K-Three were really good babies, so we didn't have to worry about them crying all damn night. It was now 10pm, and they were knocked out in the middle of the beds, not disturbing us at all. Gianna put these little soft inflatable bed rails on the sides of them so that they wouldn't roll.

"What do you think the boys are doing?" Shannon asked.

"No idea. They better not be doing too much, though, because I'll kill Kendrin's ass," I cocked my head making them laugh.

"Shannon I didn't wanna tell you this. Well, I did, just not right now, so never mind I will wait," Gianna stammered.

"What Gigi?" Shannon frowned and put her champagne flute filled with apple cider down.

"I went to dinner with KJ last week, and Kenzie was there with another girl. Some Blasian chick," Gianna explained.

"Oh really?" Shannon chuckled nervously. "We're broken up though so it doesn't really matter."

"Are you sure? You don't look like it doesn't matter," Aysia raised a brow.

I knew Shannon was lying because her whole damn demeanor changed. If she really didn't care, there would've been no shift in her behavior.

"Nope, no I'm good. I'm the one that broke up with his ass, so why would I care?" Shannon grinned.

"Because your voice is trembling," I responded.

"My voice is not trembling aight? I said I don't give a fuck!" she spat loudly. "I'm sorry, I hope I didn't wake the babies."

"No you're good," Gianna nodded. It was quiet for a few moments, and then Shannon got up to go to the bathroom. "She's lying," Gianna shook her head.

"Yeah she is, I don't know why she broke up with him in the first place," I shrugged.

"Too much drama she said, because of the Rosalind fight," Aysia answered.

Suddenly we heard faint sniffles coming from the bathroom area. The three of us hopped up and rushed to the bathroom. I twisted the knob, and when we walked in Shannon was sitting on the toilet top sobbing very lightly. Shannon only cried when she was really hurt, so this just confirmed for me that she not only cared about Kenzie being out, but she cared a whole lot.

"Shannon it's gonna be okay," Gianna walked over and knelt down beside her.

"I know girl, I was just getting a little bit of it out. I'm good." She hopped off the toilet top, leaving Gianna kneeling down, and then began washing her hands.

My girl was in denial like fuck, and I hoped she didn't keep this shit up for long. If she did, Kenzie may really move on.

Once Shannon got herself together, we decided to play a game of *I Never*, since we had about seven bottles of non-alcoholic champagne that I found. I didn't even know we had this shit at first, but I was happy to see it. Even though it wouldn't get us drunk, we still wanted to feel like we were drinking champagne.

"Okay, I never sat on anyone's face," Aysia said.

We all paused, and then the four of us threw back a shot of the non-alcoholic champagne. If you'd done the action that the person said, you had to take a shot.

"I think we've all sat on our man's face," I said and they nodded as we laughed.

"Alright, I've never ever, and thank God for this, had whack dick," Shannon said. Aysia rolled her eyes and took the shot.

"What? Brice was never good; he was just my first. Y'all bitches are lucky that you've only experienced King dick," she smacked her lips, making us chuckle.

"Almost forgot about Brice," Gianna responded with a smile.

"Umm, I've never gotten my ass ate," I grinned. Both Gianna and I threw back shots, as Shannon and Aysia's jaws hit the floor.

"Oh my gosh bitch, KJ and Kendrin eat ass?" Shannon bucked her eyes as Aysia died laughing.

"I don't think KJ meant to at first, but once he did it, he just kept going. Now every time he eats me out from the back, he gets that part too," Gianna giggled.

"Well, Kendrin's freaky ass purposely did it. He pressed my face into the pillow and went in," I cocked my head as my friends roared with laughter.

"Oh fuck, well they are brothers," Aysia panted from laughing so hard.

THE NEXT DAY...

Today was the day I would walk down the aisle to meet my love. I was beyond excited to get married, go to my reception, and then fly off to Paris, France. I wasn't feeling as sick either, which was always a plus, even when it wasn't such an important day as this one. I never took for granted the days I could just relax and enjoy my pregnancy, so today brought me joy for two reasons.

I stood in the mirror in my wedding gown and palmed my stomach. The seamstress had to basically make my dress a maternity one. She made it so that it was slightly hugging my small bump, yet still classy and beautiful. I was so upset thinking I was gonna look like a whale today, but luckily she was able to make me look like a pregnant bride and not Shamu.

"Everybody is ready Lo," my mom smiled and picked at me.

"Ma, stop I'm good," I chuckled.

"Okay I'm sorry, I'm just making sure not a hair is out of place. You look so pretty Willow," she teared up. She pulled me into a hug and then kissed my cheek. "I love you baby and I love to see you so happy. You guys have been through a lot and it feels good to see you finally settle down. I didn't think it'd be this early, but I'm still just as happy as I would be four or five years from now.

"Thank you, mommy," I giggled.

We embraced again, and there was a knock at the door. Kendrin's father came in wearing a smile, followed by Aysia, Gianna, and Shannon, in their beautiful teal dresses. I cheesed when I saw Aysia because I promised her I would wait for her to have the baby before I got married. Little did I know, that while she got smaller I was gonna be getting bigger. But it was worth it because she wanted to drop from my bridesmaid's line up, thinking she would look too fat. I was happy to have been able to prevent that.

"Are you ready?" Kendrin's father asked.

"Yes," I grinned.

My father died before I was even born, but I was happy to have another male figure to walk me. My mom's boyfriend was not an option with his annoying ass. He talked too fucking much and he was always suggesting shit that never made sense. I don't even know what my mom saw in his ass. I think she was just lonely.

We let my mom walk out so she could go sit down with the guests. I lined up with Mr. King and then my friends lined up with their significant others. Shannon and Aysia paired with Kaleeini and Kenzie respectively, so that there wouldn't be any problems. I was happy they agreed to switch because I didn't need any lovers quarrels ruining my special day.

Gianna's little twin baby cousins Antonia and Biagio were the flower girl and ring bearer, so we watched as little Antonia dropped flowers down the aisle. Gianna's mother Fiammetta, grabbed her up once she'd finished. I became nervous as I watched my friends go down the aisle and then take their places at the alter. This was really happening; I was marrying the man that I'd been crazy about for the longest. The man who ultimately turned me crazy, ever since he dicked my little virgin ass down.

Finally, the piano music came on, and Mr. King and I started our way down the aisle. I spotted Kendrin looking so fine in his white tux, with a teal blue bow tie just like I wanted. He was so fucking gorgeous and I couldn't wait to be on our honeymoon.

I finally made it to the alter, and Kendrin and I were smiling from ear to ear, like two little teenage lovers with crushes.

"We are gathered here today, to bring about the union of Kendrin King and Willow Jameson. The couple would like to say some personal vows before I have them repeat after me. Willow," the pastor gave me the green light.

"I didn't write anything down, so please bare with me," I chuckled making the wedding party do the same. "Kendrin, I don't remember a time when I didn't love you. I don't remember a time where I didn't think about you and didn't care for you. From the first time I saw you I feel like I fell in love, but was just too chicken to approach you. From the very first date we had, I knew that I wanted to be with you forever. You were everything a girl could want, from looks to personality. I loved that although a bit rugged, you had a kind heart and you genuinely cared for the people you loved. I feel protected with you, safe with you, but ultimately I feel loved. Even through the times where we may not have been on the best terms, you were always the one in my heart. I love you so much and I can't wait to see what we've created here," I palmed my belly, "and what we will accomplish together in the future." I was crying hard as fuck by then and barely got the last sentence out.

"Kendrin," the pastor nodded in his direction.

"Willow, I'm happy to see you standing across from me today. There were times where I thought I'd lost you for good, and it was the worst feeling in the world. I wasn't always the best guy, but you never strayed no matter how many times I caused you pain. The love you have for me is undeniable by anyone who comes into contact with us. Your love for me isn't conditional nor calculated, and that was something that I needed at the time that I met you; someone who would ride for me regardless of what the situation was. You may have rode for me a bit too hard sometimes," he chuckled with the wedding party, "but nonetheless it was all out of love. When I got shot that night, the first thing that crossed my mind was you. I thought about how much you've given me and given up for me, and I was upset that I hadn't shown you the same in return. Willow, I want you to know that I love you more than anything. I am so grateful for you, and I promise to always show you how much I appreciate your love and patience. I'm even excited about having twins, which kind of scared me at first, but anything that you and I create together will be nothing short of perfection."

I was sobbing so hard that Kendrin reached under my veil to thumb my tears. He pecked me lightly to calm me down, making the wedding party say, "Awwww."

"Okay repeat after me," the pastor smiled. We repeated the traditional Christian vows after him and then little Biagio walked the rings
up for us to say I do again. "I now pronounce you man and wife. And
you may now kiss the bride." Kendrin had the veil out of my face, and
his tongue down my throat before the pastor could even finish. "Mr.
and Mrs. Kendrin Draise King!" the pastor announced.

Everyone stood up to clap as we walked down the aisle to the
piano music. We climbed into a limo, and then headed to the reception hall. I was happy as hell right now. The man that I thought
would never get his shit together had finally done so, in more ways
than I could ever imagine. Nothing could bring me down in this
moment.

We made it to the reception hall, and once everyone was seated,
Kendrin and I prepared to have our first dance together. The DJ
turned on our song of choice, "Mr. Incredible" by Mya, and we began
to dance. I was tearing up so much that my head was throbbing.

After our dance was over, I changed into my reception dress, and
the party got for real started. Today was the beginning of the best
parts of my life; I could feel it.

WILLOW AND KENDRIN were married a week ago, and I still couldn't get the fact that Kenzie was out with another girl from my mind. I know I broke up with him, but I didn't expect him to already be out on dates. I wasn't even thinking about another guy, and here he was getting his fucking groove back already. I could barely live my life normally because all I thought about was him, and how we acted like we didn't spend numerous special moments with one another. We acted like two complete strangers at the wedding, and it hurt me to see two people who were deeply in love, ignore each other like that. Kenzie was my everything, and I hated to see us be distant like that.

I was lying back on my bed, fully dressed with my keys in my hand. I'd gotten dressed because I was gonna go curse Kenzie out, but then I'd changed my mind about it.

"Fuck it," I said as I got up.

I was gonna confront his ass and see what the fuck he had to say about the bitch he was with. I don't care if he wasn't my man, he shouldn't be out with her. He knows I love him and that I just needed some time, so why is acting as if he's gonna move on? He wasn't moving on to any fucking body while I still had air in my lungs!

I quickly slid my feet into some Adidas and checked the time on my phone. I had something to do today, so I wanted to get this out of the way first. I rushed down to my car, hopped in, and then sped to Kenzie's workout. I knew he would be there at this time, and that he would be done in about ten minutes from now, so probably just when I arrived.

I made it to the gym in about fifteen minutes and quickly parked my car. I saw a couple players walking out, but they just all blended together with their tall asses. I scanned and scanned looking for Kenzie, and when I spotted him my stomach dropped. I saw some girl talking to him, and I assumed that was who he was on the date with. She slipped her hand into his, and they started to walk together, making my stomach churn like butter.

As tears left my eyes, I slipped my key back into the ignition ready to leave. I couldn't do this, and I didn't wanna look dumb if he dissed me. *Stupid ass bitch*, I said to myself as I glared at the little bitch. That was my nigga that she had her little rat claws on.

"No, fuck that," I said aloud, and took the key back out of my ignition.

I climbed out of the car and then jogged until I stopped them in their tracks. The wide ass smile the girl was wearing faded quickly as hell. *Yeah, bitch, your time is up.*

"Kenzie can I talk to you for a second?" I raised a brow.

"Imani give me a moment," he exhaled as if I was some thirsty hoe begging for his time. Imani just nodded and walked to go stand by his car, making me scoff.

"You fucked her?" I sniffled. Crying seemed to be my thing lately, and I was not one to shed too many tears.

"What's up Shan? What do you want?"

"I wanna know if you fucked her," I cried.

He looked away, and then back down at me with his sexy ass. His deep caramel skin had not a blemish in sight, and his dark green eyes were sparkling so brightly. His lean muscular frame towered over me, making me feel all warm inside.

Running his hand through his short curly hair, he finally said, "Not yet." I just nodded slowly and looked away.

"So we haven't even been broken up for a month, and you're already moving on?"

"I'm just living life before I have to leave Shan."

"Leave to where?" My demeanor had completely changed.

"If you had have answered your phone a while back, you would know."

"You chose a team? Who?" I smiled and wiped the lone tear that had traveled down my face.

"Don't even trip shorty, you'll find out tomorrow like everyone else."

"You don't love me anymore Kenzie?" I sniffled as I felt an abundance of tears flow down. I could feel his love for me slowly dwindling.

He licked his lips as he stared down into my face, before he cleared his throat.

"Shannon you're killing me, man. You know I love yo' ass so don't come up here crying and shit like I'm the one who ended the relationship. You're the one who wasn't happy."

"I never said that I wasn't happy, Kenzie! You always make me happy, I just said I needed some peace. I couldn't deal with the drama."

"There ain't been any drama ever since you and Gigi beat her and her sister's ass!"

"Her sister?"

"Yeah, that was her sister Brooke, not her friend. I think they're moving to North Carolina soon. She wants to leave the drama too, what a coincidence. Maybe y'all should room together."

"You still talk to her?"

"No, we have mutual friends Shannon. Are we done here?" He raised a brow.

"Kenzie-"

"Do you wanna be back together or not?" he cut me off.

"I do but there's-"

"No buts, it's a yes or no."

"You just have to promise there will be no problems."

"I can't do that Shannon, relationships go through things. I can only promise to love you, be faithful, and have your back. I can't promise that drama won't occur."

"Kenzie-"

"Bye Shannon." He walked off towards his car and that girl, and I just wanted to whoop her ass. He wouldn't even let me talk.

"Kenzie!" I called after him, but he and the girl just got into the car.

I wiped my eyes, and then went and got into my own so I could handle some business. Today was just a trash ass day for me, and it wasn't over yet.

I made it to the clinic about ten minutes later, and quickly found a park since it was a weekday and everyone was still working.

"May I help you?" The nurse at the desk asked once I approached it.

"Yes, I have an appointment for Shannon Breaux."

"Yes, I see you here for pregnancy termination. Just fill out these papers honey, and we will be with you shortly."

I PULLED up to my parent's house and shut off the engine. I wanted to come and talk to my baby sister and see if she was still mad at me. I never got the chance to explain to her why I did what I did, so I wanted to make sure I took the time out for that. I didn't want her being mad at me because that would make her rebel, and that could get her killed. Plus I loved my little sister, and I wanted us to be cool, not have hate towards one another.

I entered the house and then jogged up the long staircase until I made it to the second floor. I made a left, and then a right, where I reached Kendria's bedroom door. Knocking lightly, I waited patiently for her to let me know when I could come in.

"Who is it?" she called out.

"KJ," I replied.

"Goodbye."

"Dria, come on man. I wanna talk to you!"

It was quiet for a few moments and then finally she snatched the door open and walked away to sit at her little vanity. She resumed doing her hair, so I walked in and closed the door behind me. I sat down on the little plush chair in her room and then looked at her pretty face. I swear she was my mom's twin, but she had green eyes like the rest of us. She stared into the mirror and brushed her long dark hair repeatedly, waiting for me to start talking.

"First, I wanna say I'm sorry Dria. I know we scared you when we did what we did," I sighed. She gave no response and continued to brush her hair. "I only did what I did to protect you. I knew he was pushing up on you a little too aggressively, and I didn't want him to hurt you."

"How did you know what he was doing? How did you even know where I was?" she quizzed dryly, placing her brush down.

I exhaled sharply and then said, "I put a small device in your purse so that I could hear everything and track you. Kendrae told me you went to a party on Beehler, and because I was worried that you would keep sneaking around, I put the shit in your bag." She snapped her neck to look at me and then shook her head. Rushing to her purse, she snatched it open and began to rummage through it. "I took it out Dria, you can stop looking. Sit down shorty and let me finish talking to you." She glared at me with her little cute self and then plopped back down at her vanity next to me. "You know what it is that I do, right, Kendria?" I asked. She nodded slowly. "So then you know that there are people who don't like me, well hate me even."

"Why?" she asked.

"Because they're jealous. They want what I have and it's so serious that they would do anything to me to get it. That even means messing with my little sister. Because they know if something happened to you I would be sick. Kendrin and I didn't do what we did so that you wouldn't be with a boy, well we did, but that wasn't the only reason. We didn't want him forcing himself on you. So when we heard him pressuring you, we quickly got to you and took you. To make matters worse, Marcel is related to some people that want your brothers and your cousins dead shorty. We didn't know that until after we killed him, though."

"Who?" she furrowed her brows.

"It doesn't matter, but I just need you to listen to me when I tell you not to do something or go to a certain place. Can you do that for me? I need you to stop lying about where you're going too, can you do that?"

"Yes," she nodded.

"Because if someone hurt you, I would ruin the whole DMV area Kendria. I love you and I only do things so that I can make sure you stay safe, not because I wanna control your life. The same with Dad and Kendrin, we're strict because of who we are, and we know people see you as an easy target. Kendrae only told on you because he knew you could get yourself hurt. So remember, we only do what we do because we love you and wanna keep you safe pretty."

"So you wouldn't mind if I got a man?"

"Umm, yeah I'm not gon' front, I would mind a lot. You don't need a man shorty, you're fifteen," I chuckled.

"I will be sixteen in two months."

"Even then, that's too young. Boys only want one thing from you, and some niggas will do the most if they don't get it, like Marcel."

"So Marcel didn't really like me?"

"I'm sure he did, but you dating him would've given them niggas who hate me access to you. And they wouldn't care how much he liked you. But Kendria you're a beautiful girl, so don't worry about that one guy. Someone who will wait to marry you before they want sex from you is what you need. Plus, Marcel was too damn old for you."

"Victoria said you can't keep a man unless you do it before."

"And excuse my language, but Victoria is a hoe just like her mama."

"You know about Victoria's mom?"

"Yes. I know that she's basically one of the girls and that you use her for your lies shorty. Now do you wanna end up like Victoria's mama? She's been giving it up to everybody and is still single."

"No, I don't. But you didn't wait for Gigi."

I chuckled and kissed her cheek before saying, "I know. But I wouldn't want you with a nigga like me honestly. However, Gigi was worth me waiting for. I love her enough that if she told me she wanted to wait until marriage, I would have," I explained and tickled her a little. She chuckled showing her beautiful smile, and the dimples we inherited from our father. "So are we homies again?"

"If you give me some money and take me out to eat."

"When?" I frowned.

"Right now. I'm hungry and I want that lobster fest from Red Lobster."

I sucked my teeth and then reached into my pocket for a knot of cash. I peeled off two hundred dollars for her, but she snatched the knot.

"Thanks!" she giggled.

"Giv- fuck it keep it," I sighed.

"For real?" she bucked her eyes.

"Yeah, but don't carry that shit all at once. Just take some every time you go out, and only the minimum of what you'd need."

"You carry the whole thing," she pouted.

"Because I got heat shorty, niggas ain't gon' get away with it." I stood to my feet.

"I want some heat."

"Get yo' little grown ass up so we can go eat," I laughed at her ass.

The good thing about our little stunt, though, was that I realized if it came down to it, Kendria knew how to put up one hell of a fight. She low key fucked Kendrin and me up. It was to the point where if she wasn't my baby sister, I would've pistol-whipped her little ass. She had Gianna giving me the side eye because of the scratches on my neck.

She put her shoes on and then I took her to Red Lobster. She was talking to me about some petty drama at her high school, and although it annoyed me I loved it. I enjoyed listening to my baby sister run her mouth about nonsense. When she was all grown up I would miss this shit.

"And do you know shorty had the nerve to ask me for your number?" Kendria rolled her eyes.

Other than Gianna and my mother, Kendria was the only other female that got sixty percent of my attention.

"I hope you didn't give it to her."

"No, I cursed her bitch ass out!"

"Aye, watch your mouth shorty," I furrowed my brows and sipped my drink.

"Mom said I'm starting to talk like you and Kendrin."

"I see that, you need to talk more like Kendrae," I said referring to my little brother.

"He curses, too!" she grinned making me chuckle.

After the food, I took her to the mall, and she insisted on spending my money as if she didn't just stick me for a knot back at the house.

"Be good, and remember to be careful shorty. No more lying," I told my sister once we got back to my parent's house.

"I know and thanks!"

She kissed my cheek and then grabbed her many shopping bags, before running to the front door of my parent's home. I stayed there until she got inside and then sped out of the gate.

I decided to go drive by my traps just to make sure everything was copacetic. As soon as I pulled onto McElderly Street, gunshots rang out. I sped off down the street as the bullets continued to hit my car like hail. I kept driving and picking up my speed until the bullets ceased.

"Are you fucking serious!" I hollered loudly as I drove home.

I wanted to go back and retaliate so badly, but now was not the time to go out like Bonnie and Clyde did.

However, I was angry as fuck and ready for war. Whoever the fuck that was, was in for a bloody ass death.

Aysia and I were in bed kissing hard as fuck; moaning and everything. I rubbed the inside of her thigh and then moved up to her pussy. I felt like an addict having withdrawals.

"Not yet Kaleeini," she whispered. "Just two more weeks okay?"

"I'm sure you don't have to wait the full six baby," I said as I started to kiss on her collarbone and caress her breasts.

"Yes you do," she moaned as I kissed her pussy through her panties, repeatedly and sensually.

"My homeboy Tesean said after three weeks he and his girl were fucking and nothing happened."

"Well I'm not Tesean's girl, so move." She nudged my head from kissing her stomach.

I rolled onto my back and stared at the ceiling. My dick was hard as hell and I had no way to fix it. I could get some head but I didn't want that. Head was not pussy no matter what way you slice it.

A smile crept across my face as I decided to fuck with her. Turning towards her, I saw she was adjusting the volume on the baby monitor. I rubbed my hand up her smooth caramel legs and began to kiss on her neck from behind.

"Kaleeini stop. You're gonna end up with blue balls because I don't feel like sucking dick for half an hour," she complained.

"You don't have to," I whispered and then resumed kissing her neck while hoping to contain my laughter.

"I'm not breaking my six weeks either."

"Don't need to," I said as I began to tug on her panties. "This is the perfect time for anal." I sucked on her ear and kept yanking her underwear. She jumped to lie flat on her back so quickly that she was smashing my hand. I burst into laughter, as I moved my hand from under her. "I hate you," she grinned and shoved me lightly. "I should've fucked with your ass and agreed to it," she sucked her teeth.

"As horny as I am right now Aysia, that wouldn't have worked in your favor."

"You are so nasty," she turned her lip up and then turned it into a half smile when I kissed her lips. "Are you busy today?" she asked.

"No. Why? What you want my time?"

"Yes, I want your time. Keeilan and I wanna spend some time with daddy."

"I told you I don't feel comfortable taking y'all out yet until I handle something."

"We can chill inside," she began to massage my back, and that shit was feeling good.

I let my neck fall to the side, as she continued to massage my neck and shoulders. Once I had enough, I lightly tugged on her bicep and moved her onto the floor in front of me.

"I need just one," I bit my lip and pointed to my crotch.

She reached up to release my dick from my boxers, and then took it into her mouth. As it got sloppier, I felt my pelvis tightening, so I massaged her beautiful dark hair. It seemed to be thicker and longer than before she was pregnant.

"Aysia you know I need to see something," I groaned as she bobbed. She stopped sucking and then removed the little night top she was wearing to expose her breasts. "Yes," I nodded and then continued to watch her suck my dick with her perfectly round breasts out.

My phone began to ring, but I couldn't answer right now. The only thing I gave a fuck about was busting this nut. Aysia sped up, and then finally I was growling and releasing. She walked away to get a warm towel for me, and my phone rang again.

"What's up?" I answered.

"Did y'all move the cribs?" Rozzie asked me.

"What? No. Why?"

"I came and everything was gone like no one lived here. Oh, I just got a message from *Unknown* saying there is a meeting at the warehouse in an hour."

"Aight see you there." I hung up and sat there for a bit as I allowed Aysia to clean me off.

I was wondering what the hell was going on, and why the traps were empty and cleaned out. If them niggas got us for our shit, I was gon' be furious as fuck. My work phone buzzed, and I saw I'd received that same *Unknown Number* message from KJ regarding the meeting.

"Baby I have to step out really quick, but I will be back ASAP to chill, okay?" I said.

She just nodded somberly, and then stood up to go get rid of the towel. I watched her brush her teeth in just her panties and bit my lip. I couldn't wait to be inside of her. Once she flossed and rinsed, she walked back out.

"What?" she asked since I was staring at her.

"You mad?"

"No," she lied.

"You're not mad?"

"Nope!" She continued collecting things for her shower.

"So when I come back you gon' be cool?"

"Yep!" She bucked her eyes, pursed her lips, and then walked back into the bathroom. I followed after her and then hugged her from behind.

"I promise I'm gon' be quick," I whispered and kissed her neck.

"Cool," she nudged me off of her. "I need to shower," she added and lightly pushed me out of the bathroom.

I didn't have time for this right now, so I would handle her when I got back. I threw a towel over my shoulder, then went to the other bathroom to piss, shower, and brush my teeth again. I got dressed in a jiffy and then dipped out. I made it to the warehouse in no time and hit the alarm on my whip once I exited.

Entering the conference room, I was caught off guard seeing over sixty muthafuckas in there. I had no idea the whole damn team was gonna be here, but then I should've known that if Rozzie was coming, so was everybody else.

"Have a seat," KJ pointed to the chair next to him and across from Kendrin. "Aight so, overnight I had the traps cleaned out because we have some new ones. These were places I'd acquired a while back just in case we needed to move. My brother Kendrin, and also Lenny will be letting you know which one you're gonna work from, get product re-ups from, and etc. I did this because them Paine niggas had gotten wind of where one of the traps was. They knew the street but not the house, so I wanted to have us relocated before they figured that out and where the rest of our houses were," KJ explained.

"How do you know they knew the street?" I frowned.

"Because them niggas had somebody shoot at me."

"You saw them?" Drew asked.

"No, but our new addition Xandra let me know who it was. Swiss also confirmed for me that they knew one of the traps whereabouts and that they had indeed shot at me. So that is why we've moved. Are there any questions?" KJ looked around the room. Everyone shook their heads no, and then KJ had Bolo and Blade dismiss everybody.

The only people in the room now were me, Lenny, Drew, Xandra, KJ, Kendrin, Swiss, and that chick Bailey. She was sitting behind Kendrin, massaging his shoulders. I just chuckled to myself and shook my head.

"Swiss and Bailey, keep your ear to the streets for information like you've been doing. Swiss, I purchased a condo for you to stay in because if people find out that you're working for me, they may come for you, and we don't want that. Kendrin did you do the same for Bailey already?" KJ asked. Kendrin nodded and I smirked at him. He smirked back and shook his head no, to say he wasn't smashing. "Now Xandra, I need you to get the addresses of Duck and Lucky's girl-friends, just in case we start having problems trying to catch them. These niggas stay with security like some bitches," KJ sighed. "I don't wanna waste any bullets on their guards, and then allow them to get away."

"Got it," Xandra responded.

"I bet they have bodyguards for when they take shits too," I half joked.

"Oh, I know they do," KJ chuckled.

"Well, they can only stay shielded for so long, and I can't wait to bring their asses out of hiding," Lenny commented, making everyone nod in agreement.

I WAS SITTING in the little office KJ had set up for me, just staring out of the window. I was still a bit bummed about losing my job, but I couldn't work there anymore. What Casey did was unacceptable, and I refused to push my pride and morals aside just to work for him. No career was worth me being violated and disrespected.

I logged into my bank account online, using my computer, and I saw my balance was only six hundred thousand dollars. I knew that was just a cumulative of what KJ had given me, but I didn't see the money I'd made while working for Casey. I double-checked the transaction history and the last deposit made was the eighty-five thousand KJ had put in there for this month. I rolled my eyes and quickly logged out because I was pissed.

This nigga was supposed to pay me. I'd worked a full week and a half, which was a little over one hundred thousand dollars he owed me. I grabbed my purse, jacket, and baby, then left out of the house to go see about my money. Did I need it? No, but it was the principle. Also, I wanted to see money in my account that I'd worked for and not just the money given to me monthly by my man.

Once I'd made it to Casey's office building, I parked my G-wagon and then got K-Three from the backseat. I kissed his little fat cheeks on the way in. He was just too cute, and it was hard not to love on his little chunky butt.

"Gianna, oh my gosh that is probably the cutest baby ever," the girl Priscilla at the front desk beamed.

"Thank you."

"He's yours right?"

"Yes he's mine," I grinned at K-Three and adjusted him on my hip.

"Adorable. How can I help Gianna? I wished you hadn't quit, it's so boring here now."

"It just um, wasn't the right job for me. Is Casey here? I need to talk to him."

"Oh, sure he is. Let me just phone him and let him know."

I nodded and waited for her to place the call. I rubbed K-Three's little hair back, and he smiled at me making his dimples appear.

"Why couldn't you look a little bit like mommy huh? I did all the work," I said in a baby voice and tickled his tummy making him yelp and chuckle loudly. I put my finger to my mouth to tell him to quiet down, while still smiling.

"Okay Gianna, go ahead," Priscilla pointed to the back.

I smiled and then made sure my mace was ready on my keys before entering. I walked into Casey's office and he smiled when I came in as if he just hadn't tried to rape me the last time I was here. I was convinced that this nigga was certified.

"Gianna, to what do I owe this surprise," he licked his lips as his eyes roamed my body.

"Casey, I need the money you owe me. I worked for seven days, and styled all three girls each day, at five thousand a piece."

"Cute baby, is it your fiancé's baby?" I closed my eyes and exhaled.

"Yes, it is. Casey, I want my money."

"Can't pay the rent?" he raised a brow.

"No, I don't rent. I just want what I worked for."

K-Three made some baby noises as he stared at Casey. I kissed his forehead to calm him. Maybe he could sense the atmosphere. If so, he was just like his daddy already.

"Oh well, I forgot to mention something when I hired you. You only get paid when I get what I want."

"What?" I frowned.

"As long as you do what I want, you get paid Gianna, and you didn't do that. It's a shame because your styling is phenomenal. I would've kept you on, but you refused to sleep with me. And now that I know you're pregnant, I'm not interested anymore. A pregnant woman is worth about as much as a bag of garbage in the working world."

"Casey, give me my money," I sniffled and wiped the tear that fell.

"Mmmm, no," he said it like he was thinking. I walked closer to his desk and maced his ass with damn near the whole container.

"Aaahh aaah you bitch!" he shouted as he fell back in his chair and hit his head against the wall. He was yelling and shouting in pain.

I rushed out and ignored Priscilla saying goodbye to me.

The whole way home, tears raced down my cheeks. I wasn't sad, I was angry. I wanted what I worked for, and he was gonna give it to me; I just didn't know how. This wasn't the last time that he'd hear my name.

When I got home, I fed and bathed K-Three before lying him down. I went back to the bedroom because I was starting to feel nauseous, and as soon as I sat down on the bed, KJ walked in with some white roses.

"What are those for?" I half smiled.

"For the sexiest, most beautiful, intelligent, caring, and fashionable woman I've ever laid my eyes on," he responded. I could feel myself blushing as he brought them to me. He kissed my lips and then sat next me. "Why have you been crying?" he asked.

"It's nothing, what do you wanna eat for dinner?"

"Gigi," he chewed his gum and stared at me, with his deep green eyes piercing through me.

"I lost my job," I replied and stared straight ahead. He scooted closer to me.

"I noticed you hadn't been leaving, but I assumed he only needed you when they had Baltimore appearances. What happened?"

I sniffled and then threw my head back, before bringing it back up and turning to face him. I didn't wanna tell his psycho ass, but I needed to tell someone. I couldn't keep it bottled in.

"My boss wanted to have sex with me. When I refused, he tried to rape me, and the only reason-" I sniffled some more. "The only reason I got away was because I told him I was pregnant. Today I went to get the money he owed me for working those seven days, and he refused to give it to me." I began sobbing harder. "He told me I needed to have sex with him to get it, but even then he didn't want to because I was pregnant. He said I was worth as much as garbage in the work world," I explained.

I picked my head up and turned to look at KJ because he was so quiet. He stared straight ahead as his nostrils flared and his jaw twitched.

"Casey Morris was his name?" he asked without looking at me.

"Yes KJ but-"

"I'll get your money," he stood to his feet.

"KJ, no ill-"

"I'm gonna get your money, and that's all there is to it," he cut me off. He then knelt down in front of me. "Are you really pregnant again?" I nodded as I began to cry some more. "Why are you crying shorty," he wiped my face.

"Because I lost my job and I don't have anything going for me career wise. And then now I'm gonna have another baby. I feel useless."

He took my hands into his and then kissed the backs.

"Gianna, you're the furthest thing from being useless alright. Don't let that bitch ass niggas words get in your head shorty. How can you be useless when I need you so much?"

"No, you don't," I sniffled.

"Yeah I do shorty, you know that. I want you but also, I need you. I love you more than anything, and my sanity depends on you sometimes."

"It does?"

"Yeah, that's why I go so crazy when you be out there acting a fool or disobeying me. But shorty don't worry about that job because I got you okay?"

"I want my own money."

"I don't mean like that, I meant I'm gonna help you."

"He had celebrity clients."

"What did I just say?"

"You got me," I smirked.

"Alright so chill. You don't need that nigga. Don't you ever think you need something from another man that isn't me. I don't care what it is, don't ever beg another man for anything baby. Now the only thing we gon' get from Casey is your bread. I got your back."

"I got yours too."

"Oh, I know you do and we should celebrate the new baby Gigi. It's something that came about from the love we have for each other."

"I guess I didn't look at it that way."

"All of the nights we made love, that's what it's a product of," he touched my flat stomach, making me smile. I stared down at him and cupped his face.

"I love you, Kendrick," I whimpered and sniffled.

"Why are you crying baby?"

"It's happy tears. You make me happy, and I just love you so much."

"I love you too, Gianna."

I sat still in the lazy boy chair, and closed my eyes just to relax. Shit had been popping off left and right, and boy was it wearing me out. This was the life I chose though, so I wasn't gonna complain. I knew it took time for me to prove myself, and I could see the finish line very closely. I knew once I took these Paine Brothers out, I would have the same respect that niggas learned to show my father. Every nigga in this game has to earn respect, and that's what I was doing now. Niggas we're learning slowly but surely that I was not the nigga to fuck with. They were learning that those four letters of my last name meant more than just being the son of a bloodthirsty kingpin. That shit meant I had heart, and that the art of winning pumped through my veins just like blood. I wasn't born to lose, and I wasn't raised to lose, but if I somehow did, I would go out with my guns blazing.

Right now every one was tuning in to the Paine versus King beef. They hadn't done much but shoot at me and try to sell on my blocks, but everything they did I nipped it in the bud. But damn, had I not been driving a bulletproof car, my life would've ended that day they sprayed my shit.

I took pride in the fact that despite who I was, I'd never been pierced with a bullet. I think it was because of who my father was, and how he'd prepared me. I knew to never leave without a bulletproof vest, and to always drive a bulletproof car. I was hated and envied by too many to be walking around with no heat, no vest, and a regular vehicle. I've been shot at more times than I can count, and if I hadn't taken my father's words seriously, I would've been in the ground years ago. I'd been untouchable, and I planned to stay that way.

Niggas hated me simply because of that. They hated that they were never able to touch me with their bullets, or scheme me out of some money. It ain't my fault I'm always two steps ahead of these niggas.

Suddenly the sound of a light switch being flipped was heard. The lights wouldn't come on, though, and my target let out a frustrated sight. I watched Casey Morris sit his briefcase on the ottoman in his room, and remove his sport coat.

Had I been a snake I would've bitten him, because although dark, the moon gave plenty of light yet he still hadn't seen me. I continued to chill in the La-Z-Boy chair in the corner of his room behind him. After removing his jacket, he turned to me and almost jumped out of his skin.

"Look you can have all the money in my wallet!" He threw his hands up.

"Sit down," I stated calmly.

"Sir, if you would just take my-"

"Shut the fuck up! I wanna talk to you." He nodded and then sat down. Bolo entered the room, and then closed the bedroom door behind him, causing Casey to panic. "You have an employee named Gianna?" I asked.

"Y-yes," he stammered.

"That's my wife."

Gianna was basically my wife, so no need to say fiancée. Casey swallowed the lump in his throat, and then chuckled nervously.

"Gianna, she-she was a great employee. Umm, we-"

"You owe her some bread."

"Do I? I thought I paid-"

"Nah, you didn't. Now how do we go about getting it? And don't try and play me or I'll shoot your dick off."

"I-in my closet is a do-door that leads to a room where I have the money."

"You tried to rape her? You called her garbage?"

"No sir I did not."

"So you're calling my wife a liar?" He stared at me silent for a bit. "Are you calling my fucking wife a liar!" I barked, causing him to jump.

"No- no sir!"

"Then you tried to rape her right?" I grimaced as tears started to fall onto his stupid ass face.

"Yes, I did."

"Lead me to the safe. If you're on some funny shit I'll kill you on the fucking spot."

We both got up, and he, Bolo, and I followed him to the closet where he put in a combination. He opened the door and it was a huge room. He tried to cut the lights on, but like his room, it didn't work. I cut on my flashlight, and there were piles of cash everywhere. This nigga had plenty of fucking money, but was trying to short my baby for a measly one hundred grand. I was more upset that he'd tried to rape her and then called her garbage. Now *that* shit had me on one.

Bolo threw a duffel bag to him, and he began filling it up with bands of $1,000. I made him count it out loud to be sure it was one hundred of them, and then Bolo took the bag. He panicked a little when he noticed Bolo and I were wearing plastic on our shoes.

"Come out," I ordered him. We all walked out and he locked it back up.

"Look I'm sorry, if Gianna wants to come back to work she can, no strings."

I smiled at him.

WHAM!

I backhanded him to floor using my gun, and he had a big gash on his face.

"Tell me how garbage and how much of a pussy you are," I hissed at him.

"I'm garbage, a-and I'm a pussy!"

Bolo and I began laughing unintentionally at his words. He looked so fucking pathetic.

WHAM! I backhanded him again.

"Tell me you're a garbage ass bitch," I demanded.

"I-I'm a garbage ass bitch," he trembled, causing Bolo and I to roar loudly with laughter.

"Let me stop fucking with this nigga man," I chuckled lightly along with Bolo.

He looked up at me sobbing, so I just a silenced the gun and popped him. He lied there in his own pool of blood, and that image was very satisfying.

"Any cameras in the house?" I asked Bolo.

"No we checked thoroughly. And Blade cut the electricity and phone wires earlier today, so even if he did they wouldn't have been working."

"Good looking."

Tonight Shannon and I were chilling at Kingin' together. Gianna was feeling too sick to come, and Kendrin didn't want Willow in the club while pregnant the way that she was. I needed to have some fun, especially because I'd been cooped up during my last few months of pregnancy, and then even after to take care of Keeilan.

Kaleeini claimed he was more than able to look after the baby tonight. I told him I believed in him, but really I only left because my baby was already bathed, fed, and asleep. I didn't trust Kaleeini with my son just yet because he was fragile and Kaleeini needed some lessons. I bought a baby doll for him to work with, but he said that was for bitch niggas. I laughed as I sipped my juice, and watched the strippers from VIP.

"So how is the baby?" Shannon grinned.

"He's so perfect. It's so funny because before he was born I was like I'm gonna be so strict and blah blah, but now I just can't see myself spanking him or anything," I smiled.

"You'll change your mind when he grows up I'm sure."

"I know, but right now he has me wrapped around his little finger."

"You look good too, I see you getting your body back, but with a little more curves like Gigi," she nudged me.

"Girl I know, my doctor said it's the breast feeding that's causing my stomach and stuff to go down. I just wish my titties stayed big," I responded making us laugh in unison.

"Gigi said the same thing. She's back to her little bee stings almost," Shannon said, causing us to crack up.

"Hey, they're squeezable."

"Yeah they are, and plus as long as KJ likes them, it doesn't matter."

"Amen," I lifted my juice up. "What's up with you and Kenzie?"

"Nothing, we're over and that's it."

"You know he's going to New York soon," I reminded her. She just nodded and tucked her bottom lip in, as she stared out at the club. "Can I say something?"

"Go ahead," she set her juice down.

"I want you to stop pretending that you don't wanna be with Kenzie so you can be happy."

"I am happy."

"You're pretending to be happy."

"They say if you pretend long enough it'll eventually be true."

"Why pretend when you can have the real thing, Shan?"

"Because I don't wanna deal with all that shit!" she barked.

"Are you scared that when he goes to the NBA, there will be hundreds of Rosalinds?" I asked. She didn't respond, she just stared into the club and bobbed her head to the music.

"Shannon."

"I know there will be, and I'm not gonna fight a new woman every time I look up. I'll pass."

"Fine. I highly doubt you will be in fistfights with groupies Shannon, but do what you want. I will fight to the death for Kaleeini. However, I know he would never have me in a position where I would be beating bitches up constantly, and neither will Kenzie."

"News flash, I fought Rosalind twice."

"Wow the same person twice. Out of the whole time you guys

have been together, you fought one girl on two occasions. And technically you started the fight both times." She snapped her neck at me and smiled. "You did. And after you and Gigi put that ass whooping on her, she hasn't sprung up."

"She moved."

"See," I nudged her and she smiled.

"Thanks, but no thanks Aysia, I'm good."

I shrugged and continued to sway to the music until a familiar face came into view. I saw it was Tamal, so I gave him a half smile.

"May I?" he asked. I noticed some big ass buff guy near him as if he was a bodyguard.

"Yeah sure," I waved him up.

"I see you didn't answer my text the other day. I was looking for a pancake house," he smiled.

I looked over, and Shannon had one eyebrow raised like *what the fuck*.

"Oh, Shannon, this is a friend Tamal, he just moved here. Tamal, my other best friend, Shannon," I introduced them and they shook hands.

"Wow, Shannon," he looked her up and down and licked his lips.

She gave him a faint smile, making her smooth brown skin beam. I saw him still watching her as she pushed her long hair behind her ears, and stared at the stripper stage.

"Sorry I didn't respond Tamal, I've been busy. As you can see, I don't have a huge belly anymore," I responded to his initial statement.

"Yeah I see, congrats. It's kind of loud in here, why don't you two come hang with me at my new condo," he offered.

"Umm Tamal, I don't think so." I shook my head.

"Come on Aysia," he rubbed my leg, surprising the fuck out of me. I never expected him to try and push up on me.

"Move Tamal, don't touch me like that."

He put his hand in my hair and then gripped it roughly. What the fuck was he doing? Was he drunk? This was not the same guy that I met in the grocery store.

"Let her go!" Shannon tried to pry him off of me.

I threw my drink on his shirt, and he gripped my hair harder, yanking my neck back to lick it. He was hurting me like a mutha-fucka, and my pushes and slaps did nothing to stop him.

Shannon started taking off on him, and then she was lifted by Bolo. Bolo and Blade then snatched Tamal up and carried him out.

"Lets get the fuck out of here!" I told Shannon.

We rushed out of the club and climbed into my Lexus. As I pulled out, I saw Blade and Bolo dragging Tamal and his big buff bodyguard into the back of a van. They appeared to be unconscious. What the hell is going on?

I sped to my house and just took it upon myself to make Shannon spend the night. I wanted to keep her where I could see her in case something popped off. Her dad couldn't protect her like Kaleeini could.

"What the fuck was that about?" Shannon yelped as I dipped through Baltimore.

"Girl I don't know what the fuck happened. It's like he turned into someone else!"

We made it to Kaleeini's and my home, and as soon as I walked in, he yanked me into an embrace. I inhaled sharply, and enjoyed the comforting scent of his cologne.

"You good?" He looked me over and then asked Shannon the same. We both nodded, so he started towards the door.

"Where are you gong Kaleeini?" I asked, making him stop in his tracks.

He pulled me close and kissed me passionately for a couple seconds, and then he let me go.

"I'm going to handle some business. Help Shannon get settled for the night. I'll be back soon. Keeilan is asleep upstairs. Kendrin dropped Willow off to watch him," he rambled off and then left.

Shannon and I rushed upstairs so I could grab Keeilan and Willow, then the four of us went to the guest bedroom. Something was going on, and I was scared as hell.

Kaleeini, KJ, and I made it to the warehouse, where Bolo and Blade had Tamal aka Duck tied up. They'd already murked the bodyguard they said they'd captured. It may not have been both Lucky and Duck, but one of them was good enough. I'd heard that Tamal was the brains of the operation, so killing him tonight would be like decapitating the snake. The three of us entered the torture room, where Tamal was sitting in the chair tied up and obviously in pain.

"Well, well, well," KJ smiled as the three of us pulled a chair up in front of Duck.

He looked off to the side and shook his head. I could tell he was disappointed that he had failed, and it was funny as fuck to me. I could've told him he wasn't gonna succeed long ago and saved him some time, and his life.

"I don't hear you talking that hot shit you was spitting just a minute ago," I said to him.

"Man fuck y'all little niggas. Getting rid of me don't mean it's over!" he spat.

"Oh, what you think your bitch ass brother gon' be able to flourish without you?" KJ cocked his head in confusion.

"Yea, I do. Y'all ain't nothing but some little bitch ass niggas! I bet you still suck ya' mamas titty to go to sleep at night," Tamal hissed.

WHAM!

KJ whacked the dog shit out of this nigga with his gun. Blood poured from his ear, and tears began to roll down his cheeks. He slurped his spit and shut his eyes tightly in order to ease the pain.

"Don't you ever in your life mention my mama nigga. I've always been told to respect my elders, but I refuse to show respect to a mark ass bitch like you," KJ gritted before sitting back down.

Kaleeini stood his feet in silence, and I knew he was about to do something crazy because that nigga did not play about Aysia. He pulled a knife, and then slowly began to push it into Tamal's leg, turning it every now and then.

"Arrrgggghhhh!" Tamal cried out, clenching his teeth together. Bolo brought out some lemon juice, and Kaleeini doused the wound, causing him to holler so loud my ears rang.

"Now honestly Tamal, I wanna know, did you really think you could come down to my city and become king?" KJ frowned and folded his arms.

"I almost did," he whimpered and bounced his wounded leg.

"No bruh, you didn't. But even then, almost doesn't count bitch. I'm the muthafucking King of Baltimore; I mean it's part of my name. Don't nobody come to my hometown and try to take over shit. You should've stayed your bitch ass where the fuck you were. You came down here to die like a dumb nigga," KJ grimaced.

Tamal was just crying, whimpering, and shaking his head by now. He was in way too much pain to care about anything else right now.

"Kendrin put this pussy out of his misery," KJ instructed.

I stood up and walked closer to him. He straightened his body and prepared himself to be shot while still sniveling. I walked off to press the button on the wall, and the chair he was in began electrocuting his ass. The three of us sat and watched him scream and shake while being shocked until he finally died.

"Bolo, clean him up." KJ demanded.

After getting rid of Tamal, I felt a bit relieved. We still needed to get Jamal aka Lucky, but shit getting one of them niggas was an accomplishment on its own. Once we got Lucky, though, we could return to more important matters. Shit, we all needed to go on vacation or something.

My phone rang, and I saw Bailey's name pop up on the screen in my car. I clicked answer, and her soft voice came through the car speakers.

"I made dinner tonight and I don't wanna eat alone," she said.

"What did you make?" I smiled and made a right turn.

"Lasagna," she giggled.

"Alright, I'm on my way."

I knew I shouldn't have been going over there tonight, but for some reason, I could never brush this girl off. She was so innocent and harmless, that I couldn't curse her out and shit. This was the last night I was gonna be so nice, though, it wasn't right to be hanging out with her alone when it wasn't for business, so this was gonna be the end of our little... whatever the fuck it is.

I finally made it to the condo I'd gotten for her, and pulled into a parking space. I gave my self a pep talk and then got out to go knock on her door.

"Just in time," she smiled and moved back to let me in.

"Smells good in here," I nodded.

"Thank you."

"I see you've done well with the money I gave you for furniture."

"Yeah I didn't wanna spend too much, though, not until KJ officially puts me on payroll and I have my own money."

"I feel you."

"I'm gonna bring the plates, what would you like to drink?"

"Umm water," I smiled.

I didn't wanna get twisted while in her presence, plus I had to drive home still. I was not spending the night.

"You don't want any liquor?"

"What you got?"

"I have Bourbon for you if you want," she offered.

"Cool, but I want water too," I called after her.

She returned a few moments later with the food, and then she went to get the Bourbon and water. We made small talk while eating, and the shit was bomb as hell. Shorty was fine, cool, and could cook. She was for sure a catch for the next nigga. *I wonder if her pussy is good too*, I thought. I wiped my face to rid my mind of those thoughts.

"Finished?" she asked and I nodded.

She picked the plates up, and I watched her walk them into the kitchen. She was wearing some little ass shorts and a tube top. Her body was out of this world, and it was the only time in a long time I wished I were single for a day so I could smash. She came back out, and slid her house shoes off. *Pretty feet too? Fuck.*

"I should go," I said and pulled my hood onto my head.

"Don't go! Just spend a little more time with me," she grinned and laid down in my lap.

I looked down at her and smoothed her hair back.

After staring at one another for a few moments I asked, "Why you be sweating me shorty?"

"Cause I like you," she replied in a low tone.

"I'm married baby, you know that."

"I do but I don't mind."

"You should mind. You're way too beautiful and you have a lot going for you. You deserve more than being a side chick."

"I know, but it's the only way I can be with you."

"I can't have you Bailey and trust me I want you but I can't." I continued to rub her hair back.

"Why not? I promise I'm not one of those crazy girls who would tell."

"Because my wife is more important than my desires."

"You must love her a lot."

"I do, very much. And I would rather let her be with someone else, before I start having side chicks and such. Just like you, she deserves better than that."

"How did she get so lucky to meet you before me," she whispered. She was staring up into my eyes as I stared down into hers, still caressing her head.

"I wasn't always like this."

"You were a player?"

"And I was a liar, cheater, all that shit," I replied and we chuckled together. "But she stuck with me, even when she should've left me. I love her and I wanna do right by her. It's long overdue."

"Can we still be good friends?"

"Of course. We're gonna be working together still, so we can homies; platonic homies."

"Can I get a kiss?"

I looked up from her, and then back down. I lifted her up and then brought her down onto my lap so that she was straddling me. She cupped my face and then crushed her lips against mine. Our lips parted, and then our tongues began to dance slowly. She moaned lowly, as she rubbed the back of my head through my hoodie. I finally pulled away, and she pecked me once more. Shit, I would never chill with her on this level again, so why not give a little farewell kiss?

"I finally know what it feels like to kiss someone who cares about me," she half smiled.

"Don't forget that shit either. I care a lot, so don't be letting niggas treat you any kind of way," I nibbled on my bottom lip and rubbed up and down her small back.

She nodded and then climbed off of me. I stood to my feet and then headed towards the door.

"Kendrin, would you be mad if another guy fucked me?" she quizzed.

"Honestly yes, but I would get over it," I grinned.

"Would you be mad if another guy fucked Willow?"

I laughed and said, "Shorty, mad is an understatement. I'd probably depopulate Maryland if my baby fucked another nigga. She's never been with anybody else and that's how it's gonna stay."

She chuckled and nodded her head, then I opened the door to leave.

I made it home about ten minutes later and the house was quiet and dark. When I got into the bedroom, Willow was sleeping in just a bra and panties. I was thankful that Kaleeini had brought her home. I went to shower and brush my teeth, then climbed into the bed behind her. I palmed her belly, and then kissed the nape of her neck.

"I love you," I whispered as she stirred a little.

I felt like God put Bailey in my life to test my loyalty to my wife. I was glad that I passed, because not only did I prove to God that I was serious about my vows, but I'd kept my promise to my wife. I was proud of myself and how much I'd changed, because Willow deserved the best parts of me, and that's what she was gonna get.

TWO DAYS LATER...

I KISSED Imani's neck as I lied between her legs. We were naked in her bed, and I was about to destroy her shit. I hadn't had any pussy since the day Shannon and I broke up, but damn was I ready to end that drought. And Imani and I fucking was long overdue.

She rubbed her small hands up and down my biceps, as I flicked my tongue over her nipples.

"Mmmm," I moaned as I began to suck them and play with her pussy at the same time.

Once I got my fix, I brought my mouth back up to hers and dipped my tongue into her mouth.

"Ooh, oh shit," she cooed into my mouth as I toyed with her clit. I brought my hand up and grabbed the condom off the dresser that I'd set there earlier. "Kenzie go slow," she whispered. *I'll start slow, but then I'm gon' beat that shit up*, I thought.

"Been a while?" I smirked.

"No, it's my first time."

I stopped rolling the condom down and stared into her eyes. Lord, please let her ass be joking right now. How did I not know this?

"Your first time?" I questioned to be sure I heard correctly.

"Yeah," she nodded.

"Wait, you've never had sex before?" I frowned.

"No, I've only done oral. Well, I've only sucked dick once and it was yours. Two guys ate me out, but that's it."

"Imani," I sighed and fell to the side of her.

"What? You've never taken someone's virginity before?"

"Only Shannon's. Imani I'm sorry I can't be your first."

"Why not?" She sat up and watched me get dressed.

"Because shorty, you're supposed to lose your virginity to a nigga you love."

"I do love you Kenzie, I always have."

"I know baby, but I don't feel the same and I can't be your first knowing that. You need to give it to someone who loves you back shorty. I care but I'm not in love." I went to the bathroom to wash my hands and splash water on my face. "Alright shorty, I'm gonna go. Come give me a hug." I leaned in her doorway. She walked over to me naked, and then stood on her tiptoes to hug me. I lifted her up and then kissed her lips once more. "Check you later," I told her and then left.

"Bye Kenzie," she responded somberly.

I hated to do her like that, but I would feel like shit if I experienced something like that with her, knowing that I was still in love with Shannon.

On my way home, my homie Tyriq called me up.

"What's good?" I answered.

"Aye man, the homie Graham said he saw your shorty leaving the clinic a while back."

"Who Shannon?" I furrowed my brows.

Did people get a kick out of surprising me and keeping secrets? I was starting to think so.

"Yeah man, he just told me right now. I don't know why his ass waited so long. He was getting some top from this jawn named Keyshia, when he saw her rushing out."

"Thanks, T, I'll hit you later."

"Fasho."

I disconnected and busted a U-turn to Shannon's house. When I arrived, I parked quickly and was happy to see her dad's pick up truck wasn't there. I didn't feel like dealing with his meddling ass.

Rushing up the stairs, I beat on the door like I was the damn police. I knocked nonstop until Shannon came and flung the door open angrily.

"What?" she asked.

She had on some tights that hugged her small shapely frame, and a little bra like top thingy. Her long hair was down, and she looked so simple but pretty. I walked in and closed the door behind me before speaking.

"Why were you at the clinic?" I frowned. She stared up at me, and then walked back to her room speedily. I was right on her heels and then I closed her bedroom door behind me once we got in there.

"Why does it matter Kenzie? We're done and you have a new girl."

"Because either one, you had an STD and I need to know how you got it and who from. Or two, you're getting birth control in which I wanna know what nigga you getting it for. Or three, you were pregnant and now you're not. Which one Shannon?"

Any answer she gave me would have me hot, so it really didn't matter which one she chose to pick.

"It wasn't the first two," she whispered.

"You killed my fucking baby? What is wrong with you huh? You really don't care about anybody but your fucking self! First you wanna break up and you didn't even care to give me a real fucking reason as to why, except for the fact that you wanted peace! That's bullshit! Just like it's bullshit that you went and killed my baby! I can't believe you wou-"

"I didn't kill it!" she screamed as tears rolled down her smooth brown cheeks. "I went there to do so and I couldn't do it," she sniffled while panting heavily.

"So right now you're...?" she nodded. I dropped down and began to kiss her flat stomach. "When were you gonna tell me?" I asked, still gripping her small waist.

"This weekend," she wiped her tears.

I inhaled sharply and then said, "Shannon if this isn't a sign that we should be together, then I don't know what is. I love you and I think we should try for one another, and for the baby."

"Okay," she nodded.

"You gotta promise me that you're not gon' flake on me, baby. I'm at a time in my life where I need someone who is gonna be solid."

She got down on the floor with me, cupped my face and kissed me.

"I promise. And I'm sorry for acting stupid. I was just worried that our relationship was changing. I want it to only change for the better, not for the worse."

"No, it's not gonna change for the worse shorty. I'm gonna try and keep it like it's always been. I may not be around as much as before, but I'm gonna keep you happy Shan." She smiled and caressed my face. "And thank you for keeping my baby shorty. I can't wait until it gets here."

"Me either. I love you Kenzie King."

"I love you too Shannon Breaux," I bit my lip and then slid my tongue into her mouth.

God has a way of sending signs, and he just sent us probably the greatest one yet.

I SAT on the chaise lounge in my bedroom, leaning over to the side. I was propping my head up with my hand, staring across the room. In my free hand was my phone. Tears flowed down my cheeks as my heart almost beat out of my chest. It was 10pm at night, and I'd been in this same position for an hour. I was tired, but not physically, just mentally. I was angry and furious, but most of all I felt betrayed. One more hour passed, plus ten minutes, and Kendrin came into the bedroom. I hadn't moved a muscle, and I was still staring at the wall.

"Lo, baby what's wrong?"

He neared me with a confused expression. Although looking past him, I could see his face from the corner of my right eye. I could see his stupid sexy face.

"Who is she Kendrin?" I asked calmly.

"Who?" he frowned.

"Her!" I lifted my phone to show him the Instagram picture that I'd ran across.

In the picture, Kendrin was standing up with his hands in his hoodie pocket smiling, as the girl hugged him from behind, cheesing just as widely. She was shorter than him, so she was leaning over in order to be seen.

"Willow that's a friend. She works with us and-"

"Liar!" I shouted and chucked my phone at him. "Don't you fucking lie to me Kendrin!" He stared at me chewing gum, and then finally shook his head and looked away. "Who is she?" I asked again. Because I didn't bother to wipe the tears away, they were drenching my neck.

"Firstly, Willow calm down, you're pregnant."

"Fuck you, don't tell me to calm down! I asked you who the fuck that bitch was!" I hollered loudly as hell, and palmed my belly. He tried to touch me but I slapped the shit out of his hand.

"She works for us, and she's a friend. Nothing happened with her. Willow! Willow! Come here!" He began to follow me as I left the bedroom.

I'd heard that stupid 'she's just a friend' bullshit too many times before. I rushed down the stairs and he was right on my heels. Once we made it to the bottom, he hugged me from behind. When I felt his hand palm my belly, it caused me to break down.

I was so tired of fighting for this man. I couldn't do it anymore. If it wasn't one thing it was another. Here I was pregnant with twins, and freshly married, and that still didn't stop him from doing me wrong. We hadn't been married a year and he was already cheating and back to his old ways.

"Willow baby please calm down, think about the babies."

"No you think about them! You don't care about them or me, and that's why you're cheating on me again! I'm done Kendrin! I want a divorce!" I elbowed him with all of my strength, but it wasn't enough to get him off of me.

"I'm not gon' tell yo' ass to calm down again Willow. Calm your fucking nerves and chill out. We ain't getting no fucking divorce and you ain't done with shit," he gritted in my ear as he carried me back up the stairs and into the bedroom.

Sitting me down on the bed, he grabbed a chair in the room and then pulled it in front of me. He reached up to push my hair behind my ears, and then wiped some of the many tears that were falling.

"Why Kendrin? I love you so much. How could you not care about someone who loves you as much as I do?" I sobbed hysterically with my head down. He got off the chair and sat next to me.

"Look at me Willow," he demanded. I didn't want to but I did begrudgingly. He grabbed my face and stared into my eyes with his beautiful green ones. "I am not cheating on you baby. That girl is a friend, and that picture is like a month old. Yes, we flirted a little but that was it. She's just cool and that is it baby, I swear to you. Everything I said at the alter that day I meant. I more than care about you, and I need you to believe me. You and my kids mean everything to me, and I wouldn't do anything to jeopardize that. Do you honestly think I would've married you to still play games?" he frowned. I inhaled his cologne and enjoyed the familiar smell of it. He always wore it and he smelled so bomb. "Willow, I'm sorry because I know I'm the reason you feel threatened every time a woman is around me, but you have to understand that I'm all about you now. I'm not the same nigga that would lie to you and have you crying all night. I'm sorry for taking the picture, especially because you have no idea who she is, but baby don't think that I don't care about you because I do. Okay?" he raised a brow and I nodded. "Give me a kiss," he said in a low tone.

"You swear you're being faithful Kendrin?"

"I swear I am. And I promise to always be. You deserve the best Willow and I wanna be the person that gives that to you." A faint smile crept across my face. "There's the smile. Again, I'm sorry about the picture."

"I accept," I nodded and kissed his nose. He bent down and kissed my stomach, making me giggle, and then he leaned me back until I was lying down. "Kendrin what are you doing?" I whispered as he spread my legs and raised my gown.

"Showing you how sorry I am," he responded in a low tone as he pulled my panties down. Putting my legs onto his shoulders, he began to slowly eat my pussy.

"Mmmm," I cooed and threw my head back some. He sucked

gently on my clit, and flicked his tongue over it slowly. "Shit," I released. Being pregnant made me sensitive down there, so I was always cumming quickly these days.

"You forgive me?" he asked and then continued to feast on my center.

"Yes, Kendrin," I moaned and rubbed his fade. He dipped his tongue into my hole, and then brought it back up to suck on my clit some more. "Oh shit, uuuh uuh mmm," I called out as he made love to me with his mouth. Holding my legs apart, he sucked faster but still gently until I exploded. He then kissed up my stomach and pushed my gown up until it was off.

"I'm sorry baby," he whispered again before tonguing me down.

I loved him and I believed him. If I was gonna be his wife, I needed to trust him and that's what I was gonna do.

TONIGHT THE WHOLE King clan and the girls, were having a huge party for Kenzie. Everyone was here that was family. I was so happy for my baby, but slightly sad that he and I would be leaving Maryland for New York soon. He decided to purchase a house near his cousins though, because when he had to travel outside of New York for games, he wanted me to come home and be close to my friends and his family; that was only when I didn't wanna travel with him. I loved that idea and was happy that I wouldn't necessarily be permanently gone from my girls.

As usual, the party was at Kenzie's grandparents home, because it was the biggest house and the safest. All parties were held there because it was less likely for some shit to go left.

"Congrats boo!" Aysia walked up to me with Gianna and Willow.

"Thank you, but you should be saying that to Kenzie," I chuckled.

"Where is he?" Willow looked around. I scanned the room until I saw him talking with his sisters, Kendlie and Kennedy.

"Over there!" I pointed.

The four of us walked over and the girls congratulated and hugged him. There were Brooklyn Nets decorations everywhere and it was so cute. I couldn't believe my baby was finally going to the

NBA. I always knew it would happen, but this party seemed to really bring the dream to life. I was more interested in the food than anything, though, because now that I was eating for two, I could really put it away.

"Okay everybody, line up and then just go down the line to pick what you want to eat!" Kenzie's mom Jessica yelled out.

Everyone began to line up as she'd directed us too. Nic, Morgan, and Christy got behind the table with Jessica, so that they could help her serve the food to us while Deija and Nic's cousin Danielle helped with drinks. There was spicy chicken, mashed potatoes, barbecue chicken, macaroni and cheese, cornbread, pasta, just all kinds of shit because all the mothers made dishes. Even Aysia, Willow, and Gianna's mothers brought food. As for my daddy, he just came to eat.

He had a little crush on Kenzie's mom Jessica, which I found to be hilarious. He could barely talk when she would try and converse with him. Tonight she looked so pretty in a short red dress and matching heels. Her freshly pressed brown hair was hanging down her back, so I know my dad was 'bout ready to have a heart attack. She and her friends were so beautiful and I hoped that I could be in shape like them after having multiple babies.

I laughed when I reached the dish that KJ and Kendrin's mom Nic was serving, because their father Kendrick was hugging her from behind. They were so in love and I hoped Kenzie and I would be that in love with one another down the line. They both had tattoos of one another's name like Kenzie and I, so I'm pretty sure we would last too.

"Please don't mind him," Nic smiled as her husband kissed on her neck. He moved her long ass hair over so he could get in there.

"Kendrick are you really gonna do that the whole time I'm serving people?" she frowned as she put some food onto my plate, and then onto Aysia's. We were laughing so hard.

"Yep!" he responded shortly and smirked at us, making us crack up.

"Oh my gosh Daddy, I lost my appetite!" Kendria frowned as she looked at her parents all cuddled up damn near.

"Baby girl, just remember if I hadn't have done this in the past, you wouldn't be here," Kendrick smiled at her and she sucked her teeth.

"And that may not be such a bad thing," Kendrae chimed in, making us all guffaw and Kendria jump at him.

Once everybody had their food, the party really started. Everyone was eating, dancing, chilling, and talking. I loved that it was so many of us. Usually, in families this big, there were rivalries and jealousy, but in this family, you could tell that everyone really loved and cared for each other.

"Ladies and gentlemen, I'd like to say something," Kenzie hit the glass with his knife. Everyone quieted down, and KJ turned down the music before sitting back on the couch next to Gianna. "As you know, I am gonna be moving soon, and this beautiful woman is gonna be coming with me. Also, she's carrying my child, which makes me pretty happy. But there is something that would make me happier," he said and then got down on one knee.

"Kenzie!" I squealed as everyone gasped, clapped, and said *awww*.

"Shannon I don't see any reason to wait, so will you marry me?"

"Yes Kenzie, oh my gosh!" I covered my mouth as I stared at the huge ass diamond.

He must've spent a large part of his twenty-one million on this one. As soon as he slid it onto my finger, we kissed and the room cheered for us.

"I love you," I said to him as we kissed repeatedly. I was crying tears of joy. I was not a crier, but this baby had me acting out of character.

"I love you too, shorty," he said before kissing me again.

For the rest of the night, everyone just chilled and relaxed having a good time. As for me, I couldn't take my eyes off of this damn ring. I could tell this was one of the many great moments I would have with Kenzie King.

KJ and I were chilling on the couch watching television.

"Refill me," I put my cup out and he poured some more Hennessy into my glass.

We were big chilling. We had alcohol, chips, cookies, and a big screen TV. All we had to do was wait a little bit, and then we could put in this last little bit of work. We were rocking all black, complemented with leather gloves and plastic shoes covers.

"What the fuck!" Jamal's girlfriend Valentina walked into her living room and dropped her grocery bags upon seeing us.

"Come in and sit down," KJ said calmly as she slammed her front door closed.

"Y'all need to-"

"Sit down." He pointed his gun at her.

She put her hands up in mock surrender, before slowly walking towards the couch. She was a pretty Spanish chick with thick hips, thighs, and big titties. She sat down on the couch next to us and stared, waiting for our next direction.

"Call your nigga and tell him to come over. If I think you're tryna play games, I'll pop yo' ass immediately," KJ explained.

I cocked my gun as it sat in my lap, and her eyes bucked. She pulled her iPhone out and began dialing super slowly.

"Man hurry the fuck up!" I barked.

Before she could finish, KJ snatched the phone from her and asked, "What's he stored as? And you better not fucking lie."

"He's stored under Lucky," she whimpered. KJ scrolled on her phone and then tapped on what I assumed to be his contact.

"Get yourself together so he won't suspect anything," I gritted.

She quickly wiped her eyes and took the phone from KJ. We sat on each side of her and listened as the line trilled.

"Hello?" he answered.

"Hey, baby where are you?"

"Getting something to eat right now, why what's up?"

"I just want to talk to you about some things, can you come over here please?"

"For what baby? I'm busy tonight. You know I'm out here looking for these King niggas. I can't do too much chilling, especially with you, because they may find where you are."

"Jamal please just come, I need you!"

"I can't Val, these niggas killed both of my fucking brothers! I have to stay out here until all of them niggas are six feet under."

KJ snatched the phone from her and said, "We killed your brother and we are about to kill your bitch if you don't come home like she asked you to."

Suddenly the line went dead, so KJ pocketed her cellphone.

"Please don't kill me. I swear I have nothing to do with what Jamal and Tamal were doing. I'm just trying to take care of myself and live regularly. I don't want shit to do with this," she sobbed.

"Shut up with all that damn crying, fuck," I scoffed and shook my head.

I had no sympathy for Lucky's and Duck's girlfriends. Just like Duck had no compassion or sympathy when he tried to come for Aysia. If he had have done anything to her, I would've turned into Ted Bundy overnight. We made sure to get Duck's bitch Cassi, just in case she tried to come back on some bullshit to avenge Duck's murder. We wanted no loose ends dangling.

We waited for about ten minutes, and then finally we heard keys in the door. Both KJ and I hopped up and stood on each side of the door, just in case Lucky tried to come in shooting like an idiot. As soon as he walked in, KJ clocked him in the back of the head with his gun. When I saw him reach for his heat, I shot him in his forearm.

"Aaahh!" his baby mama screamed and cried.

"Scream again shorty, and I swear I will blast you!" I hissed. She shut up and sat back down on the couch.

"Fuck!' Jamal hollered as he doubled over in pain, and collapsed to the floor.

"Y'all niggas really thought y'all was gon' win huh?" KJ laughed as he towered over him. "Honestly, I expected more from you bitch ass niggas. Y'all were a piece of cake to destroy, just like all the muthafuckas in the past who have come for us. Too, bad you won't live to spread the word that the King family ain't to be fucked with," he added before blowing Jamal's head open on the floor.

Valentina sat there shaking uncontrollably, as she stared down at her nigga with his head blown to smithereens. I didn't feel bad for her because I knew she was helping this nigga in some way. The way he was talking to her on the phone let me know that she was well aware of more than she let on. I popped her ass and she fell off the couch.

We let Bolo and Blade in through the backdoor, and the cleaning crew got to work, wiping down the whole house and removing the bodies. Once everything looked untouched, we collected the glasses we drank from, as well as our liquor and snacks, and then bounced. This shit was finally over.

"We finally got them, niggas," I grinned and tapped the dashboard of KJ's Cutlass.

Words couldn't express how elated I was that our enemies were finally gone. Not only that, I was proud that time and time again, we proved ourselves and didn't lose all that our fathers had worked so hard for. The King clan of Maryland was still undefeated, and it was gonna stay that way. We'd created a sub legacy in a way, and would no longer be looked at as just the sons of those King brothers.

"I know man, shit feels good," KJ grinned widely as he sped through Baltimore.

I admired my city in all its gritty glory as he did. This shit was mine and would forever remain in the King family.

"I told you we always come out on top man," I replied.

"I never doubted that we would. I mean there were times where I thought we were in deep shit that would last for a while, but I always knew we would come out victorious."

"It's in our blood to win," I dapped him up.

"Ain't it."

He dropped me off at home and then headed to his.

As soon as I got upstairs, I took a shower so I could lie close to my baby. I didn't like touching her right after I'd killed someone, or done anything within the operation. Once I was clean, I turned the heater on a little and then climbed in bed behind her. I gripped her waist, making her stir a little and then she covered my hands with hers. I was gonna sleep like a newborn baby tonight; shit me and Keeilan.

THREE DAYS LATER...

I WAS LAID out on the bed in some white lace lingerie. Tonight I was gonna end the drought between Kaleeini and I. I missed having that physical connection, and couldn't wait to get it back popping with my baby daddy. I heard the front door ding, letting me know he was home, so I walked out of the bedroom to stand at the top of the stairs.

"Welcome home daddy," I smiled and placed my hand on my hip.

I had on white lace panties, the matching bra, garters and white stilettos. Gianna convinced me to order from a sex shop because they had way sexier getups. KJ had turned my best friend into a little freak.

"Aysia," Kaleeini whispered and began to ascend the stairs.

"Do you like what you see?" I inquired as he neared me.

"Nah, I love what the fuck I see."

I giggled seductively and then turned on my heels to go into the bedroom. Like a little puppy, Kaleeini followed after me with his tongue out. I pushed him onto the bed and then pulled his shirt up.

"You are so beautiful," he commented as I moved my long hair from one side to the other.

"Thank you," I bit my lip.

I began unbuckling his pants and then pulling them down along with his boxers. Once he was naked, shoes and socks off too, I began to massage his dick. It was already hard as hell, but I still felt the need to rub on it.

"Don't tease me," he whispered as he watched me with his beautiful jade green eyes.

His dreads were hanging loosely and looked perfect against his supple caramel skin. His six-pack was protruding beautifully and I just had to kiss it before getting to work.

I gave him a smile and then began to suck the tip of his dick slowly. His moaning motivated me to do an even better job. I loved to hear him groan and curse, because that meant I was doing what the fuck I was supposed to do. In no time I had his dick bumping my tonsils, as I bobbed up and down on it.

"Shit, babe fuck," he mumbled and began to guide my head up and down his shaft.

I sped up and began to play with his balls at the same time and soon enough he was exploding. I stood to my feet and he began pulling my panties down.

"Leave the heels and these little shits on," he said referring to the garters. He turned me around and then unhooked my bra to release my breasts.

"Get on your back shorty." I did as I was told. "Spread your legs." Again I complied.

He got in the middle of the bed with me and then began gently sucking my clit. I played with his dreads as he devoured my pussy like a professional. My back arched and I threw my head back as he made love to my center with his tongue.

"I'm gonna cum Kaleeini, shit," I cried out. Suddenly, he lifted me a little and ran his tongue from my ass back to my clit. He did it again, and again, and I was floored at the way he was eating my pussy and ass like he was in an eating contest. *I can't wait to tell my friends,* I thought. "Uuuh aaah uuuuh!" I screamed and released.

He didn't slow up, he kept going until he brought me to two more orgasms. Shit! My baby had obviously been more deprived than I thought. He planted a soft kiss on my lower lip, and then got up to slip his tongue into my mouth.

As our tongues danced, he placed his dick at my opening and began to enter me. I took small breaths as we kissed in order to relax my body. Once he was all the way in, he closed his eyes and bit his lip as if it was the greatest feeling in the world. He even shivered a bit and had to pause for a second. He began winding his hips into me, while sucking and licking my nipples hungrily. My body began to quiver at the feeling of him inside of me.

It'd been so long since I had him and it was like a drug. My body had been going crazy without his touch for so long. He intertwined our fingers and then pinned my hands above my head. He pressed them into the bed and began sucking my lips as he worked between my hips.

"Fuck, I love you Aysia," he whispered as he slammed into me every now and then.

The area under me was soaking wet from me cumming so many damn times. My legs were like noodles and trembled as this beautiful specimen slammed into my pussy.

"So fucking wet," he grumbled as he began to beat it up. He pinned my hands behind my head and really started to go in.

"Uggghhhh!" we both hollered as we came hard together.

He fell onto me, hugged my body and kissed me so hard I thought our lips would burst. He trailed his kisses from my lips to my neck and then began sucking and licking it.

"Thank you for my baby shorty."

"Thank you for giving me a baby," I whispered back before our lips met again.

Once we caught our breaths, he rolled off of me and out of the bed. He slipped on some boxers and then went to the bathroom to brush his teeth.

"Where are you going Kaleeini?"

He better not be about to go any fucking where! I planned for us to spend the night in together.

He ignored me my question, and when he finished brushing, he rushed out of the bedroom. I threw the covers off of me and got out of the bed because he was about to get an earful. He couldn't just come up in here, fuck me and leave like I'm one of his fuck buddies. I stormed to the bedroom door to leave, but he slipped in and stopped me in my tracks. A beautiful smile spread across his face and he backed me to the bed to sit me down.

"Kaleeini wha-"

"Aysia, I've been trying to figure out the perfect way to ask you this and nothing seemed right. Every time I rehearsed in the mirror it wasn't good enough. So I'm just gonna come out and ask you with no forethought. I love you Aysia and I'm pretty sure I wanna be with you forever," he grinned and I nudged him. "No, I do wanna be with you forever, so will you marry me?" he slowly knelt down and opened the small red velvet box. The beautiful ring it contained almost blinded me.

"Yes Kaleeini, oh my gosh," I cheesed and threw my head back in laughter as he slid the ring on. "This means that when I gain five hundred pounds, or possibly stab you, we will still have to be together."

"Shorty, you sure and the fuck know how to ruin a moment. Give me that shit back," he tried to remove it.

"No!" I giggled as he playfully tackled me. I ended up on top, straddling him. "You're mine forever now."

"That's perfectly fine," he replied and squeezed my ass while pursing his lips. He then laid me on my back for some celebration sex.

"KJ WHERE ARE WE?" I quizzed.

"Just go with the flow shorty, and quit asking so many questions," he replied as we walked onto the elevator.

I had no idea what he was up to, and since he was so damn unpredictable, I didn't know if I should be scared or what. He held my hand in his, and kissed me a couple times until the elevator made it to the sixteenth floor. When we stepped out I noticed we were at King Records. I recognized the name, but still didn't understand what the hell I was doing here, or what KJ was up to.

We walked down a long hall, until we made it to two big brown double doors. On it was a gold plate that read *Kayden King*. His wife Christy's little sister Ciara walked by and waved, to which KJ and I did the same in return.

"KJ why are we at your uncle's label?" I quizzed.

Kayden King, a damn legend in R&B music, was KJ's father's cousin. They called him uncle, though, because he seemed more like an uncle than a cousin. He was married to KJ's mom's best friend Christy. I thought it was cool that Christy, Nic, Jessica, and Morgan all married family members. It was kind of like my friends and I, except only one if us were married so far. The rest of us were engaged though, so that was a start.

KJ knocked on the door and then twisted the knob to enter. Kayden King was sitting behind his big cherry wood desk, and his beautiful wife Christy was in his lap.

"What's good Unc'? Aunt Christy? You know Gigi," KJ greeted them.

"Hi sweetie," Christy stood up and walked over to hug me.

She rubbed the small bulge in my stomach. I was four months pregnant now and starting to show a little more.

"Hi, how are you?" I grinned. No matter how many times I'd met Kayden King, I was still star struck.

"Good afternoon Gigi, why don't you guys have a seat," Kayden said as he walked to his office door and shut it.

The four of us sat down on his plush leather couches and Christy poured some sparkling water for all of us. I was happy to be here, but I still didn't know why. KJ just said he had a surprise for me, so I was waiting to see what it was exactly.

"So Gianna, I heard you were looking for a styling job?" Kayden inquired as he sipped his water.

"Well yes, I recently had one a couple months ago, but that fell through. I'm doing little photoshoots here and there to build my resume and portfolio, but I'm looking for a career," I replied.

"Nice, so how long have you been into fashion?" he asked.

"For as long as I can remember. I'm subscribed to just about every fashion magazine and I know when all the latest fashions hit the market. I can style anything from business casual, to sportswear, to swimwear, even Goth stuff. I'm pretty well rounded."

"Dope," he looked to KJ and nodded approvingly.

"Told you," KJ replied.

"Do you have any pictures Gigi?" Christy asked.

"Yes, on my phone if that's okay," I replied.

"That's fine," Kayden nodded.

I pulled out my iPhone and then went into my styling album. I handed it to Christy and she and Kayden flipped through it to see some of the styles I did for other people. I didn't know why all this was happening, but I was hoping it led to some sort of opportunity.

"I would even be interested in interning," I added as they looked.

"Way too good at what you do to be an intern honey," Christy chuckled. She reminded me of the actress Lauren London. They handed me back my phone and I put it away.

"Gigi, the reason you're here is because I'm looking for someone to style my new artists. I have three females and one male artist that I'm gonna launch and I would need you to be their stylist for a while. New artists tend to not know anything about fashion. They're focused on making music, so they couldn't care less about their wardrobe, which is why I wanna hire you. I need you to worry about their wardrobe for them, so they can focus on their craft. Once they get to a point where they know how to look and dress on their own, we move you to the next new artist. Your job title would be the N.A.S, or New Artist Stylist. You would be helping that artist develop themselves and their image, which is a very important element in the business. These days image is everything. Your pay would be eight thousand per artist, per event that you have to style them for. Now I know you can't travel too much because of your children, so if the artist is going out of town, we would need you to prepare their outfits for the duration of the trip. Does that sound like something you'd be interested in?" Kayden explained.

"Oh my gosh, are you serious? Of course I would Mr. King, that sounds like a dream job."

"Great and if you're wondering whether or not I'm gonna show favoritism to you since you're my nephew's wife, the answer is yes," he said and we all chuckled. I didn't expect him to say that which is why it was so hilarious.

"I don't know what to say Mr. King, umm thank you," I smiled and stood up to give him a hug.

We discussed more details of the job and then I filled out some paperwork. Kayden and Christy showed KJ and me the office I'd be working out of and the styling room I'd be working in. I was so excited and I had no one to thank other than KJ; my man, lover and best friend.

"Thank you baby," I said to KJ once we got into his car. "And I appreciate that they still interviewed me and stuff."

"Of course, they wouldn't have chosen you for such an important job if you weren't good baby. Styling a new artist is very pivotal, because that sets them up for life. First impressions are everything."

"I know, don't make me nervous."

"When you start getting rich can you buy me a car?" he asked.

"Of course daddy, I'll buy you whatever you want, I just wanna get my parents a new condo first."

"That's why I love you baby, because you care a lot about people."

"I love you too Kendrick," I replied.

He kissed my lips since it was a red light. We continued on to his parent's house to pick up K-Three, and then retired to our home to relax and celebrate with lots of food, music, and sex.

My baby really came through for me, just like he promised.

'I'm just sayin, you can't hurry love...'
- Eric Bellinger

I STOOD AT THE ALTER, waiting for my baby to walk out in her wedding dress. If you would've asked me two years ago was I getting married this soon, I probably would've said no. I knew I would marry Gianna Isabella Daniels one day, but I thought I'd be much older. I must say I'm happy she put that fire under my ass and made me man the fuck up.

Getting in a relationship with her was one of the best decisions I've ever made. Now I have a son, and another kid on the way, who I'm sure is a boy as well. I already have his name picked out, just between you and I. She'd learn soon that all I made were boys.

I couldn't wait to officially call this woman my wife. We've been in love ever since I could remember and it was time we made shit official. No one but Gianna deserved to be my wife, and today I was crowning her as my queen. It was time she sat on the throne next to me.

Aysia and Kaleeini were the last of the bridal party to walk, before the pianist began to play the music for Gianna to emerge. She appeared at the end and I could see her small belly from here. She looked so beautiful when she was carrying my baby and I made sure I told her that every second.

That was something I'd learned from my father. He told me to always compliment my woman so she never forgets how beautiful she is. He said it's a daily reminder that what you saw in her from the very beginning, is still sparkling just as brightly as always. I used to think he complimented my mother everyday just to get in her panties, but now I saw his logic behind it. Every time he told my mother how good she looked that day, or how beautiful she was, she would light up like the sun. I noticed Gianna had the same reaction, and nothing brought me more joy than seeing her and K-Three smile.

Gianna and her father Gary began walking down the aisle and I couldn't keep my eyes off of her. This was finally happening and I was anxious as hell to get it done. Wow, Kendrick Jr. anxious to get married. That's what beauty, unconditional love, personality and good pussy will do to a nigga. It'll have you ready to be locked down.

Gianna finally reached me and she was smiling widely under her veil. Her father took a seat next to her mother and then everyone settled down so the pastor could speak. I wanted him to hurry up and make this shit official.

"We are gathered here today, to celebrate the union of Mr. Kendrick Dreaux King Jr. and Ms. Gianna Isabella Daniels. The couple would like to say a few words before we proceed Gianna," he nodded down to her. She was already crying, which made me chuckle.

"Kendrick, I've loved you since the first day I saw you walking down that hallway at Patterson High. Never did I think in a million years that I would be standing here at the alter with you. Some days I doubted that we would ever get further than friendship, but a part of me just wouldn't allow myself to let you go. I'm happy I didn't, because although I've never had a boyfriend before you, I don't need to be with anyone else to know you're the best thing for me. I hate to use the word perfect, but it applies so well here. You're everything that I could ever dream of in a partner baby, and I just thank you for loving me and caring for me. I love you so much, and I will be by your side forever and always," she said.

I had to pinch my nose and sniffle a little, because she did make my eyes water. I was not the mushy type but damn, this was an emotional ass event. I was not expecting it to be either.

"Kendrick," the pastor said.

"Gigi, Gianna, what can I say. Uh, It's hard for me to put into words how I feel about you because there are so many emotions. The things I feel for you was something that I thought I would never experience nor understand. To love someone who wasn't my blood so much that I would die for them, was never a feeling I thought I would possess. You changed a lot about me, Gianna. You turned a callous, somewhat reckless, ladies man into Gerald Levert overnight," I said and the party laughed. "I was never the sappy type of guy, but you brought that out of me. You showed me that being a man is being able to show love to those you care about, and being able to discipline yourself in the face of temptation. I appreciate everything that you've given me, especially my son. That was the greatest gift anyone could've ever given me, and I'm happy that it came from you. My first-born. I love you to the moon and back Gianna, and I will always have your back and protect you until the end. And I promise to never allow my feelings for you to waver in any way."

Her mother got up and handed her a tissue because she was bawling.

After Gianna wiped her eyes, the pastor said, "Repeat after me please."

"You are my best friend. Today I give myself to you. Using the love that we share as a vessel, through the pressures of the present and the uncertainties of our future. I can promise that you will always have my deepest love, my fullest devotion, and my most tender care. I promise to love you, to always strive to encourage and inspire you, to laugh with you, and to comfort you in times of sorrow and struggle. I promise to love you in good times and in bad when life seems easy and

also when times become difficult; when our love is simple, and when things become complicated. I promise to honor you and to always hold our love for each other in the highest regard," we both repeated after him.

"Gianna Isabella Daniels, do you take Kendrick Dreaux King Jr. to be your lawfully wedded husband?" the pastor asked.

"I do," she responded.

"And Kendrick Dreaux King Jr., do you take Gianna Isabella Daniels to be your lawfully wedded wife?"

"I do. Hell yeah I do," I nodded as everyone chuckled. I then slid the ring down her finger.

"By the power vested in me, by the state of Maryland, I hereby pronounce you man and wife. You may now kiss the bride."

I lifted her veil, and we smiled at one another for a couple moments, before pressing our lips together. I felt a spark shoot through me as I held her body in my arms as my wife.

"I love you," she whispered.

"I love you more shorty," I pecked her nose and she smiled.

HONEYMOON - HONOLULU, HAWAII

We were in the same house in Hawaii that we stayed in when we first got together. It was crazy to think about all that had transpired from that time up until now. We went from being friends in love, to boyfriend and girlfriend, to parents, and now husband and wife in such a short time. None of the shit felt rushed though, it all felt right.

"Can you believe that the last time we were here, that it was the beginning?" Gianna smiled.

We were lying in the bed together naked. We had a crib here, and K-Three was sleeping peacefully in it. The fireplace was burning and we were listening to jazz music like we always did at night.

"Yeah it's crazy, you were just my shorty then but now you're my wife."

"I know and for some reason I'm itching to flaunt it," she raised her ring in the air.

"I'm itching to flaunt you, too," I said and turned on my side to face her. "Everything I promised you then, I made good on. I told you I would make you my wife and the mother of my kids."

"I never doubted you."

Summertime and the livin' is easy. Fish are jumpin' and the cotton is high. Your daddy's rich and your ma is good lookin'. So hush, little baby, don't you cry...

We stared at one another as Ella Fitzgerald's "Summertime" played over the whole house. We always listened to jazz at night, because we found out that when we were babies, both of our parents used to play it to make us fall asleep. I thought it was dope that we were connected even then, even though her ass was two years younger than me. I think it helped K-Three sleep too, because as soon as we cut it on, he was calm before drifting off.

I pushed her hair behind her ear and then kissed her lips. Since she was already naked, I climbed between her legs and entered her slowly.

"Mmmm," she cooed as I began to work in and out of her, seemingly to the smooth sound of the music.

The feeling of the warm fireplace, in combination with her good pussy and the jazz music, had me feeling high. I kissed all on her neck, as I slowly slipped in and out of her.

"I don't ever want this to end," she whispered before I kissed her lips and began sucking them.

"Me either shorty, that's why we've got forever together."

GIANNA KING

CHRISTMAS EVE

ONE YEAR LATER....

It was Christmas Eve and the whole family was spending it in Munich, Germany. KJ's grandparents had a huge home out here, with plenty of rooms so it was like a damn hotel basically; literally since they had elevators, maids, butlers and every damn thing.

Everyone was in the living room just relaxing by the huge fireplace, as both the Jackson 5's and the Temptation's Christmas albums played on repeat. We had two huge thirteen foot Christmas trees because there were so many gifts. There was eggnog, cookies and other little snacks being passed around until it was time to eat. We had chefs this time, just because everyone wanted to just relax and chill. So far this was the best Christmas ever because literally everyone was here at the house. There were so many generations and I thought that was so dope.

I kissed my seven-month-old son Kendry, as KJ held K-Three in his lap. Like he wanted, we had another son. I was convinced that KJ only made boys as well at this point. I thought it was a stupid theory at first, but now it was making a whole lot of sense.

"Come here cutie!" Kendria picked K-Three up from KJ and then sat down on the white plush carpet to play with him.

I currently loved my job as the N.A.S. for King Records. The new artist were super cool and most of them were open to trying new outfits. On top of that, one of the artist who didn't even need my help anymore, decided to stick with me as their stylist still, so that was extra money in my pocket. To say I was doing well would be an understatement. My husband still spoiled me, but I had my own money if I needed it.

I smiled at Willow as I watched her pry something from her son's hand. She had twin boys, Kennard and Kennely. They were so cute and they looked just like my sons. I guess it was because their fathers could pass for twins. Although very cute with chunky cheeks, dimples, and dark green eyes, her little twins were so bad. It was so hard for her to spank them, though, because they would cry and then their little lips would tremble before she could even raise her hand. Kendrin never fell for it, so he would still pop their hands lightly, but Willow couldn't do it. I chuckled at the thought.

Right now she was back in school to get a degree in Political Science and Criminal Justice. She'd stopped for a while because of all that was going, but now she was back at it and double majoring. She eventually wanted to attend law school to become an attorney. KJ said she would be a good asset to the family.

"Oh my gosh, let me go clean his hands. Kendrin please get Kennely off the floor," Willow shook her head and then took Kennard out to clean whatever he'd gotten into, off his little hands. Her babies were so little but moved so much.

"Eggnog?" Aysia offered holding a tray.

She was about to pop any minute with her new baby. Again she didn't wanna know the sex, but she was crossing her fingers for a girl.

"Thank you." I took another one.

She finished passing them out, and then sat back down next to Kaleeini who was holding Keeilan. Aysia and Kaleeini had just gotten married six months ago, about two months after Shannon and Kenzie.

Currently, Aysia and I were in the process of opening a clothing store together. It would be a store that sold high-end brands from all over. We'd already gotten a couple designers to allow us to sell their stuff, so the store should be open for business in the Spring of next year. I was so excited to do this, especially with one of my best friends.

We were listening to Kenzie tell us about all the crazy shit he'd encountered while traveling. Kenzie was making waves everywhere. I saw his face every time I turned on the TV, looked at a magazine, or got on social media. He had so many endorsements that it was crazy. Shannon had given birth to a son who they named Kenzington. He was adorable and looked just like Kenzie. I was starting to think that the Kings men genes muted other people's.

As for Shannon, she was still in school and doing a great job too. She delivered her baby, and three hours later still popped open her laptop and took a final, which she got an A on. My girl was very determined. It was a final she took online but still. After I give birth I just wanna sleep, not take tests. She was well on her way to being a nurse.

"Okay, the food is ready for everyone to eat!" KJ's grandmother Camia called out. To be as old as she was, she didn't look a day over forty.

"Come on wife," KJ stood up with K-three on is hip, since Kendria had moved on to carrying Willow's son Kennely. The older my baby got, the more like KJ he looked. He was always grinning like him too.

"I wanna kiss babe," I looked up at KJ as I adjusted Kendry on my hip. He pressed his lips against mine and then looked down into my eyes.

"Tell me what I wanna hear," he bit his lip.

"I love you Kendrick, and I'm gonna always be down for you." He kissed me again and we walked out towards the dining area with the family.

I meant every word I'd just said. It was gonna be me and my dope boy until the end.

FIN